The Dragon Medallion

The Sage's Legacy, Volume 1

Alexa Whitewolf

Published by Luna Imprints, 2017.

THE DRAGON MEDALLION

First edition. February 19, 2017.

Copyright © 2017 Alexa Whitewolf.

ISBN: 978-1999449995

Written by Alexa Whitewolf.

To my mother, and in a more special way, to my Canadian grandmother, B.MacTier

Prologue

On a nondescript beach in the Mediterranean...

A woman walked the shores, bare feet in the sand. She wore an ivory tunic, wrapped around her body like a second skin. Long, black hair flowed down to her waist, framing the face of an angel. As she turned her profile to the moon, its light reflected off the headdress she was wearing, in the shape of a throne.

It had been eons since Isis had walked the Earth. The goddess of fertility, so revered in Ancient Egyptian times, had been, like most deities of that time, forgotten.

Once, long ago, Isis remembered having spent countless years – or what mortals counted as years – with Osiris, her husband. That was before Set, his brother, murdered him. The memory of that awful time, of gathering his parts strewn about the Nile, was a shadow to Isis' every step.

The goddess sighed, pushing away the bitter thoughts, and focused on the smooth sensation of sand on her toes, waiting for her husband. It would not be long until Osiris joined her for this hallowed day.

Her lovely face was a mask of nostalgia, a troubled gaze fixated on the moon. It didn't take long to notice the stories told by the stars. One, in particular, had caused this abnormal descent down to Earth... A tale of two youths, a male and a female, whose strength together would save the universe from things untold. Another, darker, tale preceded it, of two others who would set in motion a string of events that would alter mankind forever.

"Beloved," a voice came from behind, and Isis spun to find her dark-haired husband grinning in greeting.

Osiris, much like her, had been forced to open a portal. In the dimension they had retired to, demons and angels alike had access. What they had to hide would be much safer on Earth than in their own godly realm.

"It has been a long time since I've watched you bathed in moonlight."

Isis' lips moved upwards in a half-smile. Osiris wore a crown as well, but his was white, with two ostrich feathers on each side. The crook and flail usually by his side were nowhere to be seen.

He could have been any tall, dark and handsome man on the street, clad in the ivory tunic. Only a golden belt adorned him, cinched at the waist, somehow showcasing the masterpiece that was his sculpted body.

"And you, my dear husband," Isis replied, treading over the sand, yearning for his strength and reassurance.

As she neared him, Isis lifted her hand, and in it shimmered an orb. At first it was blurry, but after a few moments it took shape. No larger than an apple, it was the color of pure gold, reflecting the moonlight's rays.

Osiris' gaze fell to the orb, and he smiled. He recalled as vividly as if it had been yesterday the day he'd gifted Isis with the relic. With a nod, he mimicked her movement.

In his palm materialized a scepter. Its handle was also gold, the tip made from a large lapis-lazuli stone. Intricate designs formed at the base, hieroglyphs shining brightly under the moon.

"An orb and scepter to withstand time, and control all the undead," Isis whispered, meeting her husband's gaze. The ominous words echoed across the silence of the beach.

Osiris wrapped his arm around her waist, pulling his wife closer and holding on tightly.

"Let us be done with this," he said, pressing a kiss to Isis' head. "Too long have we feared the demon shall steal them."

Isis threw her head back, peering at him with hooded eyes, before consenting. "Be it so."

Osiris brought the scepter next to the orb, close enough to touch, but not quite. The power they held could be easily unleashed, and attract the wrong type of attention.

Sighing, he intoned, "May these relics never be put together by man, forever protected from their greed. Only the worthy will find them, only the worthy will handle them."

As the words were spoken, a soft brilliance enveloped the two objects. Both gods let them go, and they floated on their own. When the last words were spoken, the glow shone brighter, and then with an audible pop, vanished – as did the two relics.

"They are gone," Isis murmured, awed at the relief seeping through.

"Yes," Osiris agreed, "gone and buried somewhere even we cannot fathom. Let us enjoy this night, what is left of it."

As they walked down the beach, Isis recalled another matter. "What of the medallion and the book? They alone hold the key..."

"They will find the two they are meant to, when the time is right."

Osiris' kiss stopped any further queries from being spoken out loud.

&&&

Centuries later...

A young boy, barely discovering his powers, was sleeping. The moon shone brightly, practically a glare in warning, and it awoke him. He had to blink twice, not believing the glossy pendant in front of his eyes.

Suspended by a leather cord, it floated in midair, a few inches away from his gaping expression. The brown-haired youth lifted a trembling hand to touch it, marveling at the skill with which a dragon's head had been carved on it. Each scale rose from the gold, and the eyes – sapphire blue – glimmered in the dim light.

A time may come for you to use me, but until such time, forget what I am.

The pendant seemed to echo the warning, and as the child clasped it around his neck, sleep overtook all senses. In the morning, he would remember nothing, except that the necklace belonged to him, and would be passed on only to a worthy person.

Further away....

A youthful, raven-haired girl stared at the moon from her room. She had finished the novel assigned in school and the story had kept her awake, despite the late hour.

As her eyes wandered across the garden, she noticed something glinting in the distance. Tiptoeing in the vicinity of the house, so as to not wake up her parents, she walked to the backyard and stood frozen on the spot.

A book lay on the grass, glowing softly. As the child picked it up, she felt the ancient leather cover, and touch the dragon's head etched on it. The engraving had been artistically done, each scale slightly raised, and the sapphire eyes glimmered.

A time may come for you to use me, but until such time, forget what I am.

The girl lifted the tome to her chest, and carried it back inside. It felt like a wonderful treasure in her arms, even as she placed it on the beloved bookshelf in her room, waiting for the time when it would call out to her once more...

Chapter 1

Somewhere in the Welsh countryside...

The moon was high in the sky, its pale light illuminating the harbor. Five boats floated on the sea, as the waves breaking against them whispered stories of an ancient world. Their shapes, long and abandoned, were as much an echo of the past as everything else about the shallow port.

In the eerie obscurity, two figures advanced towards the largest of the ships, which was right out of a Viking movie.

Among the striking features was its abnormal architecture, so different from the modern boats lining the port. It was all made of wood, with ragged and torn ivory cloth sails. The shape itself was long and narrow, designed for speed, and double-ended.

Broken oars rested off the side of the boat. Their power had once permitted a full reversal of the boat in a different direction. This particular ship had one last defining detail: a dragon-shaped bow. It was, without a doubt, a long ship of the Vikings.

Aboard it, hidden in the shadows, someone waited and watched. It was a boy, no older than twelve, though his gaze alone could fool most into believing he was more mature, despite his cerulean eyes and baby cheeks. He was dressed in faded jeans and a white t-shirt too large. His feet were bare, not that it fazed him.

Though he was in the darkest area he'd been able to find, the faint ice-blue aura around his body was still enough to betray him. He shifted restlessly, but it was too late to change his mind.

Pushed by an underlying instinct warning his presence was needed at the scene, the child had arrived barely a few minutes earlier. He now curled up in a corner, keeping his form as camouflaged as possible from the viewpoint of the incoming men.

The two figures were as ancient-looking, battle-worn and yet unassuming as the boat. They approached the abandoned side of the port where it floated on the waves, and climbed aboard via a broken wood board. Their old-fashioned boots should have vibrated loudly in the silent night – and yet the eerie silence persisted.

Aboard the long ship now, both men faced off near the bow, ignoring the broken furniture and pieces of wood lying about. Neither detected the pale shape's watchful eyes, too engrossed in a conversation.

"Is it ready yet?" The abrupt question came from the most imposing of the men. His rough tone broke the silence of the night, as loud as a gavel in a courtroom.

From the corner in which he was situated, the child peered to better observe the newcomers. The one who had spoken was a rather large male. Looking closer, one could see the long, stuffed red beard covering his chin, and the muscles of his arms stiffen, as though ready to jump the other being.

"You bet. You can inform Cadmael that in two weeks, we can move ahead, according to the plan."

The second speaker, though less imposing physically, would have attracted attention in the modern world. Besides the beard, another thing could simply not pass unnoticed – the axe tucked in his belt.

Its blade flashed dangerously, as if to warn the man of the lack of privacy. Clueless, he was too preoccupied by the torrent of menacing words coming out from the mouth of his opponent to pay any attention to it.

"What? What in your bloody mind were you thinking? I was clear enough, you fool. The chieftain wants your men capable of winning a battle in less than ten days."

The same large bearded man snorted in disgust. "I warned him not to trust the bunch of you, but does he ever listen? Of course not! And I told him you're a bunch of slopes not even able to stick their fingers up their—"

"Now you go easy on us, Asger! You have to understand a force so strong isn't easy to unite under one authority, even if it is Cadmael."

Both beings squared off, and the shape in the corner finally caught the resemblance it was searching for. Although the men were surprisingly different on the outside, there was one thing similar to both of them: a tiny glow encompassing their bodies, easily visible in the moonlight.

The child's interest increased exponentially. *This can't be good! They're ghosts – and old ones – probably of Viking origin, if their clothes are any proof at all. I smell trouble...*

The boy stuck in the area, listening for as long as he dared to what was discussed. When things started to die off, he was about to retreat, unobserved, but picked up one more thing. It was enough to make him pause, and it was coming from the stronger of the two Vikings.

"You best have the army ready on time. Cadmael needs those relics – and soon. Before the prophecy comes to pass."

&&&

"Freya?" Professor Seamus O'Keeffe scowled, his tone laced with an edge of frustration.

Sitting behind a mahogany desk, he focused piercing grey eyes in a lined profile onto his pupil. The man was in his late forties, handsome in a rugged way. Blonde hair fell to his shoulders, pulled in a severe ponytail that emphasized a focused stare and square jaw.

Perched atop a roman nose was a pair of black-framed glasses. They did nothing to hide the depth of his grey stare, dark like an incoming storm. Though he was sitting, his form was imposing, with broad shoulders and a narrow waist. In short, the man was the epitome of aging well.

His determined contemplation narrowed onto the teenager sitting across from him, in a much-too comfortable armchair for his liking.

Long, raven-black hair past her shoulders, paler grey eyes, a heart-shaped face, she was nothing if not pretty. One would have guessed she was a good student, were it not for her unfocused, blank stare, as she twirled a lock of raven hair around a finger.

A talk of how ghosts had appeared on Earth a hundred years earlier didn't interest Freya as it had when she'd been only a child. She had stopped paying attention half an hour into Seamus' lecture, withdrawing into her head.

She fantasized about a world where she didn't have to listen to long lectures, where going to school was the norm, and being a teenager the best part of the day. Most importantly, it was a place where parents would kiss her goodnight and be there each morning when she woke up and each afternoon when she returned home from school.

Of course, it was all a daydream. Freya's parents had died when she was only four, and Seamus O'Keeffe, their best friend, had taken care of her since.

"Freya? Freya, are you listening to even ten percent of this history lesson?" O'Keeffe's voice grew more irritated by the second as he tried to gain her attention.

When his tone reached her brain, Freya was momentarily confused by the intrusion. Vaguely, she recalled there was something requiring her attention... With an inward groan, the teenager returned to the present and met Seamus' irritated gaze.

"I'm listening to a hundred percent of what you're saying, professor," Freya said, hoping he might have finished talking, and was ready for a break.

In reality, O'Keeffe was not only far from finished, he'd also been alerted by a mysterious sixth sense that Freya was not paying attention.

"Really? In that case, what was I instructing you about?"

"Um...well...you were....um...err..." Freya chewed on her bottom lip in concentration.

Busted! She put on a contrite expression, trying to figure out a way to get out of trouble. The young girl was ready to admit she'd zoned out, when an idea crossed her mind. *If I dare...and if I could only focus enough to do it...*

Meeting Seamus' scrutiny, Freya squinted, trying to extend the barrier of her mind forward as he had taught her, to read his mind. To her utter surprise, the elder man's mind was hermetically closed, locked, and barred.

"Freya!" O'Keeffe stood from his chair, slamming his hands on the desk. His tone was no longer patient, rather as stern and severe as a principal's. "You are not supposed to be using your powers to read my mind. How many times do I have to repeat this? You're *sixteen*, for heaven's sake, you should be able to pay attention for a few hours a day to what I attempt to communicate!"

"I get it, Seamus," she mumbled, hunching her shoulders inward.

"If you do, then why do you keep on doing this?" The elderly man stopped ranting, frowning at Freya. With a resigned expression, he asked, "Will you at least tell me what distracted you this time?"

Freya mumbled an incomprehensible suite of words.

"I'm sorry, what was that?"

"I said it's nothing important, only fantasies of teenager." The lie left Freya's lips automatically, and she avoided eye contact.

O'Keeffe exhaled heavily, then straightened up and walked around the desk until he was in front of her. "You were reminiscing about your parents, weren't you?" At her obvious shock, he had a wry smile. "Do not look so surprised, Freya. I may not be able to read minds, but I have no need of *super powers* – as you like to put it – to read you. I have known you since you were a little girl, do not forget."

"Seamus, I just can't stop thinking about them. I mean, I try not to, but…"

O'Keeffe ran a hand through his hair, already streaked with white. It came loose off the ponytail, but he didn't notice. On some men, the gesture may have looked effeminate, but with him, it only served to emphasize the rough look, like a rocker.

He removed his glasses, placing them on the table, and pinched the bridge of his nose in actual defeat. It was not the first – nor would it be the last – conversation of the sort he had with his protégée.

Since turning sixteen, Freya had become adamant about discovering more, always *more*, about her parents. In a blind quest for her own identity, she was getting too close to truths that could harm. And it was his duty, as her guardian, to continue to protect her – even if at times, it meant being much too blunt.

"I gather how hard this is for you, Freya," O'Keeffe started softly. "And I realize my history with your parents only serves to remind you of them daily. They were great people, and you have no idea how much I wish they were still here, raising you, teaching you." He paused, rubbing his forehead. "That being said, and much as I hate to sound emotionless, you have to focus and not obsess over them, at least during these lectures."

At the hurt crossing her features, Seamus tried to reason. "Freya, you have to understand my side of this. If you were a regular young girl, perhaps things would be easier. But you are not, as evidenced by your Sage legacy and the fact I am homeschooling you. Regular classes will never be in the plan for you, not as long as we have to protect this world from evil ghosts."

When he couldn't catch her eye, Seamus knelt in front of Freya and took one of her hands in his. "With the Sage Council gone, and so much of our kind dead, it is my job now to prevent anything from happening to you. Whether you like it or not, you are one of the last Sages on Earth..." He trailed off, waiting until Freya looked him in the eye. "And you are in training, which means you need to pay attention to your mentor – me. But I cannot do this alone. I need your cooperation, Freya."

When she nodded, albeit reluctantly, O'Keeffe appeared satisfied – at least enough to return to his lesson.

Ghosts had appeared on Earth a century earlier, and no one knew where they had come from. At first, people were scared of them, afraid the spirits would begin to haunt houses and such, but nothing happened. In fact, the wraiths didn't even talk – at least to most humans – and so, year after year, the generations had grown accustomed to them and begun to ignore them.

To the present day, phantoms could be observed in airports, restaurants, and all other public places, but no one paid any attention to them. Oddly, not all humans that died joined their ranks. Only souls that could not depart due to whatever was holding them on Earth became stuck.

No one knew how dangerous they could be, except for Freya and Seamus. The two of them were Sages, and had been since their birth.

People of their particular race of humans had unique powers. In Antiquity, they were able to contact the gods, detect the unseen, and perform spells and rituals. Once the ghosts showed up, Sages' powers developed.

They could talk to the apparitions, and fight them when it was required. Their bodies had more physical endurance than a regular mortal, and their spiritual strength affected the elements, which could be wielded much like magic. In times of danger, a Sage's aura would grant a specter physical form, thus making it easy to defend themselves.

Freya and Seamus had been forced to, in the past, grapple with phantoms in order to save people. The spirits, however, could not be killed, simply put out of commission for a few hours, at best. The souls that walked the Earth could not cope with violence, and whenever it was aimed at them, a disconnection happened, kicking the soul into the realm between the dead and the living. Ghosts were thus rendered immobile – similar to an unconscious human – and became incapable of anything. They would exist as empty, glowing shells, until such time as the soul returned to inhabit them.

The only thing the two Sages could do was confront them over and over, until the specters learned their lesson – or their soul was stuck forever in the in-between dimension. Luckily, another advantage of being spiritually gifted was a Sage's stamina could last for hours on end sometimes – though their bodies suffered. Some of the specters did cease causing trouble, as they got scared by their soul not withstanding violence, while others kept on going.

"Now, at the risk of repeating myself, ghosts are not all bad," O'Keeffe went on. "For a hundred years they have been walking this Earth, and at no time have the good ones tried to take over the Earth. On the contrary, we Sages like to consider them allies in the battle against evil. The bad ones are another matter altogether, and yet it does not mean we have to give up."

Freya was beginning to zone out, when Seamus' next words increased her interest.

"...although they are considered immortal," the professor said, "specters can dematerialize forever."

"You mean they can *die*?" Freya interrupted, sitting upright in her chair, mouth gaping open. They had researched this subject for months, only to come up empty. *And now, a ray of hope!*

"You are forgetting their rather permanent dead state," Seamus pointed out. "But to answer your question, yes, ghosts can dissipate back to where they emerged from a century ago."

"All of them?"

"No." O'Keeffe broke into a huge grin, eyes twinkling. "The concept is, I admit, complicated, but I went through some old texts and learned that a great spiritual intensity can force ghosts into the Underworld realm, their ultimate resting place, forever. However, this can only be performed on one specter at a time, otherwise the owner of the power risks exhaustion."

"Wait, you mentioned an owner," Freya frowned. "You don't mean...an actual *person*?"

"I do indeed." Excited by the prospect, Seamus started pacing back and forth as he kept reasoning aloud. "Of course, the man or woman in question would have to possess great moral strength to be able to perform such a thing, but it is not unheard of. In Ancient Egyptian times, there is documented evidence that—"

He was interrupted as the wall next to him blurred, and a ghost passed through. Freya leaned forward in the chair, her expression lighting up at the apparition.

Chapter 2

"Well, well, well, check out who stopped by to say hello. If it ain't dear ol' Sam!" Freya used a thick American accent, and the blonde boy was quick to mirror her delight.

Though she'd been raised in Scotland, Freya was originally born in America, and her *origin story*, as Sam liked to call it, was a source of inside jokes between the two youths.

"Frey-Frey!" As their resident investigator, Sam had a special place in both Freya and Seamus' heart, despite the little time they spent together. He was also the only person Freya had ever allowed to give her a nickname.

The ghost floated to Freya, and she stood to hug him. Though the top of his hair only reached her shoulder, his hug was full of a young man's strength. Freya pulled back and ruffled his hair, laughing at his annoyed expression.

It had taken Sam months to get used to having a physical form around her and Seamus. Because there were two Sages living in the same household – a rather large castle on the coast of Scotland – each chamber was imbued with their aura. Thus, despite not being a threat to them, Sam was vulnerable and always tangible.

The young boy had had died three decades earlier in Canada, due to an auto-immune disease that had caused his body to turn against him. At the time, there had been no cure, and he passed away without having lived his life. As a result, he spent years roaming the Earth with no purpose, stuck and unable to move to his resting place, until he ran into Freya and Seamus.

After they'd helped him with a side-problem, Sam had chosen to join them and help out. He was their messenger in the spiritual realm, their private investigator of sorts, due to his special manifestation faculties.

Aside from being able to move across huge distances in a matter of seconds, Sam was also great at sneaking in and out of places mostly invisible. It was a great skill that led to better eavesdropping and more information on ghost movements than either Sage could have gotten on their own. Most of the time, this meant he was out and about.

Snapping out of his thoughts, Sam contemplated Freya, noticing how little she had changed: same long raven hair, attached in a ponytail, same gray smiling eyes. She appeared to have grown, more metaphorically than literally, over the last month. There was an odd glimmer in her expression, speaking to a maturity only an old soul like him would understand.

Sam grew serious at what she would be put through but, as always, there was no choice. "Freya, professor, I have some important –"

He was interrupted by an irritated Seamus. "Did you never learn to knock before you enter a room?"

"Sorry, no time for social etiquette," Sam shook his head, and went on – even whilst Seamus continued to mutter under his breath. "This couldn't wait. I was by Beddgelert, in the Welsh countryside, and ran into some trouble."

"What kind of trouble?" Freya narrowed her eyes, a gut sensation warning her it was nothing good.

"Not me, per se," Sam corrected himself. "I was in one of the old piers, in Porthmadog, and was drawn to an ancient-type ship."

"One of your feelings?" Seamus enquired.

"Yeps," the boy nodded, referring to the mysterious sixth sense that always led him on some hunch or another to find situations that needed mending – and the Sages' diplomacy skills. "Well, I hadn't been there for longer than ten minutes, when these two big men walked in. Vikings. They're plotting something and bad by the sound of it."

Seamus and Freya shared a look. Only a few months earlier, the professor had been teaching Freya about the barbarians of the sea, and their successes and failures at war. The thought crossed Freya's mind that the might get outnumbered this time. *Sometimes it sucks being part of this special club of non-existent Sages.*

"The location, where is it exactly?" Seamus picked up a pad and pen, his irritation long forgotten.

"Porthmadog, England, sir," Sam said. "I couldn't make out what their principal target is. All I caught was something about a large army."

Reading their alarmed expressions, Sam sighed and explained further. "I was in one of the boats when two of the sergeants met. Their behavior implied they're not too happy about each other, though. They're meeting in the harbor next Sunday. The operation is supposed to happen mid-next week."

"Well, today's Thursday, so that means we have three days to gather some clues, and only a few afterwards to stop the Vikings. It doesn't leave a lot of time for intel-gathering and planning," Freya observed.

"It will have to do." Seamus placed his notepad on the desk, then moved behind it and pulled out a duffel bag. He stuffed a few papers and books lying about inside it, then zipped it. "Any idea who their leader is?" he asked.

"Someone they call Cadmael. An odd character too…" Sam trailed off, scratching the back of his head. "From the way those guys talked about him, it seems he's bossy and smart, some ancient war leader. Maybe a general? They mentioned some war, suggesting he fought in one of the greatest battles of the Vikings, too. He's definitely respected by his men."

"And we have no idea what they're scheming?" Freya intervened.

"Not really," Sam said, "but from what I caught, it's related to taking over the island in some way."

"This is not entirely surprising." O'Keeffe threw the bag over his shoulder and moved towards the door of his office. "To be perfectly honest, I was expecting some trouble from them. What does throw me off is this Cadmael you mention, Sam. If his war strategy knowledge is any good, it could mean some serious trouble."

"It would be a good thing for Freya though," Sam pointed out. "She can test her powers and kick some serious ghost butt." As an undertone, he added, "I seriously hope not mine."

Freya burst out laughing, and even O'Keeffe cracked a smile. He gestured for them to follow him, then locked the office behind.

"Sam, go help Freya pack. I have to test the car and make sure it drives well, then book us a flight."

He left at a fast pace, and Sam followed Freya to her room. The walk was the opposite of short. Though neither human was born in Scotland, Seamus had lived there for most of his adult life. Set with a fortune from his deceased parents, he had purchased the castle they now lived in after returning from Canada with an orphaned toddler Freya trailing behind.

At first, they'd only vacationed to Scotland, before eventually moving in a few years earlier. In the end, the old country was more suited to their needs. Plus, the quietness of the castle and the lack of ghosts – due to certain precautions Seamus had put in place – made it the ideal place to recharge after a particularly long mission.

The rather large mansion stood in a clearing, on the border of an enormous forest. It had been a laird's home once upon a time, with a small internal courtyard, and on the outside still had a fortified stone bridge. It was truly a fortress in its own right.

Inside, the castle was large enough to host tens of families. As she'd grown older, Freya had taken to the West wing of the castle, with Seamus living in the East. It suited their needs for privacy, and made for a good workout most days.

Panting as she reached the top of the stairs, Freya turned to Sam. "So, Vikings, huh? Couldn't have brought me something less intimidating?"

Sam snorted with laughter. "You, intimidated? I doubt you know the meaning of that word, Frey-Frey."

The Sage grinned, then burst into her room and started throwing clothes on the bed. Within half an hour, they'd packed and were back downstairs, joining Seamus.

Less than five hours later, Freya and Seamus O'Keeffe boarded onto a Boeing 747 with destination to London, from where they were to rent a car to Porthmadog.

A quick internet search at the terminal told them the village was located in Gwynedd, Wales, and had easy access to the Snowdonia National Park. The legendary area was steeped in Welsh mythology and legend. As Sam had mentioned, an old harbor did exist in Port, as the locals called it – lost amongst the treasures of time. Freya made a mental note to go and search for additional clues.

In the plane, she stood near Seamus, in the window seat. As she peered below at the ocean, her eyes lit up. If there was one thing she loved, it was its soothing color and large waters.

The ocean's calming strength only worked for a few moments, contrary to the past. Pursing her lips, Freya thought about her parents, and wished...for things she couldn't have.

Reading her like an open book, Seamus squeezed her palm and said, "They would be incredibly proud of you, Freya."

The teenager breathed in deeply before responding. It was done as much for air, as to maintain control and avoid sobbing – the one thing she dreaded most in that instant.

"Thanks, Seamus." she replied to the man who had known her parents, and yet refused to speak of them. Another profound breath, then she took the plunge. "Can I ask you something?"

"Of course."

"Why do you refuse to tell me more about them, about their deaths?"

O'Keeffe exhaled loudly. "I realize you believe I am keeping something from you, Freya, but I am not. Your parents were wonderful people, caring and gentle. Some things are just too hard to relieve." He paused, avoiding her gaze and hiding his anguish as best as he could.

"Mark and Evelyn were my best friends. When they perished, I reckoned I would die of grief, and how much I missed them. But I couldn't, for there you were. An innocent four-year-old girl, filled with remarkable powers. And someone had to teach you how to use them."

Seamus' stare grew nostalgic as it bore into Freya's. "I swore to protect you and not let any harm come to you. If I was to tell you all the gory details of their deaths, sooner or later my promise would be broken. And I simply cannot stand to lose you too, Freya."

Freya said nothing for a long moment, gathering her thoughts. She managed to set aside her own selfish feelings and identity quest, and thought about things from Seamus' perspective. *If only there was some way to find out more about them,* Freya mused to herself, *I would do anything.*

In the end, she was still left dissatisfied with O'Keeffe's rationale. "What if I swore not to do anything that could put me in danger, regardless of what you tell me?"

"I am sorry, Freya, but some things are better kept unveiled." Seamus' heart constricted when the teenager's face fell. Tears glistened within her grey orbs, so similar to her mothers'. But much like his brave best friend, she fought them and managed to project a brave face.

Seamus tried to redeem himself, cursing the secret that kept his tongue tied. "At least for now. I promise you, one day I will disclose everything. For now, the past is simply too dangerous to be unfolded."

Freya nodded, then let go of his hand and angled her body towards the window. Seamus watched her for long moments, but the shoulders curled inward and her pursed lips were a clear indication she was done talking.

On a last heavy exhale, she gradually drifted to sleep under his protective gaze.

&&&

In dreams, and only in dreams, the truth can be shown, or parts of it...

It was an echo, a plea, a warning at once, and Freya caught it as clearly as what happened next.

"Freya!" Someone was calling out, close by.

She spun and saw a woman waving at her. She had fair skin and silky raven hair, a tiny silhouette and huge grey eyes. In her palms was a shining globe, almost like an orb. She smiled, motioning to the object.

With a shock, Freya recognized her mother from the pictures Seamus had kept. Indescribable joy overcame her, and an urging to run for her mother's wide open arms. Her legs were like lead, heavy and unmoving, but she managed to force them onwards.

Yet as the teenager drew closer, the gracious woman drifter further away. With each passing second, her silhouette became blurry, fading away.

Freya extended a fist, trying to grasp onto – something. "No, mom! Wait! Don't go!"

She ran as fast as her legs would carry her, but the woman vanished, and Freya was left alone. She paused, letting the tears stream down her cheeks unreservedly.

"Why did you go? Why did you leave me alone?" Her words echoed in the emptiness, but nothing responded.

It was then the décor changed. Instead of being in the midst of a thick fog, Freya became surrounded by nothingness. A pitch black enveloped her, an oppressive agony eating at her little joy.

"Mom!" Freya desperately searched the darkness, but there was no sign of her. "Please come back!"

She received no answer, only a solid stillness.

"I'll do anything!" Freya pleaded, barely above a whisper.

Silence.

The tears stopped, and Freya was overwhelmed by incredible sadness. Loneliness engulfed her heart, an odd sense of loss and longing all at once. The feeling took over, and it was as though the darkness itself was moving, feeding on her.

A voice whispered around her, *Give in... Give in to me... I can show you the true path...*

"Stop!" Freya yelled, trying to shake it off, but there was nothing to battle, and thus, no way to make it stop.

Right as it became overwhelming, a light burst out of nowhere. Silver on black, it was as though a lantern was being shined in the secluded crevices of the Underworld. Far back into the nothingness, a shadow reluctantly formed.

Freya squinted at it and gasped when it came into full view. It was a dragon, but one unlike anything the Sage had ever seen in illustrated stories. This one was large, with scales of the purest silver. It had massive wings, furled onto its back, and intelligent, blue human eyes, golden flecks specking them. It was easily five times her size, almost a giant next to her curled up silhouette.

The beast turned its massive head, and one blue eye surveyed the Sage with evident reproach. Freya shivered under the menace, despite being unable to figure out what she had done wrong.

For now, the past is too dangerous to be unfolded. Do not try to search for answers, lest you wish death to await you at the end of the road.

&&&

Freya woke up with a start. She glanced around in a panic, settling once it sank in she was still on the plane, with Seamus asleep by her side, snoring softly.

In an effort to calm her fast-beating heart, Freya watched the ocean below once more, but not even the sight could pacify her. The fantastical beast's image kept coming back vividly in her mind, as did its words.

Now removed from the creature's imposing shape, she recalled a detail that had escaped her, an odd one at that. The dragon had been holding a burgundy book under one clawed paw, with its own image engraved on it.

"What does it all mean?" Freya murmured aloud, frowning at the clouds as if they could deliver an explanation.

Chapter 3

They landed at Heathrow Airport a few hours later, on a fresh Friday morning. As soon as they were allowed off the plane, Freya and Seamus hurried to get their luggage, and went to get a rental car.

While the elderly man was in line, Freya took in their surroundings, in search of unique specters. Most were old grandpas and pilots, or families that had died in crashes. Humans passed by them as indifferently as if they were statues.

As Seamus had been explaining, the ghosts had emerged out of nowhere a hundred years before. At the beginning, everyone was quite scared of them, but since they didn't talk nor try to haunt houses, the population of Earth learned to ignore them. Even now, the living didn't realize the spirits which appeared so innocent to them could, at any time, become vicious and dangerous.

Freya was about to abandon her observation when something, or rather some*one*, attracted her gaze. The person in question was a young man, not much older than herself. Brown hair, tall, nothing was unusual about him, and she herself couldn't understand the weird sensation running down her spine. Then saw it around his neck – a silver dragon pendant, suspended on a leather chain.

Freya's eyes widened as she recognized the creature. It was an exact replica of the one in her dream. And judging by her impression of déjà-vu, she'd already seen the necklace before. *But where?*

The youth, somehow aware he was being watched, was rotating his head in all directions, seeking the source. Before she was able to avoid his stare, his hazel-golden eyes locked onto hers.

"Freya Hayes, hurry up!"

Freya glanced towards the sound, noticing her mentor waving next to the rental car. When she looked back to where the boy had been standing, he was gone.

With a shake of the head, she hurried towards Seamus and the open car door. Once inside, she couldn't help her racing thoughts. *Now what the hell was that all about? And where have I seen that pendant before?*

Lost in her broodings, it was only once they passed the hotel that Freya realized they were heading to a new destination. This, sadly, also meant she wouldn't be catching up on sleep anytime soon.

"Seamus, where are we going?" She twisted in the seat towards him, slightly pouting. "I thought we were heading to the hotel."

"Not quite yet. Before we go there, or even before we go to the port, I have to show you something of great importance. It will assist you in the upcoming battle."

Freya remained silent, an onslaught of emotions assailing her without warning. The time spent traveling, and constant emotional battle against herself won, and she fell asleep.

&&&

"Freya! Freya, wake up! We have arrived." O'Keeffe urgently spoke, with a tone that awoke the teenager.

Tired, muscles sore from the flight and car ride, it took Freya a few moments to stretch, and only then did she peer out the window of the car.

To her utter amazement, it was past noon, and the area they'd gotten to was nothing like the one from earlier in the morning. Rather than buildings, cars, the smell of gas and pollution, Freya noticed something quite opposite.

In the vicinity, going on miles, were forests, majestic trees, and the high blue sky. Not too far from the road was a high green hill, rising as an ancient giant across the horizon.

Exiting the car, Freya let the sun's warmth penetrate and irradiate her body, and all her muscles loosened in response to what her subconscious mind perceived. Her worries disappeared, and only a settling sense of peace remained.

In this place, I feel... as if I'm at the beginning of civilization... Freya wondered at the vibrations coming off the hill, and the hum of power underneath. *This is home.*

Seamus was watching her expression with evident delight, before approaching. A backpack was slung over his shoulder. "Come. I have brought you here to show you something."

"But... *where* is here?" Freya continued looking around, then turned towards him.

"All this, far and beyond, is Wales. We are now in the west end of England, here where wisdom still lies." A note of reverence had entered Seamus' voice. "Come, Freya, time flies and Dinas Emrys awaits you."

Freya's eyes widened as the information sank in. She gaped at the elderly man, who was already walking towards the hill.

The teenager hurried after and reached him, out of breath. "Dinas Emrys? Seamus, you don't mean *the* Dinas Emrys, the place Sages reunited once a month, on the full moon, to join forces and grant each other the strength to endure? Not *the* Dinas Emrys, where the fledgling Sages received training... Do you?"

O'Keeffe simply smiled enigmatically, and with a sideways glance to her, said, "You'll see soon enough, my dear. Come now, we have to reach the top of this hill."

&&&

For the next little while, both teacher and student hiked in silence, each one lost in their thoughts.

O'Keeffe was debating whether or not he'd made the right decision in bringing Freya to the training location of her ancestors. Dinas Emrys was where adult Sages, who'd already mastered their spiritual power, learned to elevate their abilities and control the elements. It was a place of power, of development, but not somewhere Freya belonged – yet.

After all, he'd hoped to delay her final decision for another two years, at least. With danger mounting, it seemed an impossible hope.

His thoughts went to the book he was carrying, remembering the day Freya's mother had relinquished it to him. Evelyn's look of utter desolation would be forever ingrained in his mind, as though she was passing on a most treasured possession. He'd heard of the artifact, but the confirmation had still been a shock. And to find out his best friend had been its guardian since she'd been a child...

Seamus sighed, and forced those painful memories at bay. What lay ahead would be hard enough without the past singing sorrowful melodies of lost friends in his ears.

Though he had trained Freya, the elder Sage was well aware his lacking faculties meant he could not teach her everything. It had led to Freya being only half-developed as a Sage. To become a full-fledged one, there was a final block she would have to go through, to unleash the spiritual strength that lay dormant within.

This was the ultimate step, and Freya had one last choice. She could retreat to the existence she had longed for during the past few years and have a normal life, without her parents. Or, she could continue forth, become a powerful Sage and be proud of the legacy she'd received, and would ultimately pass on.

&&&

Freya had her own internal struggle to deal with. Seamus' quiet demeanor told her something big was coming, and she had a feeling it would be tied in to her future. At the same time, she couldn't help but fixate on the brown-haired youth from the airport, and the necklace he wore. A nagging instinct told her something about the entire situation was amiss.

A crack of a branch brought her brutally out of her reverie and she spun around, ready to defy an adversary, only to find... nothing. Freya frowned, easing out of her battle stance. Seamus had noticed nothing, and kept advancing up the hill.

For the sake of safety, Freya extended her spirit, picturing a large circle surrounding her, then gradually encompassing all her surroundings. It was a way she'd learned to scan for adversaries and friends alike, and which increased her awareness.

Despite pushing as far as she could like Seamus had taught her, Freya met no hostile feelings. She was about to go her way, when a raccoon fearfully scurried out of his hiding spot, and ran as fast as it could to the nearest shelter.

A wave of relief dawned on Freya and, sure paranoia was gaining on her, she hurried to catch up with Seamus – who was now a distance off. After a brief debate with herself, she decided not to tell him anything about what had happened or about the boy from the airport.

At least not until she had a few more facts strewn together.

It took them another half an hour to reach the top of the hill, and once there, they both remained speechless for a long moment. At their feet, a rocky, steep-sided and partly tree-covered hill emerged from the earth, defying the ancient gods and the far mountains. Emerald green and mossy rocks mingled in the landscape, creating a mix of colors that surpassed any painter's skill. And further, out in the distance, the setting sun caressed a mountain's top as a lover would.

"Dinas Emrys..." Seamus broke the silence, then inhaled deeply the fresh air. "How I have missed this place." He knelt on the mossy grass, placing a palm to the ground, and closed his eyes.

Freya sensed the undercurrents of his spiritual energy travel through the earth, and gasped. "Seamus, your powers!"

O'Keeffe opened his eyes then and gave a wry smile. "It is but the effect of this place." He stood once more, and said, "Did you know this used to be an ancient medieval hill-fort?" When Freya shook her head, he continued, reminiscing over what he knew of the hill itself. "Centuries ago, it was believed a pool in which a red and a white dragon were hiding – symbols of the Romano-Celtic and Saxon powers – was believed to be camouflaged at the deepest of its heart, making the construction of a fort impossible."

"That part rings a bell..." Freya chewed on her bottom lip for a minute, trying to remember. "Wasn't it part of a story on Merlin? Didn't he advice the king who'd eventually build the fortress here?"

"Yes," Seamus nodded, "a shaman by the name of Emrys – Merlin's alias – revealed to King Vortigern that a fortress would not be built on the hill unless the two creatures below it confronted each other in a battle. After digging, this proved to be true, and two dragons were unearthed – one white, one red. These monsters fought a fierce battle, with the red being victorious in the end. This is how the red fantastical beast supposedly found its way onto the Welsh flag." He paused, his eyes taking in the vast horizon. "Vortigern, impressed with the accuracy of Emrys' prophecy, assigned him the fort, which to this day, bears his name."

Freya waited a beat, believing her mentor would follow the impromptu history lesson with something else. When he appeared to be done, she stepped closer and touched his arm. "Seamus, why did you bring me here?"

When he turned to her, O'Keeffe's expression was peaceful, but she could read the conflict in his eyes. He met her gaze piercingly, and she proudly withstood his scrutiny. After a while, as though he'd gathered all the information he needed, O'Keeffe bent over his backpack and rummaged through it. He proudly extracted an ancient book, probably as old as Dinas Emrys itself, and held it.

Freya gaped in silent shock. The cover of the book was blood red, and a silver dragon was carved on it. The part that struck her most was that it was an exact replica of the one from Freya's dream, and from the boy's medallion.

While Freya admired the tome, Seamus spoke softly, as though to not disturb the creatures lying in the depths of the hill. "You remember what I mentioned yesterday, about the ghosts not being immortal?"

At her nod, he said, "I *was* referring to a person being able to use that power. You can do this Freya, you can become a full Sage. It all depends on you, and if you desire it enough."

Seamus paused, eyes seeking beyond the hill, to the vast horizon, then back to his pupil. "My intent in bringing you here was not for an ultimatum, though it may come across so. I hope this is the only time you will be faced with this choice, my dear. You alone comprehend what you desire, but I would be failing my duty as your mentor if I did not emphasize the fate of the world lies on your shoulders."

His eyes fell to the book, reading Freya's silent question. "Sages are no longer the force they were. With the corruption in this world, fewer innocents make it out alive. This book, it is not to be trifled with. It contains keys that will elevate your Sage abilities to places I have never seen, nor can follow. But it will also help you battle the dead souls, in the end." He raised his gaze, leveling it on Freya. "I understand this may be too great a responsibility for a sixteen-year-old girl, and I will respect your decision, should you wish to walk away."

A few seconds passed by as he waited for Freya to acknowledge his words in some way. When she remained silent, O'Keeffe knew he had to go on.

"This is an ancient artifact, much more than a regular tome. It contains secrets of great danger. In criminal hands, it may be the end. In a powerful Sage's ones, it can do miracles." Seamus thrust the book toward her, anticipating Freya's response. "You take this, and your fate is ready to be written. You refuse it, and you are free of this vocation's constraints."

What Seamus kept silent, and what perhaps was most important, was how he'd come by the book. He feared it would sway her choice, and he wanted no regrets.

Freya was lost in a daze, analyzing her feelings. She had a chance, the last one maybe, to have a normal life. But then, what *was* a normal life? Would going to school and hanging out with friends be enough, after all she had been through? After all she had *seen*?

Freya reflected on her life up to that point. Seamus had raised her after her parents' mysterious death. He had done everything possible to offer her a regular life – as regular a life could be in an world populated by ghosts – at least until she was fourteen. It was then he'd revealed the information about her powers – forcibly so.

The choice was all but stolen from them when a group of specters tried to kill the president of the United States. The ghosts were not as innocent as they were believed to be. If the spirit of one entered a human body, it could compel it to do its bidding.

O'Keeffe had been backed into a corner. Although lost, the phantoms had great strength and were too many to fight, especially for him, whose powers were not what they used to be. Seamus had been on a trip with Freya, when they'd stumbled onto the vengeful spirits. Out of instinct, Freya had jumped in the fight, helping out her guardian.

After they'd won, Seamus had revealed the truth of her legacy – what he could at the time, and definitely less than she yearned for. He'd had also taken on the active role of mentor and professor for her. Through the years, he'd trained Freya in martial arts and as much theory and practice of mastering her spiritual energy and wielding it as a weapon as he could. He'd been a full- fledged Sage once, but had lost his powers the same night her parents died – a fact not lost on the teenager. But despite the time that went by, he'd not once allowed himself the weakness of speaking of her parents.

Regarding ghosts, Seamus had no such qualms, and taught Freya everything. As she was mainly home schooled, they tried to keep a study schedule, so she'd be able to graduate high school – to what end, she had no idea. Being a Sage was the only life she knew. And though it'd been only a short two years of fighting ghosts, it had been enough for Freya to realize where she truly belonged.

And yet, what if she failed? Seamus had dedicated his entire life to being a Sage, and now was left with almost nothing. Freya dreaded having to press for answers, especially considering how their last conversation had ended, and yet...

"Before I decide anything, I need to know one thing."

Seamus hesitated, then lowered his chin in assent, indicating she could continue.

"How did you lose so much of your powers?" At his bewildered stare, Freya thought it well to explain. "If I was to make my entire life about being a Sage, it's only fair I be made aware of how quickly it can all be lost."

O'Keeffe rubbed the back of his neck, then met her inquisitive stare. "Losing one's powers can only be caused by a huge amount of wasted spiritual energy. It is rare for it to happen as it did for me... In the past, should anyone go through such an ordeal, Dinas Emrys helped recharge them on the first full moon following the event."

"Recharge?" Freya frowned.

"Yes," Seamus nodded, "there is a ritual and such involved, but it is possible."

When he was silent for a few moments longer than necessary, Freya probed, "And what happened to you? Why weren't you able to bounce back?"

"I was not able to." It was the way he responded, with such finality and resignation, and the look of desolation in his eyes that stopped her from challenging him further.

Freya surveyed the hill for a few moments, sensitive to the ancient power lying beneath, and a hum within. It was a similar vibration, though more muted, that surrounded the book. As she glanced back to it, something inside of her clicked into place.

It could've been her Sage instinct finally coming to life or simply her ancestors' call, but something within the young woman found its missing puzzle piece. Freya clenched her fists and drew her head high, determination shining in her expression.

"I've always wanted a regular life, with my parents and you at my side, in a normal world, simply at peace, and enjoying our lives. They aren't here and I probably won't be seeing them any time soon – if I ever do, that is. But they've left me a legacy, one I can't just spend or throw away. So there's only one thing I can do with it."

She paused, meeting Seamus' expecting gaze, and solemnly continued, "I can do my best and make them proud until I die and join them wherever they are."

Freya reached for the aged bundle of paper and grasped it, sensing the weight of what she'd just agreed to on her shoulders. She also knew this was only the beginning.

Of what, though? I have no idea what I've gotten myself into, and maybe it's better like this. But I'm guessing my days of getting bored are numbered.

Freya felt the power in her hands, and shivered. If it was of anticipation or excitement, she couldn't say. Yet as its heat permeated her palms, words tumbled unwillingly past her numb lips. "Will you tell me where you got this?"

Seamus hesitated for a long moment, watching her. His eyes shone brilliantly, and she could have sworn it was with tears. Finally, he sighed and said, "Your mother gave me the book. She had come upon it a long time ago, though it was not a story she admitted to often. All she revealed was that it was to go to you when the time was right, and you would figure out what to do with it."

"I'm not sure I understand...What's in it?" Freya pressed. "Didn't you open it?"

Instead of answering, Seamus glanced away, a faraway look in his eyes. The sun was setting, spilling its blood-red color onto the hills and horizon. They stood like that for a while, with Freya holding the book, before he spoke.

"Do you remember the story I used to tell you when you were little? The one about the dragon and the fair maiden?"

"Of course I do," Freya smiled fondly. "It was one of my favorites."

"Would you care to narrate it for me this time?"

O'Keeffe plea was at odds with their previous conversation, but Freya humored him. "There was once a silvery dragon –" She stumbled on the descriptive words, ones she knew by heart, and a story that was taking on an entirely new meaning, since her dream.

"Freya?"

The young woman snapped to at Seamus' concerned tone, and continued more reverently. "The monster fought a huge army, and became badly injured – enough so that he had to retire to his cave. One night, a maiden by the name of Estella stopped by his cave for shelter because it was raining outside. The beast could've eaten her right then and there, but he spared her life on one condition – that Estella would stay with him and support his healing. She accepted and so the days passed by, with Estella helping dragon regain strength, following his instructions on what to do, and what to feed him."

Her eyes flicked to Seamus to see if he wanted to add anything. His eyes were closed, and he nodded softly. At the encouragement, Freya continued the story.

"After many weeks, the dragon was finally ready to take his revenge. But Estella couldn't stand to watch her own people suffer, and so begged the monster to spare them, offering her life instead. The dragon looked at her for a few moments, amazed at the will of the tiny human. He dropped his head to her height, close enough to eat her. But rather than end her life, he said, *Fair maiden, you have cared for me and yet now you stand for your own people. Your courage touches me, and I give you this.* He took a deep breath and Estella began to shake, fearing he would burn her. And flames did come out from its mouth, but they weren't harmful, instead cool and ash-colored."

Freya's eyes widened as the truth of the words hit her, but she kept her thought to herself. "When Estella was conscious again, new power ran within her veins and she asked the beast what he'd done to her. The dragon said, *You shall be the first of your race – a Sage. The powers I have gifted you will serve later in the future to save this world you inhabit. Share them with your fellows, and use them only for good.*'"

"Yes," Seamus snapped out of his silence, "that is how we Sages inherited our powers. Estella shared those powers with ten people, among whom were her two brothers and the man she fell in love with. But those powers weren't the only gifts she received."

After checking he had Freya's undivided attention, O'Keeffe pursued, "He also gave Estella a book. It was rumored to hold secrets of immense power. He made Estella swear she would not open it unless she was in grave danger, and the maiden held her word. She went on the hill that is now Dinas Emrys and hid the tome there. Unfortunately, someone had observed her. This someone was Estella's third brother, with whom she had not shared the powers, for he was a cunning, evil man. Blinded by jealousy, he went and retrieved the book and, uncaring of the risks, he opened it. The power was too much for him to hold, and he was consumed by it. The book was never seen again...until it came to your mother."

Freya said nothing for a while as she pondered his words. The warning was clear, as was the meaning behind why Seamus had not yet opened the artifact, despite the fact it had been in his possession for over a decade.

"Don't worry." She lifted her chin resolutely, meeting his relieved glance. "I'll wait for the book to call out to me, and will only use it for the good fight."

Relief and pride shone in Seamus' expression at her words, and Freya returned the grin. They took their time walked back to the rental car, with Freya clutching the book to her chest. The certainty that whatever powers it held would be hers was euphoric, yet strangely calming at the same time.

Once they drove away, Freya watched the landscape pass by and fell back into dreamland, still holding the book.

&&&

Neither Freya nor Seamus detected the silhouette hidden in one of the concealed corners of the forest, and who'd been there during the entire conversation.

He'd observed Freya come to her decision, and was amazed by the aura of light and power surrounding her. As she and Seamus walked back to the car waiting for them, he reflected, *She may have some Sage blood in her veins, but she still has to prove her worthiness. I wonder if she has any idea what she's gotten herself into.*

Then, he smiled. It was time for him to jump into action.

&&&

After the two Sages were gone, a mass of darkness rolled from the depths of the earth, leisurely materializing into a man's body. His eyes were black as coal, tinged with red, hair somber as the night, his skin not much lighter. He smiled, showing spectacularly white teeth, in features as angular as a stone.

"Run, little Sssage, run away," he cackled. "Ssssoon, you shall provide me with the toolsss I have been waiting for. It isss finally time. You may not lisssten to me in your dreamsss, but I promissse... You *will* give in."

His stare unwavering from the departing car, the wraith transformed back into smoke. Within seconds, the smoke retreated back inside the earth, gone with no trace.

&&&

From where she was, Freya could not say in what place she had landed. The more she looked around, the more familiar the place felt. She was in a big comfy room, with a canopy bed and a leather armchair. Somewhere in a corner a fire crept, and Freya advanced towards it.

Taking a seat on the chair, she noticed the book Seamus had entrusted her with lying on a small table across from her.

The silver dragon was laughing at her, its sapphire-blue eyes twinkling in amusement. The echo of a sinister laugh taunted, "Can you really not open me? Use me! How weak can you be, not to use me?"

Freya scowled at it coldly and, before she could stop herself, reached for the antique object. The laughter immediately ceased. A power commanded her to open the book, and she wondered vaguely what was so important for her to seize.

Maybe it will help. Maybe I'll become so powerful, I won't need anyone's protection anymore.

With a trembling hand, Freya reached for the cover.

No! The declaration came from deep with her, a different kind of order.

Freya narrowed her eyes, confused on what action to take. Part of her craved what was in the book, but another part wanted to be careful.

She pondered the matter, then caressed the cover softly, before placing it back on the table.

"Whatever this holds can wait," she said to the empty room. "The power within it is not yet ready to accept me, nor am I prepared to risk it."

"Fool! Coward!" That same sinister voice accused.

Deception stung as Freya backed away, wondering if she'd made the right decision.

Yes, another voice, softer, assured her. Freya accepted its reassurance, and walked out of the room.

As she stepped out, a shape emerged in the room. It was a beautiful woman with long black hair, a honey complexion, and kohl-rimmed eyes. On her head was a crown modeled as a throne.

She lowered her gaze to the table, scowling at the fake artifact. "We knew you would escape the pits of hell, demon. But this girl will not give in, no matter what you do."

"We will see..." The wraith cackled, then the object was inanimate once more.

The goddess passed a palm over it, shuddering at the remnants of the negative corruption.

A man materialized next to her, wearing the white crown of Upper Egypt. "Beloved, do not linger. His essence is potent."

"We have to protect her, Osiris."

"I gathered as much, but she will have help. It is on its way."

Holding hands, they both dematerialized to their dimension.

&&&

Freya woke up with a start in the car. Seamus was in a focused driving mode, his gaze glued to the darkening road. In her lap lay the book, as innocent and normal as any other tome of knowledge.

It felt so real…

Shaking her head, the teenager turned to the window and watched the landscape drifting by, her thoughts flying free. *My dreams are becoming way too strange.*

Chapter 4

After their trip to Dinas Emrys, Freya and Seamus arrived at a bed and breakfast inn, where they had reserved rooms near the harbor. Its owners, a nice elderly couple, had transformed their three floor mansion into a comfy shelter for tourists. Aside from the quietness and quaintness of the place, the food was to die for – at least in Freya's opinion, who gulped down her dinner in a matter of minutes.

Freya's room was beyond what she'd expected. There was a big bed, covered in beige sheets and two large, fluffy pillows. Two armchairs – one facing the window, the other the bed – covered in cotton sheets completed the décor. There was also a bedside table with an old lamp on it. The bathroom, painted in the same warm beige color, contained the necessary for comfort.

After a shower, Freya made sure her door was locked, then dragged her suitcase to a dresser. She tried to keep her movements as quiet as possible, since Seamus' door was only down the hall from her.

In front of the dresser, Freya knelt next to the suitcase and opened it, then piled her clothes unceremoniously in a few drawers. She hid the red book in the middle one, underneath a sweater and a pair of jeans.

Then, she did something Seamus had only theorized to her about. Freya extended her spirit, this time picturing a blanket covering the treasured artifact – one only she could detect and remove. *This'll keep it safe from prying eyes.* There was no way she planned to leave the book unguarded, and she couldn't exactly carry it everywhere.

Sam – who had in the meantime materialized at the hotel too – paid her a little visit to see if she needed anything, but Freya knew he was checking up on her after her conversation with Seamus. The kid was well-versed in human emotions – too much so, at times.

To pacify him, she smiled in acceptance, then requested some peace and quiet to sleep.

The only problem was, she could not get her mind off the book and the brown-haired youth. When she did fall asleep, terrible nightmares sought control over her once peaceful dreams, of a shadow chasing her and not letting go.

&&&

The next day was the weekend, and both Freya and Seamus had to get up early to go hunting for clues. They woke up before sunrise, and after a highly needed cup of coffee, drove the rental car to Porthmadog Harbor, where Sam was to meet them.

The port itself was pretty impressive – mountains cut across the horizon in the distance, a blue sky teased above, and tons of boats lining the clear blue water. On each shore, some small houses housed tourist rental equipment.

Freya and Seamus parked a bit before the harbor, and walked the rest of the way. They met up with Sam near some empty metal containers.

"It's there that I saw them."

Wasting no time, the ghost pointed to a massive and ancient boat anchored close to the abandoned part of the pier. Hardly noticed among the new and modern ones, it seemed out of place. Freya couldn't stop the shiver creeping up her spine, and fear enveloped her in a solid grip. *That ship has battled – and killed; the aura is unmistakable.*

The sails were torn and yellow. The ship itself must have been centuries old, but was floating on the water. It was quite long, and she wryly mused, *It's not for nothing they call it a long ship.*

"No wonder the Vikings chose it as their meeting place," Freya noted aloud. "It's like a pirate ship."

And, indeed, with its torn sails and ragged body, the boat really did have the appearance of belonging to pirates.

"Be that as it may, we should go and search for anything which may better inform us about our new enemies," O'Keeffe suggested.

He scanned their environment, pursing his lips as if trying to decide a course of action. In the end, he said, "Freya, you go east. Sam, head on the west part, and I'll go to the north of the harbor. We shall meet here in five hours. The time frame should allow us some leeway to discover anything, *if* there is anything to be found."

Freya and Sam shared a look, then went on their way.

&&&

Sam was confused. Seamus had decided to split them up, and it didn't sit well with him. Since he'd been back at the harbor, a nagging feeling of something bad about to happen had taken hold of him.

But hey, he mused, *I have bad feelings about anything, so it shouldn't really surprise me.*

With each step, the sense of foreboding had crept. He felt they were in great danger and, though not afraid to die – his abilities did grant him the large advantage to dematerialize if danger became tough. His concern was more for Seamus and Freya, who had no such options.

As he passed through the streets of the port, desolately noticing the lack of, well, *anything,* Sam tried to push the annoying thought away. And yet it remained, like an annoying fly.

&&&

Seamus continued his walk, despite having a feeling their search would lead to nothing. The types of spirits he had dealt with in the past had taught him one thing – much like their very alive criminal counterparts, they didn't leave traces of their evil plans.

Unlike the shadow in their pursuit, who happened to leave *way* too many traces, and evidently was not a professional.

His leader instincts cried at having split his team, but the truth of the matter was, a divided group was the only way to realize which one out of them was being followed.

As he kept about his business, trying not to tip off the intruder in their midst, Seamus tapped into his low reserve of powers and extended his mind, searching the surroundings. He made brief contact with Freya, then Sam, and met almost nothing else except—

There!

It was faint, but it was a male essence, and from what Seamus touched before he was shut out, it was innocent. Furthermore, it had a familiar tinge, as though a connection tied him to the unknown stranger.

Shrugging, Seamus renewed his pacing, brooding on a tactic for their upcoming battle, now at ease with his discoveries.

&&&

Freya was fuming, and definitely not in a good way. For the past few hours now, she'd been ruminating black thoughts – afraid for Seamus, for Sam – all the while blaming the former for having split them.

"I mean, what's his bloody problem?"

She, too, had noticed someone trailing them. And between her gloomy dreams, and her own paranoia, she couldn't figure out if it was a good or bad presence.

Wish they'd get it over with and show themselves!

"As if we don't have enough problems," Freya continued aloud, the sound of her own voice calming in the creepy silence, "Seamus has to go and ensure we're powerless. Like he didn't grasp we were in greater danger once alone. Seriously, I don't *get it.*"

She fiercely kicked a rock that was in her way, sending it landing in the water below her with a splash. "I mean, why, all of a sudd–"

No sooner had it vanished, that Freya stopped walking immediately. *What was that? It can't have been the splash... There, I heard it again.*

Though faint, another's footsteps were clearly trailing her, and she was sure they didn't belong to an animal. The persistent itch she couldn't scratch was even more present, and the paranoia was more real than anything.

I don't like this one bit.

&&&

O'Keeffe was positive he wasn't the one being followed, since he hadn't felt a shadow for over two hours. Despite this, there was a persistent nagging at the back of his mind that his original idea was not as brilliant as he'd first thought.

He'd caught the first trickles of this the day before, on the hills of Dinas Emrys as they left. A fog of darkness had been nipping on the previously peaceful hill, but he'd put it up to his imagination and the somber night. Now, he suspected the same forces might be closer than he'd first believed.

Brow furrowed in concentration, he started retracing his steps to the meeting place.

&&&

Sam was dragging his feet towards a giant overloaded dustbin where he'd picked up a noise. He went around it cautiously, muttering to himself about stinking garbage, and –

"What the *hell*, professor!" His shout had a few rats scurry away and Sam scowled, more ashamed of his reaction than anything else. "I mean, do you *want* to give me a heart attack?"

O'Keeffe rolled his eyes. "I am sorry to point this out to you, Sam, but first of all, you have no a heart, so you cannot die. Second, at your age, it would be an unlikely occurrence. And third, you are a ghost, so a stroke would not change much, correct"

"Whoa, no need to be so harsh," Sam muttered in a slightly hurt tone.

"My apologies..." Seamus sighed and ran a hand over his face tiredly. "I've just about had it with this day. All I've located are some maps and a lost cat!" As the boy opened his mouth to interrupt, Seamus nearly growled. "No, I did *not* bring it with me! Besides, I think someone may be lurking on our heels." He muttered the latter part almost to himself, but Sam's eyes widened.

"What? I mean, who...and why?"

"Do you really believe I know who it is? No," Seamus added, lifting a palm up to stop him, as the blonde boy was about to add something, "before you mention anything silly, *no,* I am unaware of who this person is or what its purposes are. Now, did you feel you were being trailed?"

"No, sir."

"Did you hear any odd footsteps?"

"No."

"Anything suspicious to report?"

"No."

"*Nothing* out of the ordinary during your investigation?"

"No, professor."

Seamus groaned, then ruffled his hair in annoyance. "Well, did you at least *find* anything?"

"No, sorry."

O'Keeffe fell quiet, lost in his reflections. After a while, he confessed, "To be honest, I hardly imagined the Vikings would have left anything for us. It would have been incredibly stupid, even from them. However, this will complicate our task."

Silence.

"Wait, I don't understand something." When O'Keeffe gestured for him to continue, Sam went on, "If you knew we were being followed, why separate the group? I mean, whoever this is, they may harm us. Why risk it?"

"My dear boy, I was unsure myself at the beginning – merely an intuition. Then, when I felt his presence, I wanted to discern if he was a spy, if he was going after the whole group, or if he was following one person in particular. So I divided us, believing he would pursue the one he wants. I acted on instinct – something you should understand – and it worked."

"Then, if he wasn't after you or me, he must be following Freya." Sam panicked at his own conclusion. "Professor, we have to go to her!"

O'Keeffe gripped his arm, taking Sam by surprise – he always forgot that whenever in the vicinity of the two Sages, he regained corporal form. "No, we will not go find Freya. We will wait for her at the meeting place in," he peeked at his watch, "half an hour."

"Why?" The boy's eyes flashed angrily. "We can't let her fight this alone! The more reason because this being you speak of is a guy, if your words are any proof." Sam was fuming by the time he was done, trying to pull out of Seamus' grip. *Why doesn't he understand?*

"Oh, yes we can and we will." O'Keeffe's tone left no room for challenges, frustrated as he was. *Does this boy ever listen or understand what I'm attempting to communicate? I'm not speaking an alien language, not that I am conscious of.* "One, because Freya is perfectly capable of taking care of herself; and two, because she will not be pitted against anyone, and so she is not in any type of danger."

"How can you be so relaxed? And, if she's not in danger, why can't we go to her?"

"Because I only caught good intentions from this person. Arrogant, perhaps, but deep down, there is no harm intended. As for your second query, do you not think Freya would find it odd if we show up at her side, when we should be investigating?"

"Maybe," Sam mumbled hesitantly.

"Good, then it is settled. Now," Seamus grew serious, "you will not share any of this with Freya, understood?"

"Yes, professor," Sam agreed, not even bothering to understand why Seamus was requesting he keep a matter of such importance secret. Sometimes, the mind of the old man was a dangerous place to try to figure out.

"Good," O'Keeffe said, satisfied. "Now, do you have any other questions, or can we go head the meeting place? We are running out of time."

"Actually, I do have one last –"

"Yes?" Seamus intervened impatiently.

"What about the lost cat?"

O'Keeffe exhaled dejectedly, trying to calm his nerves ready to explode. The ghost, however helpful, tended to be incredibly annoying at times.

&&&

Freya had been walking in circles for hours, trying to investigate the tiniest trickle of information. She knew the presence was at her heels, but was not about to invite it to the party. If it decided to show itself, fine. If not, the better for Freya, since she had less issues to look forward to.

Although, I do need some exercise... She pondered the matter, smirking to herself. *And it's been a while since I've been able to practice some fighting moves.*

With a shrug, the teenager decided to simply close her mind in order to ensure the stalker, if it had any special abilities – one could never be too safe in the current times – would be unable to read her thoughts and figure out she knew it existed.

&&&

Far in the background, hidden behind a corner, the demon narrowed his eyes when the Sage's mind became inaccessible to him.

So, she is well versed in playing... Interesting.

He lifted a palm and, with it, the mangled piece of paper he'd picked up from the ground. It was blank, but not for long. He passed his other closed fist over it, and an ashy smoke enveloped it, before writing appeared.

Satisfied with his work, the demon let it drop. The piece of paper was carried by the wind, aided by his wicked influence, and floated until it was near the Sage.

Not much would be accomplished by what he had done. He was definitely not a step closer to getting the relics, but at least he would determine how powerful this little human was.

The demon was about to leave, when he picked up another's scent. He sniffed the air, and the narrowing of his eyes became more pronounced. *Another one...? Impossible!* He wanted to get closer, inspect it more, but his time was running out. With a last annoyed glance around, he dematerialized.

&&&

Freya glanced at her phone again, rolling her eyes as she noticed it was time to head back to the meeting place. Her foot stepped on something and at the crunching sound, she froze.

A piece of crumpled paper was under her shoe, half of it fluttering in the wind. Freya picked it up, and her heart sunk.

On it, in cursive writing, was a message not open to interpretation.

"COME AT MIDNIGHT, ALONE, ON THE LONGSHIP AT THE END OF THE HABOR. THE TRUTH WILL BE REVEALED ONLY TO YOU. SHOULD YOU MISS THE MEETING, YOUR QUESTIONS ABOUT YOUR PARENTS WILL BE LEFT UNANSWERED FOREVER."

Freya read it twice, her jaw clenching. *All you tried to protect me from, Seamus, is coming right to me, whether you want it to or not.*

The young Sage didn't need more than the mention of *questions about your parents* to decide. She also knew sharing the information with O'Keeffe was out of the question. *What he doesn't know can't hurt him.*

She folded the piece of paper and placed it in her jeans' pocket, certain of her decision. Not once did she question how someone would have recognized her, or where she was from. All that mattered was she finally had a clue to her past.

As Freya watched the sun's reflection in the water, something smooth caressed her left leg. More than surprised by the contact, she jumped and peered down. Her features instantly softened noticing the tiny fur ball at her feet.

The kitten was the size of her palm, with beautiful white fur and large, green eyes. Freya bent over to pet it, kneeling by its side once the little animal kept rubbing on her leg for more attention. Enjoying the luxuriating feel of its fur, she stayed like that for a few moments, before using her faculties to figure out it was, in fact, a female.

"Are you lost?" She scratched under kitten's chin, laughing softly at the purring emerging from her throat. The small beast had a purr loud enough to wake the dead.

Shaking her head, Freya knew she was lost. "Guess what, little one? You're coming home with me tonight." She picked the cat in her arms, rubbing her nose in its fur. "You're so adorably soft... But what should I call you? Well, you're white, which in the Antiquity symbolized purity, and you showed up of nowhere, so I'll call you...Artemis. Yes, Artemis."

The kitten purred again, emerald eyes shining, and Freya grinned. She noticed the time and hurried towards the meeting place, no longer caring about the presence. In fact, she'd forgotten all about it.

&&&

Seamus and Sam were waiting for Freya, their anxiety growing by the second. When she emerged around a corner, running towards them, relief dawned on them.

"Finally! You gave us one of those frights, Freya!" O'Keeffe admonished half-heartedly, too relieved she was safe to really mean it. "Have you found anything?"

"No, nothing."

"Well, as I mentioned to Sam, I wasn't expect–" Seamus stopped and his mouthed opened in disbelief at the little head emerging from Freya's arms. "*What* is that?" He pointed an accusatory index to the little fur ball.

"That, sir," Sam spoke for the first time since Freya had arrived, "is a cat. They're mammals, popular pets for humans, and–"

"I know very well what a cat is, young man," Seamus glowered at him, before spinning to Freya. "What I cannot wrap my head around is what *you* are doing with the same cat I ran into and ignored this morning?"

Freya and Sam gaped at him, then the latter erupted in laughter.

"You have to admit, the irony is hilarious!" The boy chuckled one last time, then sobered up at Seamus' persisting glower.

"Never you mind!" O'Keeffe shook his head, muttering under his breath. "On second thought, let us not bother with explanations."

At Freya's pleading manner and Sam's amused expression, he groaned, "I give up. You can keep it, as long as it doesn't get in my way."

With a small cry of joy, Freya jumped in his arms and kissed him on the cheek, squeezing the cat between them. She pulled back as the little animal hissed, and proudly announced, "Sam, Seamus, I'd like you to meet Artemis."

The elderly man rolled his eyes. "Let us return to the hotel before you decide to adopt all the stray cats hidden here. We have a battle coming, and a plan would not be amiss."

With one last glimpse at the fur ball, he shook his head and stalked off. *Cute it may be, but an annoying pain in my behind it will become!*

&&&

Freya was in a dark place. On each side, as far as the eye could observe, large statues rose like looming soldiers. Each one was three times the size of a human being, made of gold or silver and adorned with ritualistic jewelry. They reminded her of the statues in the temples of Ancient Egypt, and yet... Something was different.

As the Sage peered closer, she noticed each statue had the features of someone she knew, or had knowledge of. She passed in front of them, and they vanished one by one, replaced by nothingness.

Shivers crept up her spine, taking hold of her heart. Fear was not a sensation she was used to, as it rarely – if ever – touched her. In that moment, it leached on like a hungry vampire, enveloping her like a cloak, paralyzing her.

Keep going, a voice in her head begged, and so she did.

One last step, and Freya was released into a meadow, surrounded by a hill, and the chill of a wintry landscape. A white blanket of snow covered the ground. The sun was rising, and everything shone like diamonds.

She heard a crunch of snow, and glanced to her right, and the hill. Atop it, a tiger emerged into view. It was white with black stripes, and eyes the color of emeralds tainted with gold. The sun behind it made their interesting color stand out even more. A surge of admiration, of reverence, filled the Sage to the point she wanted to kneel down and worship it.

The animal sat down, as though waiting for someone, and watched her expectantly.

Freya hurried to climb the hill, plagued by a sense of familiarity. Within moments, she was at its level and met the feline's scrutiny. In its depths, she could read all the intelligence and love it had accumulated over the years.

The tiger spoke in a deep tone, its words echoing in her mind. *I have waited long for you, my daughter. Your powers weaken in the face of what awaits. To succeed, you need to decipher the book, or you risk losing not only the battle, but your friends.*

Freya frowned at the words, and a new kind of shiver ran down her spine. "Where am I? And how come you're here?"

You are sleeping. My presence in your dreams is because you have called for me.

"No, I didn't. I would remember if I had," Freya said, frowning in confusion despite her words.

The feline unveiled its fangs, and she had the weird hunch it was smiling.

It began to fade away, but she could capture its words as loud and clear as if it had been sitting near her. *Your mother would want you to open it, to be strong. Thwart your demons, daughter, and* open *the book.*

"Wait! Who are you?" Freya demanded, desperately scanning her surroundings, even though the animal itself had dematerialized.

I am all and nothing, the answer echoed. *I am power and weakness. I am Tyr.*

&&&

Freya woke up with a start, her pulse racing like she'd run a marathon.

She got out of bed and ran to the dresser, pulling open the drawer and uncovering the burgundy book from the pile of clothes. As she touched it, a faint zap hit her fingertips, and she withdrew her hand.

The young Sage rocked back and forth near it, tears streaming down her cheeks. "I can't open it, Mom, I can't! Not yet!"

&&&

The tiger, Tyr, materialized in front of the gods.

Isis stepped out of her husband's embrace, getting closer. "You chanced much, meeting the Sage in her dreams, Tyr."

The entity bowed in acknowledgment. *Thank you for allowing me this.*

"I can allow you more," Osiris admitted. "You can trespass into the realm of the living, but at a high price to your soul, each time. Keep that in mind."

It would not be the first time I choose to accept your offer, Osiris, risks and all. The feline inclined its large head at the ominous words, then stepped away.

"Why did you not tell her the truth?" Isis challenged.

The feline twisted its head to the side and sighed aloud. *Seamus has not divulged anything to Freya, and I cannot make things harder for him. After all, he is right – her parents are well and truly gone. In a way, the less she discovers about them, and their end, the better.*

Isis watched Tyr walk away, then turned to Osiris, burying her face in his chest. He tightened his arms around her, attempting to reassure with his embrace.

"I cannot help but suspect we are playing with something we cannot catch," Isis murmured.

"But we will," he assured her firmly. "The demon covets both relics. We *will* catch him, and send him to the depths of hell and beyond."

The promise in his words was enough to settle her...for the time being.

Chapter 5

The air was cool, and the breeze coming from the sea refreshed Freya's soft features. She was in the harbor, almost near the long ship, and it was close to midnight. Inspecting it now, she began to doubt her abilities, and wished she was back at the hotel, in her cozy bed, sleeping.

Half an hour earlier, a hungry Artemis had awoken her. Morose because of her recent dream – *But was it really a dream?*– Freya had felt hopeless. But then, remembering the note, her zeal returned with a vengeance.

If there was one chance, even one so slim, to find out more about her parents, she'd seize it, no matter how high the danger. Uncaring of the risks, she decided to take her chances and discover for herself what she was willing to lose for the truth.

After feeding Artemis, Freya pulled on a pair of black sweatpants, a hoodie and combat boots, as the outfit would support her efforts to blend in. She tied her hair in a ponytail and, leaving a bewildered Artemis behind, took off at a jogging pace.

Freya arrived to the pier in little time, since it was running distance from her B&B – at least for a Sage. She hadn't meant to tire Seamus earlier by suggesting it, but at night, there was no point in raising hell with the sound of a car engine.

Shivers of anticipation ran down her spine when she stepped past the modern boats, in the eerie quietude, and entered the more abandoned side of the port.

As she watched the boats and ships surrounding her, Freya wondered if the whole idea had merit, or if it'd been a mistake. A twig snapped nearby, pulling her out of her thoughts. It was followed by a ragged breath, then a silence that was more worrisome than reassuring.

Freya froze, anticipating the blow to come, preparing herself to take a stand. But as quickly as it appeared, the noise evaporated.

After waiting for a few more moments, Freya was pulled from her trance by the waves brushing the ships. Seeing the water so peaceful and calm, she wondered if the sound had been simply a trick of her imagination. *I definitely need to get more sleep. I can't fight an army of Vikings half-asleep* and *by myself...*

&&&

The demon was hiding in the shadows, sneering to himself. *So she took the bait, and showed up!*

He observed the teenager for a few moments, tasting her fear and hesitation in each step. It would be so easy to snuff her life out, but he had other plans. *If only I had perceived it would be this easy...*

He sent a gust of wind filled with intent towards the long ship, where the Vikings were busy hiding and plotting out of sight. He had no interest in their puny intrigues. But he did have interest to get them to notice the Sage, and *soon.*

&&&

For the umpteenth time, a nagging feeling warned Freya it was time to get out of the port. She glanced around again, now by the longboat, and couldn't detect anything out of the ordinary.

She's been pacing about the area for the last ten minutes, and it was well past midnight. No one had showed up, and the entire area appeared deserted.

With a dejected sigh, Freya had to admit the truth. *This meeting was a hoax.* She started walking away from the longboat, when a raspy tone stopped her dead in her tracks.

"Leaving already?"

The question was followed by several barking laughs, coming from all corners. The Sage extended her senses, scanning the area, and could have smacked herself for letting her guard down. *Great, now I've done it!* In the time she'd been pacing, ghosts had managed to surround her.

Freya was preparing to run, but even as the idea formed in her head, shadows emerged from the secluded corners – *glowing* shadows. And they were covering all the ground between her and the rest of the port. Unless she wanted to swim, she was stuck.

Get out of there! The warning came in her mind, echoing like in the dream. Freya froze, stunned – and half-afraid she was losing it. *There are too many of them, and more are coming!* Its tone was more intense than before.

More of them? You've got to be kidding me! Freya spun in a circle, taking them all in, then groaned in dismay. *Guess there's only one way to solve this. I just hope it won't last too long, Artemis must be hungry.*

A groan echoed in her mind, but Freya chalked it up to her imagination. Resolutely, she turned to take a stand against the hidden stalker – the one who'd spoken first. "Now why would I be leaving? This looks like a great party and personally, I've always been a bit nocturnal."

Another laugh, this one coming from her right.

Freya freed her mind, encompassing the five-mile radius to figure out what kind of an army she was up against, and barely stifled her shock. *Well, I guess I can bid adieu to my night of regenerating sleep. With twenty ghosts to fight my way through, I won't be getting back to my room before dawn. If I ever get back to the hotel in one piece, that is.*

Then, an idea popped in her mind, and a smile spread on Freya's features. It was something Seamus had once told her about facing large groups of foes – *You can use their strength against them, because you're smaller, quicker and more flexible. Be like water, and you can win.* She inhaled deeply, and waited for them to strike.

A huge man with a long beard advanced, an axe in his closed fist. Freya bent at the knees for balance, feet spread for support, ready to take him on. Then, with a cry, the man jumped on her. She stepped to the side, her lithe form slipping easily out of his grasp, and he landed on the ground.

When he stood up, sputtering and fumbling in anger, Freya took advantage of her aura giving him corporeal form, and sent her knee straight into his lower region. She then rotated, adding a kick to the stomach, watching in satisfaction as he fell. The burly man lay unconscious – hopefully for a long time.

She stood up from her battle stance, and challenged the ringleader that remained hidden. "I thought you were going to tell me about my parents."

There was a pause – an informative one. It was long enough for Freya to realize how naïve she'd been.

"I am," the leader tried to recover. "Only, it will have to wait until after you've defeated my men. See this as a reward for your hard work."

Great, just great, Freya thought. *Of all the ghosts in the universe, I had to fall on a stupid one.*

She had no time to reply out loud, as another specter replaced her previous attacker, this one better balanced. He charged, his head bent, before Freya had time to get out of the way. The impact of the head with her stomach caused her to stumble backwards, and she lost her balance. As she hit the ground, making contact with the back of her head on the cement, she could've sworn stars floated above.

Freya shook off the daze and jumped back on the balls of her feet. *If I ever meet that dragon in person, I'll have to thank him for the physical endurance he gifted my kind.*

Her extra abilities enabled her to continue fighting, but there would be only so many times she'd be able to get up again. She hadn't yet mastered the skills of a full Sage, which meant she had no backup for herself.

Ignoring the dizziness trying to overcome her, Freya punched the ghost in the nose, then under the jaw, making him lose his balance. With a last punch to the stomach, he fell on the ground and stayed there.

Freya was about to pause for a breath, but another opponent approached. If these had been normal boys, a brawl with them would not have broken a sweat. But each ghost was larger and burlier than the last, their Viking bodies annoyingly strong. Twice the strength was required to face them, and it was depleting her resources.

The hit on Freya's head oozed blood, and it trickled on the side of her temple. Out of the corner of her eye, she saw the rest of the Vikings hold back, but ready to jump in at a moment's notice.

As thought upon thought crossed Freya's mind, the ghost kept advancing, now only a few feet away. He was taking his time, noticing she was immobile, shoulders slumped.

The stupid hit to the head, I should've known better....

I won't be able to make it, nor see Seamus or Sam ever again...

The man stepped closer, then closer, and closer...

Freya bowed her head, clenching her fists and trying to draw on reserves of power.

You cannot give in!

As she remained frozen, the same voice murmured, but it didn't sound as if it was in her head, more like in her ear. There was an oddly vibrating quality to each word. "Whatever strength you require, may you obtain it from me. Whatever grace you need, find it in me."

Freya's body shuddered and a wave of intensity, of adrenaline, surged within her. The tired gleam in her eyes was replaced by a furious one, and her body regenerated strength, muscles no longer at the point of exhaustion.

The incoming Viking, however, lacked a keen sense of observation, and didn't notice the change, instead creeping closer. When he was about to punch her, Freya charged.

Her fist connected with his big, abnormal nose, infused with newfound strength. One blow was enough to crack the bone, to her utter shock. The Viking's eyes widened in surprise, and their gazes collided for a brief second. No longer soft, Freya's glare was piercing, her jaw clenched in determination.

He had no time to defend himself. Freya's knee next connected with his ribs, and another crack echoed. The ghost stumbled back, clutching his chest. With another perfectly placed punch under the chin, he flew backwards and landed in the mud.

"Never send a man to do a woman's job," Freya said, smirking. "I understand why now. If all of you brutes fight like him, then you have no chance to win against me."

"Get her, *now*!" The leader ordered, anger clearly evident in his tone.

All the phantoms hidden bounced forward, ready to confront Freya. However, as the first one came close, a ball of white fur leaped in front of it and he was greeted with an incredible sigh – a tiger.

The feline was not recently escaped from a zoo, as the hum of power, the odd glow surrounding it, indicated an aura of the spiritual world. It had black stripes over thick, white fur, and stood protectively in front of the girl.

Freya, sensing something, had leapt back, and was clear of the animal's path. It was only after her action that she realized its position – instead of facing her as if to battle, the tiger was defying the pack of ghosts. It was only a few moments later that it communicated mentally to her.

You should not have come here.

Freya hesitated, torn between gaping in utter shock, to re-plying, and finally went with her instincts. Mentally, she con-veyed her own message, *I get it, but the need to know about my parents was too great. And I don't care about the risks.*

You should.

With that, the animal roared, and all the ghosts stepped backwards. When it roared a second time, they seemed to de-cide fighting another being like them would be useless, and re-treated. Only the leader's voice remained.

"Well, well, so you've got yourself an ally. A powerful one, at that." When Freya was silent, he went on, "It really is too bad you couldn't experience my men's great skills of battle–"

He was cut off by the fuming Sage, who stepped past the tiger. "I've really had it with you! First you drag me here on false grounds, then I get attacked – not that I didn't see that coming, but *come on*!" She scowled at the darkness. "If you judge your men's skills of battle so great, then come fight me yourself, and let us end this once and for all."

Freya's eyes flashed dangerously in the night, burning through the darkness with their piercing glare. A moment later, she sensed the last of the presence vanishing with no trace.

"What a coward," Freya scoffed, then turned towards her savior. "I guess my dream was no dream, after all. Tyr, is it?"

The tiger only stared back, as though waiting for more.

"Any idea who was behind this?"

No, but what I did gather is it wanted you! And you came here, all alone, walking straight into his trap!

Tyr's green eyes blazed, the gold specks within them shin-ing molten anger, and Freya realized it was furious. She tried to defend her actions with all the dignity she could master when she had blood all over, her clothes were full of mud and she was extremely exhausted – but no sound left her mouth.

The tiger's glare softened when it noticed the weariness in Freya's expression.

Come on my back, and I will bring you back to your room.

"I can try to walk..." Freya's whisper was only half-intended, and quickly rejected by Tyr's dark look.

Not an option.

Freya pursed her lips, but agreed nonetheless, conscious that Tyr was right. Whoever the entity was, it had saved her butt, and that deserved a measure of trust.

Without further argument, she climbed onto the animal's back, surprised to notice it could hold her weight with no effort. Lacking anything better, she wrapped her arms around its large neck, digging in, and closed her eyes.

When there was no movement, she opened them. They were passing through the streets at top speed, buildings flashing by, but with no sound to speak of. Before she knew it, they had arrived at the B&B, and all Freya could remember from the trip was the sensation of freedom and the wind slapping her awake.

She thanked Tyr, then shifted from foot to foot restlessly. "I..."

We will speak, but later, child. Get some rest first.

With one last look, Freya nodded then ran inside and took a hot shower, wincing as it hit her bruised body. Afterwards, she bandaged her cuts and went to bed, falling into a dreamless sleep as soon as her head touched the pillow.

&&&

Outside the B&B, Tyr waited to ensure its protégée was asleep. Once it was sure of the fact, the tiger took its previous shape, and trotted inside the B&B.

Chapter 6

The demon waited until the Sage and her protector were gone, before dematerializing as well.

Useless ghosts! he cursed angrily. The wraith wanted to remain behind, to act out *his* brand of fighting, but the pull was too strong.

He was only allowed a few moments to stay into the world of the living from the Underworld. Anything more, and he would be stuck within. Still, it had been enough.

Clenching his teeth, he reflected that the few moments alone had served their purpose – he knew who was assisting the Sage.

&&&

Not too far away, in the harbor Freya had left, the ghosts had re-materialized. They were sitting in a circle, waiting for their leader to come back.

After Freya's departure, the leader had reappeared, and summoned them. He wanted the girl because of her powers, and they were instructed to figure out another way of capturing her – alive.

Yet as they debated, the ringleader had other things on his mind. He was now on the long ship, in a fierce meeting with his own boss, Cadmael. All the specters could see were their glowing figures atop the boat, and so they waited...assuming the meeting was going fine.

However, things were far from *fine* between the two head Vikings.

The leader who had remained invisible during Freya's altercation was standing up, head bowed. He was about five foot ten, with long, brown – almost reddish – hair, braided in two loose braids, and a huge beard, of the same color. His eyes were of a hideous orange-green color, the kind no one could stare into for a long time.

His features were scarred like someone had taken a knife to his face, and one could barely imagine what he had been like in his youth. The hideous expression, completed by a huge crooked nose had gained him the name Asger.

For now, however, it was him who was afraid, his shifty eyes glued to the second person atop the long ship. Cadmael was the opposite of Asger. He was taller, over six feet, with fair, blonde hair, and a beard half the size of his partner. His nose was rather preeminent, in a lined expression, with a built body. Rumor had it he possessed all the qualities of a leader – except mercy.

It had not been his size or booming tone which made him the ruler of the Viking army, the one feared by all. It had not even been his leadership skills.

No, it was his eyes. The man had eyes of iron – the cold and burning kind. His stare was piercing, and the Vikings serving under him whispered that he could read minds, both mortal and immortal, with a single glance. It was thus he knew how to sort out the liars from the group.

True or not, the rumor was widespread enough that a certain myth had formed around the Viking, and most of his acolytes were too afraid to challenge him.

No one knew exactly how Cadmael had returned, for he'd been gone for nearly eleven centuries. Neither did they discover how or why he'd disappeared. Legend had it that, after trying – for his attempt was unsuccessful – to steal a boat with merchandise from the East, he'd vanished into thin air, never to be seen again by mortals.

Cadmael had re-emerged only a few months earlier, and had claimed the universe was not to be ruled by mere mortals with new technology, but by them – ghosts. As proof, he'd shown his army an axe, and his new and improved speaking skills.

"In the past," the chief had said, "we spoke not this way, but in our own dialect. To own this world, we have to speak its new language. We will not be labeled as barbarians any longer!"

He acknowledged having been gone for so long because he'd had to sacrifice his life in order to gain faculties which would permit them to win. And he had foreseen the future. A future in which they would be the rulers of a great nation. Among other things, Cadmael had also promised the return of ancient Viking ways.

The phantoms, only too happy of having their leader back, merrily obliged – even to the point of mimicking modern language, with some help from their chief's new spiritual assistance.

In the months that followed, Cadmael had kept busy plotting the war that was to take place in less than a week. Now, learning about the girl and her abilities, he was unhappy – he didn't like surprises. He'd heard talk of beings that could hurt them, but he wouldn't have deliberately provoked one.

Ignoring Asger's pitiful form, he walked a few paces away, and used his hard-earned powers. His eyes glazed, then became fully white, as he sought the future. The trance lasted only moments, before his piercing gaze was back – along with a terrible scowl.

Cadmael had foreseen the girl and her companions fighting him. No matter his efforts, these humans wouldn't join him. He looked at the ghosts below and, without bothering to consult with Asger, headed towards them.

"Hear me as I say this, for I have looked into the future," he said, his deep, cavernous voice echoing for all to hear clearly. "They will not join us, these new foes you have met. The mortals, as well as the ghost. They have to be eliminated."

"But, Cadmael, the boy...We cannot kill him..."

The ghost shut up as the chieftain moved his icy scrutiny to him. When he stepped closer, the spirit started trembling. "Please..."

His plea came too late. Cadmael raised his axe, and struck him. The acolyte froze, before dismantling in little pieces, like a mirror being shattered. By the time the leader tucked the axe in the wide belt at his waist again, nothing remained of the phantom.

He enjoyed the silence, the fear across his men's expressions for a few moments. When he spoke again, his tone was the iciest of winds. "I have the ability to send you all back to the beyond, do *not* dare challenge me!"

The men cowered away, trying to keep space between them and their leader.

"I do not recognize who these people truly are, but tonight was a chance to rid us of a problem. And you failed. You *all* failed. But more importantly..." He spun to Asger, who'd followed him. "All you had to do was exhaust the girl, then send a pack of your men to finish her off."

Cadmael's expression was cold, devoid of any emotion – lethal. "Fool! *You* failed me, most of all! She should have been dead in less than twenty minutes. No one can last that long against us, especially not a mere mortal foolish girl."

"Y-yes b-but–" Asger stuttered. "S-she had assistance. A tiger. It scared the men and–"

"A *tiger*?" Cadmael clenched his fist, resting it on the handle of his axe. His eyes burned – of a killing fire. "Are you *mad*!?"

Asger whimpered pitifully at Cadmael's angry tone. The chieftain saw how he avoided his gaze, fearful of the punishment. But his words had set him on a rant, and it was time to teach his henchman who led the operation.

"We are immortal! We *cannot* die! Not unless *I* kill you! Do you understand what this means, you pitiful sight of a scumbag? No creature whatsoever can hurt us, let alone kill us!"

Asger held up his palms, mumbling under his breath about the tiger's roar, and the power he'd seen in the girl's eyes. "It was frightening, so piercing and intense it almost reminded me of–" Asger stopped abruptly, cutting himself off as if he'd been about to say something worse.

Cadmael narrowed his eyes on the ghost, then glanced at the rest of his army. *It would not do me any good to kill this fool. But it does not mean I cannot have my fun.*

When Cadmael spoke, he did so calmly – almost *too* calmly. "Of...? It reminded you of *what*?" Asger trembled, biting his lips to avoid further words from tumbling out, and Cadmael lost his patience. "Spit it out, if you wish to live! Who did she remind you of?"

"Well, she kind of reminded me of –well– you," Asger finished lamely, then shut up and cowered further away, seemingly waiting for his death sentence.

No one dared talk about Cadmael, least of all himself. But that didn't mean he hadn't heard the rumors, the whispers about the camp. The ghosts gossiped about his abnormal attributes, so well-depicted within that stare, and how he could destroy them in the split of a second. They raved how there was no one stronger than him in the entire world – ghosts and human alike.

Rather than be furious at Asger's comparison, which clearly indicated there was someone else out there as powerful as him – *a girl!* – Cadmael remained remarkably calm. He turned his back on Asger and began pacing.

Idiot, stupid, useless, irresponsible, big-mouthed, nothing! Why did I ever trust him with this mission? It is of no use! The scheme is ruined, and the girl has escaped. I shall have to come up with a way to get her and her pesky friends out of the way before I make my next move.

"You have disappointed me, Asger," he announced out loud and stopped pacing.

&&&

The henchman had been brooding over what Cadmael would do to him if he learned of the failure. He was expecting a major outburst, and then dissipating into nothingness. Or some other way of torture the chieftain would devise.

After all, it was said Cadmael had a lot of imagination when torture was involved. Asger had been expecting anything, except the heavy silence that followed his stupid, *stupid* words.

The *unknowing-what-is-going-to-happen* silence.

The *I'm-deciding-your-sentence* silence.

The *you'll-be-dead-(again)-by sunset* silence.

The silence was only making it worse, keeping him hanging, unsure of what would happen next. It was frightening, a new torture in itself.

Asger was lost in his thoughts when the chief spoke. It was so sudden he started – brutally. And the calm tone Cadmael was using didn't predict anything good. So, he waited. He could do nothing but wait and hope for mercy – though it was highly unlikely, considering his leader's merciless side.

"You have disappointed me *very* much," Cadmael continued in the same soft-spoken and indifferent voice that would've sent shivers down Asger's spine, if he'd been alive. "You had one task – to protect our interests and eliminate any possible threat. And you were incapable of achieving that."

"I–" Asger tried, but then gave up. He knew what was coming – his punishment. And an unpleasant one, for all intents and purposes.

"The girl was ready to be eliminated. She was practically crying for you to do so. And what do you do? Do you go and catch her? No, you had to *toy* with her. You simply had to go and show her how great you are!"

Asger cringed. As the leader's tone rose in sound, their remaining companions observed the two silently. No one would protect him, it was obvious.

"And what happens? She escapes! Under your very nose, by the way. And with an animal, a *pet*, nonetheless." Cadmael stopped for better effect, then shook his head. "So easy to do, and you ruined it."

"I'm sorry," Asger whispered.

"Unfortunately for you, an apology is useless to me," Cadmael said in an icy tone. At the words, he took out his axe, and let his finger follow the blade.

Asger paled visibly, even for a ghost, as he remembered the comrade Cadmael had sent to the grave with only a touch of the axe. *So this is the end.*

Cadmael advanced threateningly towards the glowing shape. Asger didn't back away, nor did he try to run. *I may have screwed this up, but I'm no coward. At least not a visible one.* Just as he could imagine the iron making contact with his ghostly shape, Cadmael hissed distinctly in his ear.

"You have one last chance. Go get the girl, and I will allow no mistakes this time."

Then he stepped back.

Asger glanced up fearfully. "W-why?"

Cadmael narrowed his eyes, then lost his patience and angrily yelled, "Do not *dare* challenge my decision! I have spared your poor miserable life, you rat, because I may require your assistance. Do not fail me, or you will regret the day you were born. Forget not – I grasp the power to kill spirits *and* torture them."

Asger gulped, stepping away. Just as he was about to leave, he thought of one pertinent thing to ask. "Alive?"

Cadmael seemed to consider this. He fell silent for so long, Asger reckoned he'd entered in a trance – or something.

&&&

Little did he know, Cadmael was reflecting hard on this particular decision.

The fool! He does not grasp what he talks about! How could her gaze resemble mine? It would be utterly impossible, for it would mean she can wield the same abilities I can. And yet, what am I going to do about it? Kill her, or have her brought here alive so I can decide for myself?

He hesitated, even as the obvious choice was evident. *Alive, I could try and use her. After all, teenagers are always changing sides. Dead, she would no longer bother me, and we could go on with the plan...*

Cadmael sensed Asger sigh, and spoke his decision before the fool could say anything else. Moments later, he watched as the henchman departed his sight.

"Perhapssss we could chat," someone said from behind.

Cadmael froze, eyes widening as he sized up the indistinct shadow.

"About the Sage."

There was a pause as the Viking leader registered his opponent's dark skin, the blacker than night eyes with red specks, the overall aura surrounding him. *How interesting... A demon, in my own backyard? This, I have to hear.*

"I am listening."

Chapter 7

Freya was sleeping, when she felt a presence in the hotel room. She opened her eyes, now face to face with –

"Tyr." Her heart thudded in her chest, and a slow smile spread on her face. Waking up to a tiger bathed in moonlight and leaning over her bed should have scared Freya into the next decade. Instead, a quiet sense of happiness filled her, at being in its presence.

She kept her voice at whisper-level, in fear Seamus would get wind of their conversation in the quietness of the B&B. Her mentor had always been a light sleeper, and she didn't want him asking questions, mainly because she wished to keep Tyr to herself – at least for a while.

Luckily, the tiger appeared to get her train of thought, and didn't ponder the Sage's unspoken wish. Instead, it delved straight into the previous night's disaster. *It was foolish of you to go there alone, especially when it was so late and you had no protection.*

Guilt overcame Freya's original delight of seeing Tyr. "I'm sorry."

You could have been hurt, or worse, be dead by now if I had not been connected to you.

Freya blinked. Once. Twice. "Come again?"

Tyr let out a noise half-way between a groan and sigh, before explaining, *We are connected spiritually, my being to yours. I can sense your emotions, and watch through your eyes if you concentrate. If the emotion running you – anger, fear, love – surpasses normal boundaries, then it may influence me, but the connection only works one way.*

The tiger paused, as if debating on revealing more, then said, *You can speak to me telepathically at any time, try to send me an image of the place where you are, or grant me some of your vital energy if I myself have a lack of it.*

"So... You're my guardian angel of sorts?"

If it is easier for you to think of it that way, then yes. There was a glimmer of amusement in its two-tone cultured eyes.

Freya pondered this new information, recalling the voice she kept hearing in her head, the sensation of being watched, protected at times. It was not something she was about to contest. Then the last thing the entity said caused her to frown.

"Why would you lack energy?"

Tyr threw her a long look. *I am not a part of the realm of the living, but rather of the spiritual. The come-and-goes between the two dimensions demand a certain amount of vitality. That is why I have to return, to regenerate. It is easier and less draining for me to show up in your dreams, and share what I need to. But if, as today, my physical form is required, then I have to come.*

Freya remained silent as she let the entirety of the explanation sink in. So she had a guardian angel that could talk to her and care for her, but if somehow it needed strength, then she had to provide it. However, in doing so, her faculties would be weakened for the moment.

Another thing, Freya.

Her attention focused on the tiger.

If you are to be hurt, it will not have a permanent effect on me, since I live in a different realm. However, if I am the one who should be hurt whilst on Earth, you will sense a loss, a weakness second to none. If you are not sufficiently strong, it may completely drain your powers – and your life.

Freya's heart sank to the bottom of her stomach. Of all the fears in existence, that was one thing she dreaded – having her abilities taken away. Especially since she'd made the decision to become a fully-trained Sage, and dedicate her entire life to saving the world. But what good could she do, if she ended up like Seamus, without her powers? She wouldn't be able take action to the extent she did now.

And yet, as she glanced at Tyr, Freya couldn't make herself reject the offered friendship. The previous night alone, she'd felt a growth in her abilities. And then there was the book, and all the potential it brought. A faint hum vibrated in her stomach, a reinforcement of sorts as though her source of strength was too close.

Freya tilted her head to the side, and smiled. "I'll risk it."

The tiger's jaws opened and ferocious teeth shone in the moonlight. *Very well.* Then its golden-green eyes grew serious. *That being said, what you did today was foolish of you. With me as your helper in this mission, I cannot stress this enough – reckless behavior is not to be tolerated.*

Freya inwardly groaned at Tyr's oncoming lecture.

"But–" she began, but was cut off.

No buts. Do you not care about the world? Do you not care about saving it? Or Seamus?

"I *do*, okay!" Freya furiously hissed back, her guilt replaced by a wave of anger. "And I said I was sorry, what more do you want?"

For you to stop acting so childish, and be more mature!

Even as the words were spoken, a pang of sympathy for Freya shot through the entity. She had been robbed, for lack of a better word, of her childhood and adolescence, as she would not experience what it was like to be carefree. A little attitude and irresponsible behavior was to be expected, after all. *And yet...*

"Well, I can't stop myself, okay? Whenever I have the slightest chance of discovering anything – even the tiniest thing– about my parents, I don't care about the risks!" Freya was struggling to hold back tears.

Tyr was sympathetic, laying its head on the bed. *Calm down, child. One day, you will discover everything.*

At the animal's words, Freya's eyes gleamed with hope, but the tiger looked away, shattering it.

For now, you will have to settle for what you do know – that your parents loved you and would have sacrificed their lives to save yours. This is why you have to be careful. Risk it all if you want to, but be certain you are ready to take responsibility for any-thing that may follow – and be able to survive it.

Freya inclined her head in understanding, her outburst gone, and blinked back her tears, inhaling deeply. "Tyr, I was won–" By the time she'd cleared her vision of the blurriness and remembered another question, she was alone in the room.

"Great," the teenager muttered aloud. "I had another chance to ask Tyr about the presence I keep feeling, and yet *again* forgot. Ugh."

As she leaned back on her pillows, eyes shut, the tiger's teasing echoed in her head.

You will find out, do not fret.

Not even five hours later, she was awoken by a frantic Sam.

"Freya? Come on, wake *up*!"

Groggily, the Sage sat up in bed, but immediately regretted it. Her back ached all over, with the beginnings of a headache stirring at her temples. The cut on her forehead was hidden by her locks of raven hair, but it throbbed. Her legs were painfully sore, and she had some difficulty to move her left arm.

With a stifled groan, Freya fell back on the pillows.

"Ouch!" The cry escaped before she could stop it, even as she bit down further cries of distress.

Hell, even my fingers ache. That was some brawl I put up with last night. Note to self: stay away from large, obnoxious Vikings.

"Are you all right?" Sam questioned, worry evident in his expression.

Freya turned her head sideways – at least *that* didn't hurt – and smiled. "Yeah, I'm slightly sore. Didn't sleep too well last night." As an afterthought, she added, "What are you doing here, anyway?"

Sam was scowling at her, evidently not fully believing her story, and shook his head as her question snapped him out of his musings. "Here? Oh, right! Seamus wanted me to tell you breakfast is served downstairs until ten o'clock. You should hurry if you want to eat something."

"Huh?" As she squinted at the alarm clock over the bedside table, Freya held back from swearing. It was nine thirty, and she could bet the elderly man was worried, and he had reason to.

She didn't oversleep, usually waking up at seven o'clock to go for a walk or quick jog, depending on the mood.

Not only would that be impossible today, but the thought alone was enough to cause her to cringe. With another stifled groan, Freya stood up once more, wincing at the soreness in her ribs, and biting down more cries of anguish.

She didn't notice Sam eyeing her carefully. Neither did she make out his gasp when he saw the huge, violet-colored bruise on her knee. When Freya tied her hair up to go shower, the cut on her forehead was revealed, and his jaw dropped.

"Freya..." Sam started in a forcefully even tone, as if struggling against panic, "what did you *do* last night?"

Avoiding his alarmed stare, she said, "Me? Nothing, of course." Freya tried her best innocent smile over a shoulder, then walked into the bathroom. "Shit!" Her reflection in the mirror explained why her friend looked so shocked – not to mention the noticeable bruises.

Sam's worried face joined her in the mirror. Freya knew he considered her like a sister, and her silence would only serve to fuel that over-active imagination of his. But she couldn't tell him what she'd done – not really.

"What happened to you?" Sam's soft voice caused her throat to tighten, recalling how last night she'd feared ever seeing him again.

Tyr was right. That was stupid.

"Umm..." Freya trailed off, unsure how to respond. "I fell in the bathroom and was knocked out for several hours?" The bad lie came out more as a query.

"Don't give me this bullshit, Freya Elizabeth Hayes!" The Sage winced at the sound of her full name. "You tell me – and tell me *now* – what happened to you!"

Freya was shocked at Sam's outburst. The twelve-year-old rarely got anywhere near being angry, but the concern in his gaze almost had her spill the beans. Almost.

"Nothing, okay? I got these bruises from falling in the bathroom." As he was about to mention something, she added, "Now, if you don't mind, I would appreciate it if you'd get out of my room so I can change and go eat."

Sam seemed about to protest, but instead said, "Fine, but I won't give up until I figure out what you're hiding."

With one last suspicious glare, he passed through the wall and went to find Seamus. He didn't hear Freya's saddened whisper. "I wish you'd just drop it, Sam."

Once the ghost was gone, Freya let out a sigh, and went to shower. Ten minutes later, she was rummaging through the dresser for some clothes to wear – preferably ones that would cover her bruises. She finally decided on a long sleeved, dark purple shirt and a pair of blue jeans.

As she searched for her old sneakers, she stumbled upon a ball of white fur.

"Oh, Artemis, I'm so sorry." The cat scrutinized her with pleading green eyes, and Freya realized she hadn't been fed since the previous night. "You poor thing, you must be starving."

Her gaze fell on the convenience store bag from the previous day, when she'd stopped to get supplies after adopting the cat. Opening a can of food, she dumped its contents in a small bowl, refilled the other water container, and sat on the edge of the bed, listening to Artemis purr as she ate.

A growl from her own stomach startled Freya out of a daze, and she winced. "Guess I'd better go eat something too," she said to the cat. "I have the feeling I'm going to need energy to face today."

She found her sneakers by the bathroom and headed out the door, making sure to lock it behind.

&&&

Downstairs, a worried Seamus was waiting for Sam to return.

In the morning, after waking up, he'd decided not to disturb Freya yet, and let her sleep some more. However, two hours later, she still hadn't shown any sign of life. Considering it was unlikely she overslept, he'd sent Sam to check on her.

The quick check-up became ten, then close to twenty minutes, and now he was alarmed that something might have happened to both of them, to delay them in such a manner.

When the familiar boy walked – or rather floated – around the corner, Seamus let out a huge breath. The relief changed to anxiety at Sam's frown. As soon as he was near the table, O'Keeffe demanded what was wrong.

"Nothing, professor," Sam said, but Seamus' expression darkened in disapproval at the obvious lie. Uncomfortable under the man's intense stare, and beyond worried for Freya, he decided honesty was his best bet. "Well, it's Freya."

"Freya?" Seamus' gaze shifted over the boy's shoulder to the corner he'd come from. "What about her?"

"Well, she's kind of tired, sir. Actually, not exactly tired... I tried to wake her up and it took about ten minutes for her to even give a sign of life."

The lines on O'Keeffe's features deepened further.

"Then, when she finally woke up, she acted funny, even for her."

"Funny? What do you mean by that?" Seamus was trying to maintain his cool, but the idea his protégée might have been involved with some kind of trouble was getting him antsy.

"Well," Sam said, "she was in a lot of pain, but wouldn't admit why. Then, when she dragged herself out of bed, she had this huge bruise on her leg and a cut on her forehead. Both are pretty recent. When I asked her about them, she said they were from tripping in the bathroom last night."

"And?"

Sam chewed on his bottom lip, hesitating. He peeked over his shoulder as if to make sure they were still alone, before speaking again. "Well, I mean, she's lying. I haven't a clue what she really did, but it's obviously something she doesn't want us to know."

"This is indeed odd," Seamus leaned back in his seat, rubbing his chin. "It's practically impossible to get a cut on the forehead by falling in the bathroom – unless she hit herself on the sink?" When Sam shrugged, the mentor narrowed his eyes. "No, I believe you're right, Sam. I'm going to ask Freya about this."

"Ask me about what?"

Both of them started at the sound of the familiar voice. Freya had approached them silently and overheard only the last part of their conversation.

"Good morning to you too, Freya."

The teenager seated herself at the table and Sam handed her a toast she took gratefully. She also piled on her plate some omelet, bacon and a glass of orange juice, the entire time trying to ignore the ache in her abdomen.

I should probably go to a doctor, but I doubt it's that serious...

O'Keeffe and Sam watched in fascination as Freya devoured the contents of her plate. The professor had already finished his food, while the ghost didn't need to eat, so they were left observing. After she was done, Freya leaned against her chair and met both of their bewildered expressions.

"What?" Freya arched an eyebrow.

"You –" Sam began, then stopped and shook his head in amusement. "Never mind."

Overcoming his own surprise, O'Keeffe said, "You must have been really hungry."

"Well, yes," Freya smiled sheepishly. In truth, the previous night's fight had made her ravenous. And, sadly, the hunger was barely assuaged.

She looked at her plate, frowning and debating on going for a refill. Pros and cons weighed in her mind if she chose to follow through with more food. Particularly worrisome was the fact she'd be alerting her companions that something *was* wrong, since she rarely ate such large portions.

"Very well," Seamus' tone had her gazing up expectantly. "I see you have recharged your batteries. I believe it is well past time we have a chat, you and me."

"Of course, but umm..." Freya quickly scanned the rather more crowded breakfast space, and suggested, "Can we go upstairs instead? Sam, are you coming too?"

"No, I, uh, have to go check something," the boy lied, keen to avoid what would be either a very uncomfortable – or very angry – conversation.

"Okay, then," Freya shrugged, then the two Sages left.

Once inside her room, Freya closed the door and spun towards Seamus. "So, what did you want to talk to me about?"

O'Keeffe crossed his arms over his chest, and stared her down. "Where did you get your bruises? And I want only the truth."

Freya's expression immediately hardened. "I don't mean to be rude, *professor,* but that's really none of your business."

"None of my business?" Seamus echoed, his tone going flat as it always did when he was angry. "I am in charge of you, Freya, and responsible for whatever happens to you."

"Seamus..." Freya softened her voice, something that usually worked, and said, "I don't want to talk about it. What's important is that I'm alive and in one piece."

"Freya," O'Keeffe started warningly, then stopped. He was evidently trying to be patient – and failing. "Explain what happened. *Now.*"

Something in his inflection caused the teenager to listen – though reservedly. Scowling, she revealed how she'd found the message, snuck out at night, went to the bay and figured out it was a trap, and fought Viking ghosts by herself. Freya told him everything – except about Tyr. That was one thing the Sage was not ready to share with anyone.

Based on his frown and suspicious regard as she skimmed over the part about her escape, Freya guessed O'Keeffe was aware of something missing from her story, but refrained from enquiring. For that, she was grateful.

After she finished her tale, Freya waited.

"You went there all alone, at midnight?" O'Keeffe burst out in an angry voice. "Are you *out* of your mind!?"

This was so predictable. Freya had to stop herself from rolling her eyes. After listening to his rant on her irresponsibility for a few minutes, she snapped back.

"Well, I didn't exactly have a choice. Since you won't tell me about my parents, I had to go and get my own answers."

If she would have slapped him, Seamus wouldn't have looked more shocked than he did in that moment. He remained speechless for a few minutes, before his shoulders hunched and the tension left his body. He pinched the bridge of his nose, groaning as though in physical anguish.

Under Freya's eyes, he appeared to have aged. Though he didn't show his forty years usually, in that moment they were evident in the lines of his face. Guilt crept up her spine for causing him hurt, for being an obnoxious kid when he needed her to be more mature. *And yet... It's now or never.*

Freya watched as Seamus sat in the armchair close by the window, and gave him a few moments to compose himself. As he grasped his head in his hands, ruffling his hair in a gesture of frustration, she couldn't hold back anymore. "I want the truth. *Please.*"

Seamus raised his head and pleading grey eyes, their usual shine gone, in his despair. The desolation, the pain within, was so intense, Freya was taken aback.

O'Keeffe shook his head, sorrow evident in his expression. "I am sorry, Freya, but I cannot. Not yet."

Noticing she was about to burst, he added, "No, *please,* Freya. There are some boundaries even you have to respect, now that you are older. I understand this longing you have of knowing about your parents. And I can even comprehend the danger you would put yourself in to discover more."

He paused, then stood up. "Not that I agree with it. And while this may seem cruel and unfair to you, I made a promise to your parents when they died. And that promise was to wait until your eighteenth birthday."

Freya's jaw dropped at the new information. "*Eighteen*? But that's two years from now!"

Seamus only stared back, waiting for the acceptance to sink in. Freya opened her mouth to argue more, to press while she had the advantage. Then Tyr's words floated back to her, about being more mature and no longer doing reckless things.

With a shake of her head, Freya dispelled the last of the tension in the room, and smiled wryly. "Well, whoever said life was fair, right?" When O'Keeffe smiled, she added, "But I won't drop it, you must know that. If the opportunity comes to find out more – through you or from the outside – I need to try."

"Hoping that you can break me eventually?" Seamus chuckled, and nodded. "I understand, fair is fair. Only, please, be honest with me. We have gone so many years together with good communication, and I do not wish to lose that in your teenager years." He stepped closer and lifted her chin with his finger. "And try not to get into trouble...in the meantime."

Freya searched his gaze, then nodded. "I promise."

When Seamus opened his arms for a hug, to seal the deal and put the dispute behind them, Freya readily went in for his bear squeeze. No matter what, he was her rock, her guardian, and she trusted him to know what was best.

Sam bursting through the wall interrupted the moment. "I have bad news."

His anxious expression announced something worse was heading their way.

Chapter 8

"What's the matter?" Seamus and Freya both spun to Sam, all tenderness of the moment gone at his announcement.

Sam hesitated for a brief moment. In the time they'd been up in the room, he'd jumped over to the pier to check on their bulky foes. He was now wondering if his quick incursion had led to a mistaken conclusion. *Might as well go for it, now that I've almost told them.*

"It appears the Vikings are moving," he said. "I went to try and gather some info, and boy was I surprised when I saw they'd doubled in number!"

Freya and Seamus shared a look, even as Sam continued. "Last time I went, there were a few dozen, at most. Now, there are about a hundred of them, maybe more. And they're patrolling the harbor – discreetly, of course – to make sure no intruders can get in."

"How can there be so many?" Freya asked, finally regaining use of her vocal cords.

"An even better question is, how do the humans not notice them?" O'Keeffe added.

"My guess is they're hiding under the decks of abandoned or temporarily empty ships in the port," Sam revealed. "As for their size... I wish I had more info, but I slipped out quickly, before they could notice me."

"Is there anything else you picked up?" O'Keeffe interceded, calm despite of the situation.

"Yes. From what I've heard, a second long ship is on its way here, with about twice as many Vikings on board." When Freya paled, Sam said, "It's supposed to arrive tonight."

O'Keeffe frowned, his mask of impassibility breaking as a worried gleam appeared in his eyes. "If the long ship gets in the bay, there are no way we can stop them. Not unless we have an army to spare." Addressing Sam, he said, "Any idea when exactly the boat will arrive?"

"No, I couldn't stick in the area to learn more. If I'd stayed one more minute, I'd be history by now." As an afterthought, he added, "I may already have been spotted."

They were all quiet for a few moments, before Seamus snapped out of his stupor and announced, "This does not leave us with much of a choice. We have to do our best to stop the long ship from arriving, or else this will not end well."

"Yeah, but how?" Sam wondered.

"Well..." Seamus moved away, pacing as he reflected aloud. "We definitely cannot go to the authorities – and forget the military! – To announce that an army of dead Vikings will attack them. They would conclude it's a joke."

"I agree," Sam crossed his arms. "Freya, do you –" The ghost stopped mid-sentence, not finding the Sage. "Freya? Professor, where's Freya?"

Seamus glanced around, snapping out of his thoughts. "I–could have sworn she was right here. She must have slipped past us without either of us noticing," he muttered, half-wondering if she was up to no good again. He had to dismiss the idea, hoping the trust he was allowing her would not work against him.

"Until she comes back, we'd better figure out something to do."

O'Keeffe had to agree with the boy, as the pressing matter of the fate of the world took precedence over a missing teenager.

&&&

After hearing the long ship would arrive that same night, Freya decided to go for a walk. She didn't wish to interrupt Sam and O'Keeffe's discussion, so she quietly slipped out of the room, heading out of the B&B, and into the indoor garden.

What the Sage really wanted to do was find a quiet place where she could contact Tyr, to figure out if the entity had any ideas.

Scanning her surroundings, she breathed in relief that the small garden was empty of people, despite the fresh air and sunny day. Freya headed towards a little bench under an oak tree, in the far end of the garden. Ignoring the splendid array of roses, daisies and peonies nearby, she sat down and prepared to focus.

"Tyr," she called aloud, feeling foolish for talking to herself.

To her surprise, the tiger responded in her head immediately. *Yes, child?*

Freya hesitated, unsure of how to voice her request, then finished with, *I think we may have a problem.*

Has this anything to do with the long ship fully loaded with Vikings that is set to arrive tonight in the harbor?

Err...Actually, it has everything *to do with that.* To say Freya was surprised would be an understatement. However, she didn't let the barrage of questions assailing her – How did the feline know? Could it work both ways? Could it see anything? – occupy her thoughts, as she would have plenty of time for those later.

Wise decision, the tiger commented.

But I didn't –

Realizing Tyr must have followed her reflections all along, Freya scowled and decided once more against challenging it. For the sake of expediency, and all.

Okay, well, since you know everything already, can you help us? We need to find a way to stop the ship from entering in the first place.

Yes, I would emphasize that is your top priority right now, the feline agreed, yet offered no solution.

Freya hesitated, before admitting, *We obviously can't go to the government, since they would laugh in our faces.*

Precisely.

We can't request cooperation of any form the army for the same reason. Actually, we can't go to anybody, period, Freya realized with a sinking sensation. Tyr's silence only strengthened the knot in her stomach.

We could evacuate the city, the Sage suggested after a long pause.

You would evacuate London? Tyr sounded incredulous.

It was Freya's turn to remain silent, wondering about the feasibility of that plan.

I see that as a highly improbable possibility, but please, continue. I am curious as to how exactly you would go about it?

The irony in the guardian entity's tone was not lost on the teenager, whose scowl deepened. *We could simulate an attack, and the government would have to listen. Then, once the city's emptied, we'd wait for the Vikings.*

And then what? Tyr challenged, almost afraid of the response.

Freya hesitated for a moment, wondering what else there could be, then said, *And then, well, I guess we'd fight them.*

&&&

"Ponder long and hard before you do anything foolish, Tyr," Osiris admonished, walking closer to the massive tiger.

In the ballroom of their palace, the familiar was spread over the golden tiles, in front of a massive fireplace.

The god had been listening in to the exchange with the Sage with an alarming sense of foreboding. Tyr's molten golden-green eyes appraised Osiris. *She will kill herself over this, if I do not intervene.*

Osiris' gaze softened, but his worry was palpable. "You cannot travel so between realms... You alone grasp what you will be risking."

It will be worth it.

"Because she's your –" He stopped at the warning gleam in the feline's eyes, then sighed. "Nothing I do or say will change your mind."

No, Tyr said as though it had been a question, not a statement. *But your blessing would be welcomed.*

Shaking his head in defeat, Osiris crossed the last few feet and placed a glowing palm on the tiger's muzzle. "By the grace of Ra, may you be protected. May your journey be steadfast, and successful."

Then, he left to find his wife – and the wrath he was sure to endure for being so soft-hearted. Isis would *not* be happy.

&&&

Tyr was silent for such a long time, the Sage was under the impression the connection had dissolved. As she was about to retry, the tiger spoke.

The plan is doable, but at a huge sacrifice to yourselves. Are you open to critics?

I'm all ears.

There are only three of you. If the ship gets here safely, they will be over three hundred Vikings, maybe more. Even with your powers, you could not battle all of them. You would be exhausted before long.

Freya nodded – all things she had considered. *Okay...Anything else?*

As a matter of fact, yes. If – and I do emphasize if *– somehow you managed to get out of the feud alive, you would be accused of simulating an attack on London and, needless to mention it, the consequences would be grave.*

You have a good point, Freya admitted dejectedly. *That part, I didn't think about.*

Tyr tried to state the obvious, without hurting her feelings. Eventually, it settled on, *It is easy, with the realm you live in, to forget the* real *consequences of the* real *law that oversees your actions.*

Agreed. Freya dropped her head in her hands, massaging her temples. *You have some valid points, and I'm not stupid enough to think we can overcome all these cons. So do you have a better idea?*

Not quite, was the protector's retort. The statement was not entirely true, but Tyr was interested to see if the Sage had any other solutions, before offering the only one that could work. After all, this would be her conflict to resolve.

After a short silence, Freya said, *Besides running away and leaving London to defend itself, I can't come up with any other options.*

Would you do that?

No! Freya denied without hesitation. *Never. I may get exhausted and die, but I won't go down without a fight.* With a smug smile, she added, *And I'll bring down as many of those Vikings with me as I can.*

I am glad to hear that, Tyr purred, satisfaction oozing from its tone.

But it won't get us far, Freya deplored, trying hard not to sound defeated. It was not an attitude she was used to. Her past foes had been, if not easy, at least easily dealt with.

Do not underestimate the formidable strength of sheer will, the entity said mysteriously, ready to assist the Sage.

You have an idea?

Better yet, I have a plan. The way I see it, you have two options – leave, or stand your ground and die.

Right... Freya grimaced. *Might I point out how* un-*helpful that is?*

Either that, Tyr ignored her, *or you could let me handle the ship and you take care solely of Cadmael and his immediate minions.*

Freya was momentarily stunned speechless. She tried not to raise her hopes up, but it was hard to do when the perfect solution was served on a platter. *Could you really do that?*

Assuming I get some important information first, yes I can.

Such as?

The exact placement of the ship, for instance. I can only view your world through your eyes, so if you send me on a mission, I require the exact location where I would be going.

I can do that. All we need to do is...go to the port, get past the guards, search for a map, and then communicate to you where they are. Then, we only have to–

–take a stand against the rest of them, the tiger finished for her.

Sounds like a plan to me. Unused to showing emotion after the last few years, Freya had to struggle against the onslaught of tears. *Thanks, Tyr.*

If it keeps you from taking foolish risks....then, anytime.

Freya smiled despite her tears, then stood up off the bench. *Take care tonight,* she pleaded with her guardian.

You too, at the harbor. There is more than one threat awaiting there.

With that mysterious warning, the connection ended. Freya stretched a bit, her muscles sore from sitting down, and set off to find Seamus and Sam.

She didn't notice the pair of eyes following her, nor the smug manner of the stalker.

&&&

"Professor, sorry to break this to you, but this mission may very well fail," Sam groaned.

For the past half an hour, they'd explored all possible ways to stop the Vikings, but no solution was good enough.

"Not while I'm alive, it won't!" Freya bounced into the room, her expression alight with excitement.

"Freya, where have you been?" Seamus stood up from his spot by the window, concern etched across his features.

The teenager waved the interrogation off with her hand. "I went for a walk. Now, listen, I have an idea."

There was a shocked silence, then... "I knew it!" Sam whooped.

O'Keeffe and Freya watched in surprise as the boy did a little victory dance. When he saw them staring at him, Sam stopped and gave a sheepish smile. "Well, what I mean is that whenever you retreat, it's either to kick some butt or to come back with a plan."

Freya eyed him closely, then laughed. "You know me well, ol' Sam. So, would you like to hear it or not?"

Seamus and Sam watched her expectantly.

"All we need to do is sneak up on the boat and discover the exact location of the second long ship. Then, confront the bad guys that are already there."

Seamus widened his eyes at the scheme, even as her disappearance started to make sense. *She has help...but who? An enemy? A friend?*

Not an enemy, a soft, melodic voice said in his head. *Not a menace. You have nothing to fear, Seamus. Read Freya's aura.*

Seamus' eyebrows rose in suspicion, but he nevertheless did as suggested. He'd been a Sage for too long to ignore such occurrences. He focused on Freya's face, and looked past her physical form, to spiritual. To his surprise, she was bathed in an angelic aura, unlike her own colors of purple and gold. As though...

She is *protected,* he realized. *And not by any mortal.* No one answered in his head, but the original declaration had done well to settle his mind.

It was not unheard of, since the ghosts had emerged, for both angels and demons to be drawn to a Sage. On the contrary, tales in his own youth and training confirmed the aura around them was like a beacon to forces of the supernatural. To witness it firsthand was awe-inspiring, but not the end of the world.

With a shake of the head, Seamus went back the situation.

"Are you quite serious?" he asked. "We cannot take a stand against a hundred phantoms by ourselves."

Freya put both hands on her hips. "Do I look like I'm kidding, Seamus? Now, as far as I'm aware, this is the only plan we've got, and it's already four o'clock. You can either follow my lead, or let London deal with this problem alone."

O'Keeffe sighed, none too pleased. The plan had certain loop holes, and was far too dangerous, in his opinion. *And yet, we have no choice.*

"What about the long ship?" Sam interceded.

Freya smiled mischievously.

"I don't like that look," Sam muttered, backing away.

"Let's just say I've got it covered."

Nicely put, Tyr laughed in her mind.

"They won't be bothering us," she went on, making eye contact with Seamus. "*Trust me*. Have I ever failed you?"

"Well, no," both O'Keeffe and Sam had to admit.

"Okay then, what are we waiting for?" Freya lifted her wrist and tapped her wrist watch. "Time flies, and we better hurry to get to Porthmadog pier."

She left the room to her own and changed into something more practical for camouflage – black slacks and a t-shirt. Five minutes later, Freya joined Seamus outside his room, and an impatient Sam.

"Car rental again?" Freya asked her mentor, grimacing.

He gave her a look. "Yes, and you too. I gather you had your little adventure last night, and can get to the port faster than me. But we are all in this mission, and let me be clear – we leave *no one* behind. Is that understood?"

Freya nodded. "Fine by me."

She linked her arm with Sam's, and followed Seamus down the stairs to the car.

Chapter 9

By the time they reached the port, the sun had set, and everything was quiet – more so than the last time Freya had come. Seamus parked the car in a secluded corner, as far as possible from the ships, to maintain their escape route.

"I'm going first, to check if the coast is clear." Sam passed through the door of the car and floated away.

Freya waited until he gave two thumbs up, then exited the car with her mentor. She led Seamus through concealed corners and shadows of boats, attempting to get to the long ship unseen. With each step, her instincts were alerting her that someone was trailing them.

And this was no ghost, as she couldn't detect a glowing silhouette. Furthermore, when she attempted to touch its conscience, it was too tangible.

Besides, Freya thought wryly, *since when do spirits have shadows?*

For the moment, she focused on getting herself and Seamus as close to the boat as possible, while hoping to remain unnoticed.

"Where the hell did Sam disappear to?" she whispered. The boy should have re-joined them by now.

They detoured to get closer, and ended up walking beside the forest near the harbor, in the wilder part. Just as they were switching to the more industrialized side, passing by some large containers, Freya got wind of sounds coming their way.

Ever the paranoid heroine, she gripped Seamus' arm and pushed him between two of the bins, intent on surprising the stalker. Freya herself hid in an isolated corner in front of some bushes, from where she could survey both her mentor and whoever was coming their way, whilst remaining invisible.

A few moments passed, then a rumble of voices reached her, before their shapes did.

It was two glowing figures that appeared around the corner – and Vikings, from their manner. Freya curled in a ball and lowered her head, her raven hair camouflaging her fair profile, blending in with the darkness. Starting an altercation wouldn't be ideal, as they had to keep the element of surprise.

I hope Seamus is well-hidden.

She overheard the specters chatting about something or other, though between the thick accent and the distance, she couldn't understand what was said. As the two Vikings neared, Freya was able to finally disentangle some of their conversation.

"I saw somethin' 'ere," one of the ghosts said. With the darkening light, Freya could only see that he was short and stout, with large arms, a square jaw, and the ever-present red hair and beard.

"And I tell ya, ya ain't seen nothin'," the other refuted, rather irritated. They could have passed for brothers, but this one was blonde-haired. "Prob'bly a cat. Damn those beasts! Always roamin' 'round huntin' for food."

"Yah, ya ar' prob'bly 'ight," the first one said. "I ain't lookin' for anythin' anymor.'"

With that, both men departed the same way they'd come. Freya let out a relieved breath. She was getting ready to check if Seamus was all right, but decided to stay hidden a bit longer in case.

Crack.

A twig broke.

Freya's head snapped back to the bushes in the background. It was gloomier now, more so than when they had arrived. Hiding had wasted more precious minutes they didn't have. Narrowing her eyes, the Sage sought a shadow or anything that would betray an intruder.

Nothing.

Must've been a bird or something, she reassured herself, not quite believing it. *Well, there's one way to find out.* Freya extended her senses on a five mile surface. She caught Seamus' familiar vibe, one or two birds, but as she concentrated on the bushes, she couldn't pick up anything abnormal.

Except perhaps a faint beating of a heart.

Just as she was about to concentrate harder, there was a light touch on her shoulder. She jumped out of her hiding place, and it took all her mastery to not scream. She spun and –

"*Sam!*" she hissed furiously. "How many times do I have to tell you this? *Don't* sneak up on me like that!"

"Sorry, Freya," he smiled sheepishly. "I couldn't resist."

"Well, next time, try *harder*! Honestly, you're worse than a child!"

He rolled his eyes at her outburst, grinning widely. "Hate to point it out, but I *am* a child."

At Freya's pissed off glare, Sam hastened to add, "Okay, okay. I'll try not to spook you anymore, but I'm not promising anything. Now come on, I have to share with you and the professor – where is he, anyway? – what I learned! It's quite interesting, if you ask me, and –"

"Shh!" Freya silenced him with a raised palm. "Not here, after!"

Without waiting for a response, she gripped him by the arm and with one final suspicious glance to the bushes, led Sam to Seamus' hiding place.

As they neared, O'Keeffe whispered, "Finally! I was wondering where you two had gone off to." To Freya, he said, "Those ghosts walked right past me. If all of them have their brain, we might have a slight chance of outnumbering them."

Freya chuckled softly.

Sam, however, was not at all amused when he declared, "Not if what I eavesdropped on is true."

Freya raised her eyebrows in surprise, but before she could ask anything, Sam wondered, "And what was *that* all about?" He pointed behind him where, about twenty meters away, were the bushes.

"What was what about?" O'Keeffe frowned.

"Nothing," Freya shrugged, even now getting the feeling of being watched. It was unsettling, to say the least. "I thought I heard something odd back there, and I didn't want to risk our conversation being overheard. Now, will you spill already, Sam?"

The boy's expression sobered. "Two people were chatting in the main cabin of an abandoned boat. They sounded so different, Frey-Frey. I mean, picture some badass villain and his henchman, that's pretty much the best description." Freya started tapping her foot impatiently, and Sam hurried to add, "Anyway, one of them – and they were both ghosts, eh, I saw their glows through the window – called the other one *Cadmael*."

"You're telling us Cadmael, the leader himself who planned to the Vikings to war unless we stop him, is *here*?" O'Keeffe asked incredulously. *Why would the leader himself show his ace card so soon? It makes no sense.*

"I'm afraid so," Sam confirmed.

"We have to go near the cabin," Freya declared.

"What!?" Both Sam and Seamus turned to her in shock.

"Think about it," Freya said, frustration lacing her voice. She was pretty sure Seamus was about to launch into another lecture about not being reckless. "What better place to discover what we need to, than where the leader himself is posted? Cadmael and the other guy are probably there to check some last details of their hideous plot."

"So, let me get this straight," Sam said. "You want to go and *spy* on them?"

"Yes," Freya folded both arms across her chest. "With a bit of luck, we're going to learn more about their plan, too."

"Professor," Sam pleaded, "please say no, this is insane! At least let me go, alone."

Seamus hesitated, sharing a look with Freya. He could read in the depths of her grey eyes her stubbornness on this matter, but also a nagging instinct hinted she was right to consider the option.

"No, Sam," he shook his head in the end. "As much as I hate to admit this and allow Freya's dangerous idea, I must admit, this is the surest way. So please, enough time wasted, lead us to the main cabin."

Sam did as he was told, zigzagging through complicated shortcuts and the less ghost-populated areas, while muttering under his breath. They couldn't sneak upon the boat itself without being noticed, so the youth thought outside the box and found another way.

After close to twenty minutes of walking, they reached a nearby boat, larger in size. They climbed on aboard, and blended with the shadows.

Sam headed to the area of the main cabin, then pointed across. "That's where Cadmael is." They had a perfect view of the little enclosure on top of the long ship, barely twenty feet across from them, and the glowing shapes pacing back and forth within.

"This is the best vantage point to see when they leave," Sam whispered, afraid his voice might carry across the quiet water. "Once they do, Freya, you can jump over, landing near the cabin."

She nodded at the plan, then turned to Seamus. "Once I have what we need, you have to help Sam create a distraction. I'll use it to jump into the water and swim back to shore, and meet you guys back at the B&B."

Seamus ran a hand over his face, then glanced at the distance between the two boats, and down into the waters. He wanted to do his duty, point out how perilous it was, but instead inclined his head in agreement.

"We should stay hidden in the meantime," he suggested, then pointed to some untouched barrels across from the cabin.

Shuffling and bending as low as they could to the ground, all three headed over, and hid between. The large barrels, darkened by age, stank of an unidentifiable smell. Freya scrunched up her nose, shuddering at the idea she could be sitting right near a thousand-year-old corpse. Some of these boats had never been searched, let alone emptied by locals, so the thought alone was not crazy.

The one advantage was their new hideout brought them even closer in distance to the main cabin, and Freya could catch bits of conversation floating to their ears.

"Guys," she whispered, "as soon as they get out of the cabin, I'm going in to search for a map."

"Very well, Freya," Seamus reticently agreed, "but be careful. At the first sign of any danger, get out of there."

She gave him a thumbs up to signal it was okay, but then, remembering he couldn't see her in the darkness, said, "I promise."

Then, she listened. It wasn't long before she could understand what Cadmael and the other specter– whom he referred to as Asger – were talking about.

"Yes, chief, everything is ready." Sam had been right – Asger really sounded squeaky, like the perfect henchman. "The long ship should be here in less than two hours."

"Are you sure nobody noticed the boat approaching?" a louder, stronger person intervened.

Freya shivered at its sound. She couldn't see Cadmael, but from Sam had said, the guy was feared by his army. The thought crossed her mind that he really must have been a great chief in the past, which meant he'd be an even more powerful foe to her.

And merciless.

Asger spoke next, answering Cadmael's previous question. "Positive!"

"Good. Those Brits won't grasp what hit them. They certainly don't expect an army of ghosts to try and beat them at their own game."

Their own game? What does that mean? Freya wondered. She was about to check with Seamus and see if he'd heard it, too, but more talk distracted her.

Cadmael was saying, "Asger, you have done well. Come with me to inform our troops of the preparations necessary. In two days, we will strike."

Some sounds could be perceived from the cabin, and moments later, the two ghosts passed through the wall. Freya was unmoved as her eyes landed on Asger's hideous expression. However, when they fell on Cadmael, she recognized the worthy opponent in him.

The hard lines of his face, evident despite the glow, spoke to the power he wielded – and the sacrifices made to acquire it. Even now, the man was immense, a certain arrogant stride to his walk – a leader indeed.

Have fun while you can, Cadmael. I'll personally make sure your plot fails, Freya vowed with a resolute expression.

As soon as they were out of sight, the Sage exited her hiding spot. She backtracked a few meters, then ran at full speed and hurled herself in the air. Her lithe body shot through the distance between the two boats as quick and silent as an arrow.

She landed on the wood softly, rolling over a shoulder, and stooped behind more barrels.

Taking a moment to gather her breath, Freya then peeked up, to where Sam and Seamus were hidden. The boy's thumbs up was the signal informing her no one was the wiser to her arrival, and, with a curt nod, she hurried into the cabin.

The door opened surprisingly easily, and Freya hesitated for a few seconds before finally entering. The slight pause in her steps was due to the old adage that enemies don't leave their doors unlocked unless it was a trap. *And yet... These are ghosts, after all. Not like they have a long list of enemies, they're dead already.*

Freya's grey eyes scanned for anything in the small space, but found nothing of great importance. Just as she was about to turn and continue the search on the outside, something under the bed attracted her attention. It was the corner of a beige parchment sticking out.

She pulled it out and saw, with relief, that it was a map. Eyeing it carefully, she examined it for the long ship's supposed location, and noticed a circle. She put her palm above it, and concentrated hard.

With her mind's eye, Freya traveled the distance between her and the ship. She was floating in the sky, and below was the ship making its way toward land, with a mass of glowing forms on board. When she let her hand drop, the coordinates were clear as day in her head.

She inhaled deeply to make up for the energy depleted, and opened her mind's eye. This time, she was searching for a connection. Tyr's reply was quick, as though it had been waiting for her the entire time.

Do you have the location?

Yes, Freya said. Without further ado, she let the image invade her mind, and unlocked it for the tiger. *See for yourself.*

There was a quick intrusion, gentle as a feather's dove, then, *I will advise you when it is done. You will not hear from me until then, but help may come in other forms.*

The tiger's imprint in her thoughts left, and Freya folded the map. She placed it in her pocket for safekeeping, and headed for the exit.

As she got out of the cabin, however, her proud grin slipped off, replaced by an astonished stare.

Barely ten feet across from her was Seamus on his knees, hands and feet bound tightly with rope. He was unmoving, his unconscious shape curled up. Sam, next to him, was paralyzed by something. Both were guarded by twenty solidly built ghosts.

From their midst, one man came forward, and Freya recognized him immediately.

"Asger," she hissed, using the name Cadmael had during their meeting.

"Well, well, well, who do we have here? If it isn't the dear missus who escaped us last night."

As he spoke, however, Asger's voice changed. It was no longer the same squeaky tone Freya had heard when he'd been facing Cadmael. Rather, it was the voice of her nightmares – the ringleader that had trapped her the night she was saved by Tyr.

Chapter 10

Neither Sam nor Seamus could protest Freya's decision of going in the cabin alone, for fear of the wind carrying their words inside, and endangering them all. So they waited.

After a while, the door opened. In the pale moonlight, O'Keeffe and Sam gaped at the most hideous creature they'd ever set eyes on.

Long arms, a short body and feet, the creature resembled a mutant gorilla, except uglier. Its appearance was completed by a prominent tummy, a mass of orange-brown hair surrounding a round facial structure and, hidden under large eyebrows, two little piercing orange-green eyes.

O'Keeffe's gaze fell on the other person – or rather, ghost – accompanying it, and shivers of fear ran up his spine. He now had the proof Cadmael was indeed at the head of this plot – the blond hair, iron-like eyes, large body and imposing figure left no doubt.

As the two phantoms got off the long ship, their steps brought them dangerously close to hearing Seamus' ragged breathing. At a warning glance from Sam, the elder Sage slowed down his breathing, and waited anxiously.

Cadmael stopped in his tracks, his cold gaze narrowed on the surroundings. He sniffed the air like a dog would, then turned to Asger and whispered something. Both men continued on their way, and Seamus slumped against the barrel in relief.

He leaned forward, squinting through the darkness to Freya's hiding spot. As soon as the two ghosts vanished around the corner, she stood up and headed to the cabin.

Both O'Keeffe and Sam were aware Freya was the least noticeable of their group. Slim as she was, she concealed herself with the shadows even better than Sam. Seamus was far too old to have the same reflexes as twenty years earlier.

Seamus had faith in Freya, and in her ability to defend herself, should it come down to it. But even so, he held his breath when she reached for the door to the cabin. What if there was another ghost inside? What if it was locked?

To his utter amazement, luck smiled on their path. The door opened as soon as Freya gave it a light push, and she cautiously entered inside.

Something's not right, Seamus thought. *This is much too easy.* He glanced at Sam out of the corner of his eye, noticing the boy was wringing his hands together.

Before he had a chance to mention anything, Sam spoke first. "Professor, something's not right. I mean, if Cadmael and that Asger guy were plotting something important, they wouldn't leave the door open."

"Exactly what I was thinking," O'Keeffe said. "And I believe Freya is of the same mindset as us."

"Then why did she go in?" Sam pointed out.

Seamus shrugged, rising from his position and shifting in the shadows. "For one thing, she has never let a minor detail stop her. And second, Freya realizes we are here to guard her back. All we can do is wait and keep our eyes wide open."

"Okay..." Sam wasn't convinced, but retreated back to observing the cabin, a slight frown on his youthful expression.

Minutes went by, then longer moments. When Sam could no longer handle the inaction, he stood up and moved out of the hiding spot. "I'm going to check it out," he threw over a shoulder to the elderly man.

Seamus opened his mouth to call him back, but instead whispered, "Would you at least remain cautious?"

Sam barely gestured and, swiftly as a cat, floated over the water and advanced toward the door's cabin.

No sooner had he left, that Seamus felt a chill come over him. "Should have brought that extra pullover," he muttered under his breath. He crossed his arms over his chest, trying to hold the warmth within his long-sleeved shirt, and waited stiffly.

He only had one moment of warning – one precious moment that was wasted. A piece of wood connected with his neck, and he fell on the hard floor, unconscious.

&&&

Sam advanced swiftly towards the little window of the cabin, trying to remain in the shadows as much as possible. When he reached it, he peered inside and saw Freya in full investigator mode, walking towards the ragged beds.

Relief filled him as he realized she was alone and not in any danger. With one last glance, he backed away, and hurried back to the other boat, and Seamus.

"She's okay, she's not–" His head rotated right, then left, trying to spot the old man. "Professor? Seamus?" he whispered, getting a weird vibe of déjà-vu.

Due to his ghost status, and his lowered senses, he didn't feel the other presence approaching him. He spun on his heels – too late.

Before him stood five Viking ghosts, all ready to fight him. Sam let out a nervous chuckle, trying his best not to show fear.

"Well, I see you guys joined us for the party."

One of the men – the closest – grinned. "Funny... Little man, we can do this the easy way or the hard way."

It took Sam a second, then he burst out laughing at the absurd situation. The fact they were actually threatening him, when he was immortal, struck him as beyond hilarious. In-between hiccups, he said, "You *do* realize I'm a ghost, right? What do you think you can do to me?"

The Vikings' calm stares struck Sam as odd, and he ceased his laughing all the same. He couldn't see Seamus with them, which only meant he'd gotten captured. Worry had him bite his bottom lip, and he whispered, "Where's Seamus?"

"We – how shall I put this smoothly? – handled him." They shared a cackle, enough to put Sam in an uncomfortable mental spot.

Okay, new plan, Sam decided, eyes darting, scanning for an escape. *I have to make them talk, to gain time...Maybe I can de-materialize and warn Freya...*

He began backing away, but didn't get far. His back connected with something sharp and pointy.

An axe?

The same Viking who'd spoken before said, "Time to say good-night."

Next thing Sam knew, electricity ran up his entire body. His limbs became paralyzed, and his entire body felt heavy, and off-balance. In front of the Vikings' amused gazes, Sam fell on the hard floor, his eyes frozen in fear.

"Good," a second ghost said. "Now we wait for the girl."

"What about these two?" another one asked.

"We'll bring them with us. They'll be our bait to...negotiate."

Their evil laughter carried across the sea, getting lost in the wind's wails.

&&&

Freya's eyes skimmed over Sam and Seamus, desperately looking for signs they were unharmed. Then her glare landed on Asger. She shivered as she remembered that night – the night she'd almost died, had it not been for Tyr's assistance.

Now, she had in front of her the author of the trap. If she'd been alone, she would have jumped Asger and settled the score, her way. But her friends' capture made her think twice before acting, and she was unwilling to put them in further danger.

Freya needed a plan, and fast. The only thing she could think of was to try and gain some time.

"Who are you?" She took a step forward, straightening her back and meeting Asger's glare head-on. Her best bet was to challenge the Viking, while trying to find a way to release Seamus.

And hope to hell Cadmael doesn't decide to join this party.

Her mentor's capture seemed the easiest to undo – all she had to was cut his bindings once he woke up. But Sam – she had no idea how to undo whatever had been done to him.

"My name is Asger, leader of these men and right hand to chieftain Cadmael."

Freya snorted, before spitting distastefully, "What did he promise you after doing his job?"

Apparently, that was not the right thing to ask, as Asger's features contorted in anger. Freya could only assume that was the emotion caused, but it was hard to read his facial expression with so many scars.

"Cadmael has not promised me anything. I am only here to serve him. To be his loyal ghost and assist him to conquer the New World."

Freya snorted. "Do you really believe all that crap? You honestly think his scheming will succeed?"

"The chief is wise," Asger frowned at her ignorance. "He has more power than you poor mortals could ever imagine."

"Oh really?" Freya asked doubtfully. "Such as fleeing?"

Asger smiled – if the awful grimace could be called a smile – and said, "That, or making ghosts disappear."

It can't be!

Freya tried to school her expression, but she couldn't help her eyes shift to Sam. The boy was frozen, but as he looked past his aura, she could see he was still there – somewhat. But it was as if he'd been thrown in a container of iced water.

The Sage clenched her jaw, trying to fight against the despair threatening to consume her. If the Viking leader had somehow managed to get the ability before she did, that put him at a huge advantage. Something tightened around her chest, cutting off her breathing. *He can't possibly know how. Please, Tyr, it cannot be true!*

There was no response from the tiger, which was an answer in itself. Freya's heart sank, and her pulse sped in response. *NO!*

&&&

In the darkness, the demon sneered, reading the Sage's aura easily. *And to think I imagined her as a threat,* he laughed to himself. Then his eyes narrowed and he sent a wave of darkness to the teenager. *All to better finish her off – then I can start re-building her to my liking.*

He watched in satisfaction as she stumbled back – then fell to her knees. The Sage's shoulders curled inward, and he knew what she was feeling. The onset of despair, the devastation of failing, the hopelessness...

It will not be long now.

She bent over her knees, panting, and the demon smirked. He retreated further into the darkness, to better watch the ghosts finish her off.

&&&

Asger's crooked smile widened, and he already tasted victory – he knew defeat when he saw it. He'd had a feeling she didn't know everything Cadmael could do, but he hadn't thought it enough to convince her so easily.

Now she lay on her knees, panting as if she couldn't catch her breath. To wound the girl even harder, he taunted, "Giving up?"

&&&

At the ghost's words, Seamus' eyes snapped opened. The throbbing ache in his head made it hard to focus, until his eyes fell upon Freya, and widened in disbelief.

No!

The girl he'd raised, and trained, could not be the same one on her knees in front of the Vikings. It was unimaginable!

I refuse to believe it!

In one glance, he realized she was outnumbered. Furthermore, his own capture and Sam's was enough to grant the ghosts the upper hand. And yet... Something else was pushing her down.

Listening to instincts that had more than once saved his life, Seamus inspected past Freya's aura, and detected the corruption encompassing her. His eyes narrowed, and he opened his mouth in warning. But it was as though his body, and abilities, shut down at once. He couldn't assist her in this any more than Sam could.

Freya's on her own.

He could only hope she could unearth the strength trapped with her, and come out the winner – for all their sakes.

&&&

Freya's head was heavy, her chest hurt, her entire body couldn't muster a single motion of defense. The abilities that had been a part of her since she'd been a child were muted, in a fog. The glow within her, the palpable heat she'd felt her entire life, the same one that had been developing over the last years, was gone.

Defeat is near, the voice of her nightmares hissed. *Might as well give in...*

Give in...

Give in...

No! Tyr's warning rang in her head, but it was faint. *Stand up and fight, Freya, like you were trained to do.*

Freya was too tired to respond. She felt the tiger poking around her head, and was acutely aware of the entity's fatigue. *The long ship...* Vaguely, she recalled Tyr had been on a mission, but the hopelessness overpowered everything else.

Leave her alone! Tyr roared at the void of darkness within her, and Freya flinched.

And yet, despite the agony, the weight on her shoulders lifted, dissipating. She could almost picture the tiger battling against everything that was holding her down, her fierce guardian angel.

Fight! Tyr commanded in her head.

Dimly, Freya became aware of something else, like a nudging. She'd always been conscious of her Sage abilities, to some extent. As a child, they were like fireflies in her stomach. When she'd grown up, it became the sensation of a center holding her together, deep in her chest.

And when she'd touched the book – the ancient artifact Seamus had gifted her – Freya had felt the vibration answering within her. Now, whatever had been in a low-powered mode hit her full-force, running through veins, filling her with stamina and adrenaline, shattering the darkness – the weakness.

My powers, I can feel them.

Freya blinked as if coming back from a daze. She stared at the ground, at her outstretched palms. Her breathing was regular now, and with each lungful of air, her head cleared. *There's no need to panic. If Cadmael can do what Asger says, so what? He doesn't know my strength either.*

She clenched one fist, feeling the spiritual energy burning its way to her fingertips. The breeze surrounding her changed its tempo, almost matching her heartbeat. The waves in the sea nearby slowed, as if waiting for an order. A lamp, far in the distance, flickered – the Sage could sense its fiery determination. And earth... Freya dug her other hand in it, reveling in its grounding influence.

Freya was as conscious of the elements as she was of her own breathing. *Is this what full-fledged Sages feel? This...rightful sense of belonging in the world?*

No answer came from Tyr, but it wasn't needed. Freya slowly got to her feet and straightened her shoulders, lifting her chin defiantly. She met Asger's incredulous stare, and the blaze within her stroked higher.

The vibration filled Freya, as she stood facing foes she should not have been able to take a stand against by herself. And yet, she didn't doubt her abilities – not for a second.

"You thought you could break me," she said, enunciating every word. "And guess what? You were wrong."

Whatever had poisoned her, defeated her, was long gone now. The flames only stoked Freya's passion, and she refused to bend down. The Sage extended her palm, and shouted only one word as she focused the entirety of her spiritual energy on her friends' captive forms, "Release!"

&&&

Sam hadn't been unconscious. Frozen as he was, his eyes had followed and seen everything that happened – including Freya, almost giving up. He'd tried to struggle against what had captured him, not understanding how he'd been paralyzed, or with what.

Then, he was free. His glowing shape rose from the ground, floating above. Two of the closest Vikings stared at him, and took a step back. Sam's eyes took in the ghosts standing in a semi-circle, and the hideous Asger – whose attention was focused on Freya. Seamus was a few feet away from the leader, bound on the ground.

The boy peered in the direction of the Viking's glare and gasped. Freya was standing there, but it wasn't really her. He'd never seen her eyes burn like that, and a silvery light surrounded her. It was her words he'd heard, he realized, when she lowered her hand.

She freed me.

A zing of invisible energy withdrew from around him, as if it'd been covering him, and Sam floated towards his friend.

&&&

Seamus, taking advantage of his captors' disinterest in him, was struggling with his ropes when they loosened at his wrists. Out of the corner of his eye, he sensed a burst of energy and looked up in time to see Freya lower her hand.

Shock hit him, shortly followed by pride. What he'd waited for, the energy Estella herself had received in gift long ago, had finally risen within his blossoming protégée.

If it wasn't for these stupid oafs, I could dance for joy! A sobering idea occurred to him, and as he stood up, he inspected Freya with his mind's eye, now free of incumbents as well. He could no longer see the darkness, only the glow around her.

The mystery of those shadows feeding on her will have to be figured out later.

The fire in Freya's eyes left no doubt about it. She was back, stronger, and it was all that mattered. He looked to the left and his eyes encountered Sam's, who was already heading towards Freya.

Seamus followed suit, unafraid to show his back to the Vikings. None of their foes were foolish enough to try and stop them. It was as if they were paralyzed, much like Sam had been. He and the boy ghost took their places behind Freya, intending to protect her back from any cowards.

&&&

Freya ignored her companions, focusing on Asger.

"Scared, are you?" Her tone was low, filled with an iciness neither Sam nor O'Keeffe had ever heard her use before.

Asger didn't answer. He merely stared at her, refusing to believe what was in front of his eyes. His jaw was slightly agape, eyes narrowed in disbelief.

"Yeah, you're scared, all right," Freya taunted. "You thought you had me cornered. It was a good idea, too. Luring me into the cabin and kidnap the two people I care most about, behind my back. You thought I'd be so scared for their lives, that I'd surrender – and I almost did. Too bad you underestimated me, *like last time*."

Asger's orange-green eyes widened, and Freya smirked in response. The glow around her body shone, and she sensed the impatience in the wind, in the air. The elements responded to her spiritual energy, encouraging her to use them.

Not yet.

The Sage glared at the Viking. "Yes, *Asger*," she spit his name as if it was something unworthy of her. "I'm well aware it was you, that night. And despite all your bravado, I wonder if you really grasp what you were talking about when you mentioned your chief Cadmael could make ghosts disappear."

The monstrous creature spoke, though its voice was not as self-confident as it had been. "I do! He can send us to nothingness. Even your little friend."

Freya didn't show a sign of being surprised, let alone scared, this time. Instead, she arched an eyebrow. "And do tell me, was it through him that you immobilized my buddy Sam? I *am* curious."

"Cadmael has power," Asger hastened to add, as if hoping he could scare the Sage with words once again. "He gave us a stick that can paralyze all mortal and immortal beings. With that kind of might, he will win, and rule the world!"

The Sage stepped closer, and Asger backed away.

"Wow, you're pretty pathetic if you think that's the case," Freya said, crinkling her nose at him. "You really believe that? Your master won't have all that ability, trust me." At Asger's evident surprise, she went on, "Or didn't your precious ruler tell you that in order to keep on killing ghosts, his strength will be drained?"

It was a shot in the dark, a fable woven from Seamus' teachings – but part of Freya believed there was some truth to what she was saying. Her conviction shone in her words, unsettling the Viking leader even further.

Asger stuttered something, but Freya cut him off, taking another step. "Do you honestly think that all ghosts will like being ruled by a tyrant? They'll fight back, as will the humans. And your dear Cadmael will need something – or some*one* – to get new energy from."

Freya had no idea where half the stuff from her mouth was coming from. It was as though someone was feeding her what to say, and yet she couldn't stop it. It must've been working, as Asger clearly looked taken aback.

"Yeah, you have every reason to be scared. Who do you think he'll turn to, this precious chieftain of yours? His loyal henchman, of course."

Asger backed away again, glancing around as if looking for an exit.

Freya clenched her fist, fury at his capture of her friends blazing through her. "What's the matter, Asger?" Her voice lowered further, and she tilted her head in amusement. "No more threats? Cat got your tongue?"

She lifted her hand, sensing the spiritual energy like a wave, gathering in her fist. At the same time, Asger caught another Viking's eye, and nodded. "Get her!" His shout echoed across the men, who stood frozen for another beat.

Then, they moved as one towards the Sage.

"Freya, let's go!" Sam's shout behind didn't faze her.

In fact, Freya showed no surprise. She widened her stance, and waited. When the Vikings were only a few feet away, she prepared to battle. At her back, she heard Seamus order Sam to leave, but the ghost argued.

A strike from a Viking drew her attention elsewhere, and she lost track of the conversation. When she next glanced over her shoulder, Freya noticed O'Keeffe fighting with a burly ghost.

Before the Viking's fist could make contact, Seamus grabbed it and pulled it forward. The heavy-footed Viking was dragged into the elderly Sage's aura, and became fully solid. The shift caused him lose his balance, and fall forward. O'Keeffe finished him with a knee to the neck, and the specter remained on the ground.

Groaning, Seamus rolled his shoulder and turned to Freya. "I am not as young as I used to be, my dear. Please tell me you have a backup."

The Sage bit her lip, but a yank on her hair stopped her from answering. With fire burning in her eyes, she spun and knocked down yet another foe. Her next attacker was even easier to dispose of, and she finished him off with a strong punch to the nose.

Her spiritual energy and high adrenaline meant she wasn't getting as tired as the previous night, when she'd been fighting Asger's men alone. Still, the same couldn't be said for Seamus.

Out of the three of them, Sam was the most in trouble. He was doing his best to avoid fists and punches, but he was only a ghost, and mostly a kid. The Vikings' large bodies outweighed him ten to one, and they seemed to recognize the fact, as a few converged on him at once.

Freya came to his rescue, jumping in the fray and knocking out a phantom with a punch that sent him flying. She contemplated her fist in surprise at the fierce strength, then reciprocated on the another ghost.

Once she cleared a path, she answered Sam's thanks with a slight smile. She glanced at Seamus, noticing in the momentum that another pack of spirits was heading to attack.

O'Keeffe groaned beside Freya, and she refrained from doing the same.

"Sam," she didn't look to him as she spoke, "You have to go. *Now!*"

"No."

Freya turned to Sam with narrowed eyes. "Since when do you stick around to fight?"

The young boy squinted at the incoming enemies, and a flicker of fear passed his expression, before his determined expression met Freya's. "We're a team, and we said not to leave anyone behind. I'll help, even if only as a distraction."

With a shake of her head, the Sage abandoned arguing with him. She had more pressing matters to deal with than a stubborn ghost.

Rather than wait for the Vikings to reach them and corner them, Freya jogged ahead and jumped in their midst. She began grappling with them, losing contact with the world as for each blow sent, she concentrated all her intensity into her fist.

And still, the elements beckoned – and she resisted. It wasn't long before a fog rose from the ground, enveloping the specters and separating the three companions.

Freya was holding her ground against two particularly obnoxious Vikings when one of them was blown into the air, disappearing in the fog.

A second later, a cocky male voice, tinged with a slight British accent, quipped, "I *did* plan to hold off but... Need any help?"

Freya spun around, eyes rising to the newcomer in shock.

Chapter 11

N*o way!*
    Freya stared at the young man perched on barrels, hovering over her. His familiar brown, wavy hair and chocolate-colored eyes tinged with gold twinkled with amusement. A corner of his mouth was pulled in a contagious grin.

It's the guy from the airport!

On the heels of that thought came another. As if on cue, Freya's gaze lowered to his neck, where the dragon medallion dazzled.

A hard object connecting with her back earned her a grunt of pain, and Freya fell on the floor, stunned – and angry at herself for letting the newcomer distract her from the battle.

Ignoring the ache spreading across her back muscles, she rolled over the ground, trying to avoid another hit. The Viking stepped closer, gripping a rather large wood board, and aiming it for her head.

Before he had a chance to strike Freya a second time, a strong fist collided with his chin, sending him flying twenty feet.

Freya scanned the lean, muscled back of the stranger, before he turned with the same twinkle in his eyes, and offered her a hand to get up. She hesitated for a moment, then accepted it, and was immediately pulled upright by a pair of strong arms.

Their bodies collided, and he grabbed her waist to steady her. Freya peeked up at young man, the golden gleam in his eyes mesmerizing despite herself. Up close, his brown hair was cut short, but a few locks fell casually in his eyes. Despite his youth, his features were already lined into the man he would be, his build athletic under the black shirt he was wearing.

What the hell is up with me, as if I haven't set eyes on a kid my age before! Freya scolded herself. As if on cue, the stranger spoke.

"You can stop staring whenever." His voice was deep, and she was annoyed at the effect it had on her.

Obviously, he's past puberty, Freya mumbled to herself. With a jerk, she released herself from his grasp, and moved a good foot away. Ignoring the weird sensation in her stomach, Freya tried to scowl at him – noticing, for the first time, that he was taller than her.

Her mouth opened for a question, but her eyes flickered across his shoulder to the shadow creeping towards them. *I hate owing anyone...*

Freya waited a few seconds, and when the specter was about to strike, she pushed the other teenager out of the way. Then, her knee connected painfully with the Viking's abdomen. Freya landed one last hit on his neck, and the man fell to the ground.

A quick glance around confirmed they were alone – for now. She focused on the young man, beaming in spite of the blood and dust covering her. "Now, we're even. I hate owing debts."

She eyed him curiously, and opened her mouth to ask who he was. Before a word could get out, he pointed behind her ominously, "Incoming."

Freya wheeled around, only to find yet another ghost heading their way. Over her shoulder, she threw, "Mind if I finish this?"

"Not at all."

As Freya assessed the approaching bulky Viking, she mentally extended her senses and scanned the area for Sam and Seamus, cursing at having been distracted enough to lose sight of them. The darkness, along with the developing fog, made vision difficult further than five feet.

She focused her attention on the still-advancing spirit, blood boiling inside her. "You really don't get enough of this, do you?" The muttered curse escaped on a hiss, and she followed through by using her opponent as a punching bag.

The frustration over her altercation with Asger, over getting distracted, over the stupid boy's annoying smirk, all came out through her fists, until the man fell to the floor, groaning.

Freya could finally breathe. That is, until the stranger tapped her shoulder, and said, "Quite foggy out here, yeah?"

Her spun around, tossing a lock of hair out of her blazing eyes. Irritation swirled just underneath the surface and she scowled. "Who *are* you?"

"Brennan Taggart," he said, his teeth shining in the night as he smiled.

"Brennan, huh?" Freya put both hands on her hips, sizing him up, before taking a deep breath. "Now's not the best time for presentations, but I guess manners go first. I'm Freya Ha-"

"Freya Hayes, I know."

"Of course you – you *do*?" Freya's eyes narrowed, and suspicion crept up her spine.

To her extreme annoyance, Brennan only nodded. She tapped her foot for a few seconds, waiting for more, but all he did was fold his arms over his chest and grin.

"Ok, let's get a few things straight here," Freya inched closer, pinning him with her stare. "I have a lot of crap to deal with right now, so straight answers would be appreciated." She paused for emphasis, then pursued. "That being said, my questions are fairly easy – how do you know my name, how can you see *and* fight ghosts, and why in *hell* have you been following me?"

The last question was more of a guess, considering she had no proof other than the odd familiarity of his presence. *Then again, that may be a trick of my imagination.*

Brennan pursed his lips in response to Freya's interrogation, unsure as to how much he was ready to divulge, and so early on. He sized the girl up, noticing the tension in her body, as though preparing for another fight.

I need to get her to trust me.

"What can I say?" He ended up shrugging. "I'm a jack of all trades."

Freya's eyes burned with lightning in response – clearly, she was not amused. Brennan held up his hand to ask for a minute, then nodded to himself. "Tell you what. How about I fill you in on all that later, *after* you've found your companions and stopped worrying about them?"

Freya's jaw dropped, and her eyes widened. "How did you know?"

Unsettled by the vulnerability in her eyes – and everything else his senses were picking up – Brennan forced a light tone. "Well, you're not exactly hard to read, if you get my meaning."

She bristled at the arrogance in his tone before he was even done speaking. "Now listen here, you–" Freya jabbed a finger in his chest, but was cut off by Brennan.

He grabbed her wrist and moved it away – where it couldn't harm him – then pretended to examine their surroundings in a bored manner. "So, why exactly are we battling a bunch of angry ghosts at night, on an abandoned ship?"

"I'll explain later," Freya snapped. "Besides, *you* don't have to stay here. I can manage without an arrogant guy getting in my way."

"You didn't look like you were mastering the situation just then," Brennan pointed out, referring to the fight he'd witnessed a few minutes earlier. "Besides, I like saving damsels in distress."

"I *don't* need to be saved!" Freya growled and shoved him, clearly pissed off.

Putting out his palms in mock surrendering, Brennan tried to pacify her. "Okay, okay, no need to go all mental on me."

Taking deep breaths to calm herself, Freya threw him a dark look. "Fine! Since I can't get rid of you, then do something useful and stand guard for a few minutes while I locate my friends."

"Sure thing." Brennan glanced around, then pointed to a spot on the side, between two larger barrels. "Why don't you try there, and I'll stand guard at the front?"

Freya stepped over to inspect the spot, and grudgingly had to admit Brennan was right. Closing her eyes, she sat on the floor and focused on picking up O'Keeffe's and Sam's auras.

Sam was easy to find, as he was close by, and in dire need of help if the ghosts she sensed surrounding him were any proof. Seamus proved to be a little more difficult to locate.

As she searched for him, Freya sensed an odd zap in the air. Since her newfound connection to the elements, it felt wrong, as if the air was being manipulated. The whole thing almost had her open her eyes, and risk losing track of her friends.

With a huge effort, Freya blocked it out and gritted her teeth, focusing until she managed to pinpoint her mentor's co-ordinates. He'd somehow ended up on the other side of the port.

Satisfied she'd mapped their locations in her head, Freya stood and headed to Brennan.

"I found them," she said.

"Good, then we can go, round them up, and get the bloody hell out of here." The entire phrase was spoken with the same amount of emotion as if he was ordering tea and biscuits.

"*We?*" Freya glared at Brennan, then walked past him. "I don't recall inviting you."

He snorted, then his footsteps echoed in her trail. "Sure you did."

Freya was about to protest, but reconsidered. If he could fight ghosts, if he was another Sage... *Another body would help. Even if I'd rather use him as a distraction than a partner, but whatever.* She planned to take advantage of the offer and get answers to her questions.

For the time being, Seamus and Sam's well-being took precedence. *Brennan Taggart, and his many mysteries, will have to wait.*

As they neared Sam's location, Freya did her best to keep in touch with his aura – vibe, as she called it – and answer her companion's questions.

"What kind of ghosts are these? They're incredibly, err, aggressive."

"Well, they're Vikings," Freya started, before adding wryly, "and not smart by the looks of it."

"No kidding," Brennan snorted.

"How come they didn't attack while I was scan-searching for my friends?" Freya asked, hoping he hadn't noticed her slip. If he *wasn't* a Sage, it was best she keep her abilities under wraps.

"The fog makes it difficult for them to see us, I suppose." Brennan's guess was as good as hers, yet the way he said it had Freya's senses tingling.

He's lying. Yet when she paused to look at him, he didn't shift under her assessment. "Right..."

They walked a few more minutes until they reached the scene of the conflict. It was another boat, half a port away, and Sam was cornered by three Vikings. Though they couldn't do anything to hurt him, his recent experience must have made him wary. He was attempting to keep his distance – unsuccessfully.

"Hang on, Sam!" Freya yelled, then sprinted in his direction. Brennan's heavier footsteps echoed soon after, as he brought up the rear.

The Sage slammed straight into the first opponent, nearly tackling him. Out of the corner of her eye, she saw Brennan engage with another, and dispose of him with a few vicious punches.

By the time they'd tackled their respective adversaries, the third ghost had vanished.

With a disgusted shake of the head, Freya moved aside and hugged Sam tightly. When she trembled in her arms, she blinked furiously against the onslaught of tears.

Twice in one night. This was way too close.

"I'm so glad you're okay," she whispered in his hair, kissing his forehead.

"Me too, Freya." Sam pulled back and sniffled, trying to be brave. "I'm mostly glad you saved me, otherwise I'd be dead a second time."

Freya forced a smile past the lump in her throat. Sam's curious expression distracted her from the guilt threatening just in time. He peered under her shoulder and she rolled her eyes, guessing he was trying to figure out her new companion.

"Sam, meet Brennan. He saved me from adding another bruise to my collection."

The two boys shook hands, warily at first, but then they recognized in each other a fellow friend – at least, judging by their matching pleased expressions.

Boys! Freya fumed internally, but held her tongue.

"Where's the professor?" Sam asked after a few moments.

"A bit further from here, I'm afraid. And I think he may be in danger."

Sam was alarmed at the bit of news. "I have no idea how we got split up, Frey-Frey. One minute the both of you were around me, the next this blasted fog came up and you were gone. We need to get him back!"

Freya nodded and squeezed his shoulder, attempting to fight down her own panic. Seamus was the closest thing to a blood relative she had left, and she wasn't about to lose him.

But I can't do this alone. Sighing, she turned to Brennan. "You coming?"

He searched her gaze for a moment, then slowly grinned. "I'd never miss out on an adventure."

They walked cautiously through the fog, trying to make as little noise as possible. After they'd crossed half of the port and were closer to Seamus, Freya caught a tap in the atmosphere surrounding them – again. She stopped dead in her tracks.

"Something wrong?" Sam asked.

Freya didn't answer, spinning instead quickly to Brennan. So quickly, in fact, he didn't have time to conceal his expression, and she read him like an open book.

She recalled the zap from earlier, while she'd been scanning for Sam and Seamus' locations. It had struck her as odd that they'd gone from full-on ghost onslaught to no ghosts attacking them, all in the span of a few seconds. As they headed to Sam after, she'd begun to wonder if they were being protected by an invisible shield. Then Brennan had distracted her with all his talking...

The zap in the air was now more noticeable – perhaps because she was focused on it. Reading Brennan's expression, the widening and alarmed set of his eyes, Freya was now convinced it was coming from him. The only question was... *How? Is he really another Sage?*

Seamus' lessons said Sages had become extinct in the mid-nineteenth century, as the old arts were lost. Fewer recruits tapped into their potential, and eventually, uncherished, the powers returned to the earth that had relinquished them. It was highly improbable this new stranger was one of them, and yet, the mystery was nagging at her.

Despite her confusion, Freya kept an impassable mask, and instead gestured for Sam and Brennan to keep going. "It's nothing." She'd deal with it, but later.

They kept on their silent trek for a few more minutes, until they ended up full circle to where Freya, Seamus and Sam had entered the port. Noises from afar froze their steps, and Freya expanded her spirit, feeling shadows in front of them and searching for Seamus.

After a few unsuccessful attempts, a slow victorious smile spread, and she moved closer to Sam and Brennan.

"Good news is, I've picked up his location," she said.

"Great!" Sam practically bounced up for joy. "How are we going to get to him?"

"That's the bad news..." The Sage hesitated, glancing at Brennan. "He's surrounded by enemies."

Sam was quiet, waiting for an idea to form in her mind. Brennan was evidently not so inclined, as he pressed, "There must be a way to get in."

Freya lifted a finger to silence him, followed by a warning glare. They couldn't barge in like they'd done for Sam, as the number of Vikings was closer to twenty than three. Additionally, the fog put them at risk of losing each other – again.

"I might know a way," she admitted, recalling one of Seamus' stories.

She'd been avoiding it for the last hour, but the elements were there – at her beck and call. When he'd first introduced Freya to the Sages' history, Seamus had mentioned the powerful beings could control elements. He'd stressed that such strength was only wielded by full-fledged Sages, due to the spiritual energy needed for the task.

Thinking back to her fight with Asger, Freya wondered if what had happened to her, and Tyr's gentle nudge, could have lifted her to the level of a trained, adult Sage. *Is that why the elements are so keen to listen?*

No answer came from the tiger, and she sighed.

I guess there's only one way to find out.

"Anytime now..."

Freya threw Brennan a scowl over one shoulder, then faced the fog. She extended her hand, reaching deep within herself for the same fire that had fuelled her before.

When she caught it, she stoked it higher, fanning the flames within, until she was able to open her lightning-filled eyes. Her tone was low as she ordered, "Dissipate..."

For a few seconds, nothing happened. Then, the fog began to vanish, revealing what it was hiding all along. Two dozen Viking ghosts, and a rather tired-looking Seamus.

The Sage caught Brennan's sharp intake at the sight, and had to concur with his shocked expression. *Just how many of them are there?*

Chapter 12

Freya snapped out of her horrified daze and realized the dilemma they were in. She spun to Sam, panicked, and yelled, "Disappear! Now!"

Sam looked hurt, but Freya didn't let it distract her. "Listen, you can't stay here. I know you want to help out, but believe me, you're only going to get in the way. Please, *go*!"

The ghost hesitated for another beat, his eyes flickering to Seamus, then Brennan. Their expressions both reflected the same message so he did as they pleaded. The last thing Freya saw of him was his resigned features dissipating into the night.

She then eyed Brennan.

"Are you sure about this? There's still time to back away – for you, at least."

Brennan narrowed his eyes as though offended, then his expression relaxed. His smile, however, didn't reach his darkened brown eyes. "You kidding? I can't wait to kick some butt!"

So I was right, Freya thought. *He's one of us – a Sage.*

She smiled to him gratefully, then took a step towards the Vikings. "Release Seamus and I promise you won't get hurt...much." The last part was added under her breath.

Brennan chuckled softly by her side, throwing her an amused side-glance. The Vikings shared broken-teeth grins and cackles, seemingly finding her statement hilarious.

"Or what?" The biggest of them threatened. "You'll *hurt* us?" He had scarred features and pale blue eyes, and one of his arms was shorter than the other.

Freya glared at him, clenching her teeth. *You're so dead, buddy, just keep laughing.*

"Go easy on him," Brennan teased.

Without even realizing what she was doing, Freya looked over her shoulder at him and winked. She then faced their opponents.

"Give us a break, you're a girl!" The shout came from another Viking, and a few laughs encouraged him.

"I'm astonished," Freya rolled her eyes. "You actually have some brains to notice *and* state it. It's been how long since you've been around females? Centuries? Must be getting rusty..."

This only enraged him. Without a warning, he launched at her, axe in hand. Emboldened by her success with the fog, Freya didn't budge. Instead, she raised her palm towards the Viking, then closed it in a fist.

He was stopped in midair, as if paralyzed. Freya stared in awe at her hand – the upgrade in her abilities was truly amazing.

A flurry of activity raised her attention back to the group. The Vikings recovered quickly from their surprise, and launched a full-on attack. She waited until they were close, then bent her knees and launched herself in the air, propelling herself as far as she could with her leg muscles.

As the first Viking was shorter than the others, she was able to get to his height, and use his head – and his companions' – as stairs. She hopped over them, aiming for the center where Seamus was being kept.

After a kick to the last one's head, Freya landed in their middle, only a few feet away from Seamus. She punched, evaded and kicked her way through the remaining Vikings still in her way, and Brennan fought and kept the ones on the outside of the circle entertained.

In a matter of moments, Freya had reached Seamus' side, and started untying him. She scanned him to make sure he was in a state to run, once freed. Aside from his obvious bruises and fatigue, and his overall disheveled state, Seamus appeared to be in good shape.

"How are you feeling?" Freya peered at him, concerned nonetheless.

"A bit tired," his faint smile implied as much, "but fine nonetheless."

"Glad to hear it." The knot finally came undone, and Freya stood. "Come on, we should go. Brennan may need back up."

"Brennan?" O'Keeffe repeated while standing up, holding onto Freya's shoulder for support.

Freya put her arm around his waist to support more of his weight, and began walking towards Brennan. He was a few meters away, clearing a path by getting rid of another Viking.

"Brennan Taggart," she said in response to O'Keeffe's question. "He saved me today. I'll explain later."

Seamus gave a shake of the head, too exhausted to ask questions. Focusing on putting one foot in front of another was hard enough without dropping due to his headache.

They reached Brennan as he delivered a round kick to the last ghost, then straightened up and watched the Viking topple to the ground. Freya raised her eyebrows in amusement.

"I see you have everything under control."

"Nothing I can't do," he winked, that same arrogant tone to his voice.

Freya rolled her eyes as Brennan introduced himself. "Brennan Taggart."

O'Keeffe raised his hand automatically to shake his, then his eyes met Brennan's and he froze, staring in shock.

&&&

Hells be damned!

The demon was in a rage, having observed the confrontations. He'd barely restrained himself from showing up to put the girl in her place. It was too soon, *much* too soon, and for the two relics he craved, patience was a virtue.

One I do not always have...

He scowled, watching the two men being introduced. The boy was an additional problem, if what he scented off him was true. An annoyance that not even Cadmael could oppose, if the prophecy was true.

Turning his back to them, the demon was about to leave, retreating to his lair. But before doing so, he sent one last wave of energy, to wake the specters up from their recovery period...

Let them deal with that!

&&&

"Seamus?"

Freya's concerned tone brought him out of his reflections. As if waking from a long dream – or memory – Seamus shook his head and finished extending his palm. "Seamus O'Keeffe."

The two men were shaking hands when Freya paled and stumbled backwards, almost dragging Seamus to the ground with her.

"Uh-oh," she whispered.

"What?"

Freya didn't bother with an explanation, instead pointed to something over Brennan's shoulder. He spun to check it out, and stepped back at the sight greeting him.

The ghosts they'd fought were getting up – something that shouldn't have been possible. They were looking around, then their hideous faces turned to the teenagers as one.

"How are they doing that?" Brennan asked, scowling.

Freya glanced at him. *I shouldn't be surprised he knows this much about ghosts... But still, he's right.* What they were seeing was impossible in a normal setting. The ghosts' soul had to recover, and that could take a few hours, at least. To top off their bad luck, more ghosts were advancing from the port, quite decided to capture them.

"Got a plan B?" O'Keeffe asked no one in particular.

"Yeah," Brennan mumbled. "Run!"

The three of them turned their backs to the little army – which was now only twenty meters away from them – and took off as fast as they could. The problem was they were being surrounded faster than they could outrun them, and Freya wasn't about to leave Seamus behind.

A quiet space... Seek a quiet space...

O'Keeffe listened to the suggestion in his head, acting before any of the two teenagers could. He led Brennan and Freya behind a large container, out of sight for the moment, then stopped. He leaned against the metal, panting for breath and holding his side.

Use the boy, a voice came to Freya, and she frowned at the female tone, so unlike Tyr's. *I do not wish you harm. He hides many mysteries, this Brennan, but one alone can help you both out of this mess.*

The Sage hesitated, unsure of what to believe. Then she recalled Tyr's words, advising her that help would still be given to her, but not necessarily in the form she expected. On a hunch, she decided to trust it.

"We're a bit pressed for time, Freya," Seamus muttered, glancing nervously at the corner.

The spirits must be getting closer, he thought, trying his utmost to find a solution that eluded him.

Freya, meanwhile, inhaled deeply and faced Brennan with a serious look. "Whatever you're hiding, now's not the time to lie. There's only one way we get out of here alive, and it's tied to you and me somehow."

"I'm not lying about anything!" Brennan denied, crossing his arms of his chest.

"Cut it out!" Freya hissed, stepping closer, uncaring of his personal bubble. "I *know* you're not saying everything, which is all fine and dandy. But you have something that can get us both out of here!"

When he seemed at a loss, Freya started having second thoughts.

Grab his palms. Think of home.

"Give me your hands," she ordered.

Brennan did as he was told, his gaze unreadable. As their skins touched, an electric zap crossed their fingertips, leaving them staring at each other in shock.

Freya shrugged it off and kept her eyes locked onto Brennan's. "Seamus, I get the impression you'll want to get closer for this."

The elderly man hesitated, then joined a closed fist atop theirs. Freya threw him a grateful look for not arguing, especially considering her previous reckless suggestions. Seamus smiled, and she read trust in his expression – trust in her, that she'd get them out safe.

"You should picture the hotel's garden," Freya said to Brennan. "And don't bother denying it, you were there," she added tersely.

Brennan clenched his teeth, the only indication he was annoyed, before nodding tightly.

"All right."

What now? Freya challenged internally.

You already grasp the power, and what to do with it...

Freya realized it was true. Now that the limit on her abilities was lifted, she could access anything she put her mind to, from within. Brennan's eyes shone with determination and a slight hint of fear, as though he could read her mind – and intentions.

Freya's tug was the signal. Eyes wide open, focused on Freya's grey ones, they held tightly onto each other. Then, the Sage started muttering. The sound of her voice was soft at first, then, like a wind picking up, it grew in strength, and Brennan was able to catch her words.

"I bind you to me, elements high and below, I bind you and command you, assist us to get home."

She clearly pictured in her mind the gardens in which she'd spent hours talking to Tyr. It was the safest spot she could think of landing – *if* what she was trying to do would work.

The port environment faded to the outside, and she saw something else. It was greyed out, like a movie in bad quality, but it was Brennan hidden behind a corner of the B&B's garden, watching her. She was leaning on the bench, her expression worried –the time she'd been talking to Tyr about the long ship.

And he was there!

A soft shine around Brennan's neck drew her attention, but she couldn't break eye contact. Out of the corner of her eye, she noticed the brilliance getting stronger, until it surrounded them.

Just as the ghosts passed the corner, the air rippled above their heads, and a vacuum formed. Freya sensed its potent essence drawing her in, as could Brennan. He faltered, almost breaking eye contact, but her tightening grip brought him new resolution.

"Let's do this," he said.

In mere moments, the channel sucked all three humans within. Fog surrounded them, and Freya and Brennan could barely keep eye contact. They strained, however, not keen to guess what could happen if they lost each other from view.

Seconds later, they found themselves in the hotel's garden, stunned the idea had worked. Freya and Brennan let go of their hands and stumbled away, eventually falling on the grass.

O'Keeffe fought against his own dizziness, but managed to stand up.

He stepped to his protégée with a quizzical gaze. "Freya, did you just transport us through space?"

She didn't reply, too busy trying to catch her breath. As she was about to stand up, the Sage turned to her companion, noticing Brennan was on his knees as well, coughing and trying to inhale air deeply at the same time.

Freya crawled by his side, placing a palm on his chest. The dragon medallion was dull now, its sapphire eyes unseeing. The Sage pressed her hand, sensing Brennan's panicked heartbeat. Their gazes locked, and the panic in his softened, then vanished. He managed to inhale properly, and touched her hand in silent thanks.

"I'm okay," he panted in response to her inquisitive stare.

Unsteadily, he stood, and Freya did the same, checking out Seamus. With Brennan's help, she helped her mentor to his hotel room.

When the door opened, they were met by Sam's anxious spirit.

Chapter 13

"Finally!" Sam breathed out in obvious relief, heading to greet them. Since he'd rematerialized at the B&B, the pacing and anxious waiting had nearly driven him up the wall.

"Not to worry, Sam," O'Keeffe smiled indulgently, "no one can get to me while Freya protects me."

Sam hugged him tightly – an unusual sign of affection – then shrugged the emotional moment off, and eyed Freya. His glance flickered between her and Brennan, who was a few feet back, giving them space to mingle.

"How did you guys escape?"

Freya glanced at Seamus, who headed over to the armchair and dropped in it. "Funny story, Sammy boy."

"Freya teleported us here," Seamus interrupted. His tone was blank, as if he didn't quite believe the situation. "I cannot begin to fathom how she thought of it, but I believe she will regale us with the details later."

Sam sighed and tried an easier question. "So, mind sharing how you two met?"

Freya glanced at Brennan, then back to Sam. She shrugged and took a seat in another chair, while Brennan sat opposite her.

"Bit of a long story," she said.

It was a poor attempt at trying to stop the talk from happening. She wanted to get Brennan on his own, and find out exactly what he was hiding.

The attempt was thwarted by Brennan without a flicker of contrition. "Not *that* long," he contradicted with a half-smile.

Seamus stood and went over to the little table, where a few packs of instant coffee awaited. He gestured to them, but when the two teenagers declined with a shake of the head, made himself a cup.

Satisfied with his fortifying beverage, O'Keeffe resumed his seat. Despite his movements, he hadn't missed the glare Freya directed to Brennan, nor the overall tension between the two.

"All right, fine," Freya began, rolling her eyes at her companions' curious stares. "I was fighting a ghost – as usual – and as I ended it, someone asked if I needed any help. When I turned, Brennan was there. I recognized him–"

Freya bit her lip, throwing a glance to Brennan. His eyes visibly widened at what she'd been about to reveal.

"Yes?" Seamus asked. "Would you mind finishing your thought, Freya?"

She hung her head in shame, not fooled by his calm tone – her mentor was annoyed she'd kept another important detail, and probably worried about what else she was hiding.

Averting her eyes from his, she said, "Then I guess the story should start when we first landed... Back at the airport, I felt something. I can't exactly explain what it was, more like an insistent nudge."

Freya raised her head, tentatively meeting Seamus' dark grey look, and was relieved it had softened. She hoped he'd realize she'd kept things from him not out of spite, but because she was unsure how to deal with the information.

To her relief, Seamus gestured for her to continue.

"Well, when I paid attention to my instincts, I saw Brennan in the middle of the airport." Freya pointed to the youth in question, who was finding the ceiling quite interesting. "He caught my eye because of the necklace with the dragon." To Brennan, she added, "You'll have to explain to me why you're wearing that, later. Anyway, our eyes met, we were both stunned... And then I lost sight of him, and we left."

Sam, who was floating in midair above the little table, stopped in confusion. "And you didn't mention this before because...?"

"I'm not sure," Freya shrugged. "I guess I was waiting for the right moment."

Sam accepted the evasive answer, but Seamus wasn't as keen on dropping the subject. "Freya, is there anything else you want to confess?"

The Sage hesitated for a brief moment. She wasn't sure mentioning Brennan and his connection to the intruder pursuing her for the last few days was necessary. Despite the fact she'd picked the same vibe from Brennan as from her mysterious stalker, there was the other matter of the bad luck that seemed to stick to her lately.

First I get caught in that stupid trap and Tyr has to rescue me. Then this entire operation goes haywire... If I didn't know any better, I'd swear someone is out for my skin.

The sobering reflection was enough to give her pause. *But can it be him?* Freya took a moment to size up Brennan, but there was nothing in his aura that confirmed it.

Am I wrong, Tyr?

She wished the tiger would signal her, but nothing from that realm replied. Whatever was holding back the entity, it meant she was on her own, with only her instincts to trust.

Analyzing everything from the moment they had landed, Freya had to admit the matter of Brennan's capabilities was unsettling... They were so similar to hers, it was confusing. *Maybe Seamus can shed some light on that, at least. Might as well share part of what I've gathered so far.*

"Actually, yes," Freya responded, eyes flicking to Brennan, noticing the tension radiating off his tightly bound body. "There's also this presence I've felt for the past few days. I have the weird feeling that it was following me, or one of us, at least."

&&&

"I see..."

Seamus' tone wasn't forthcoming, no matter how hard Brennan tried to read the old man.

Brennan did his best to not show a reaction, but even he was aware of the tension within. He had no proof of it, but he was under the impression the girl knew more than she was letting on. It was not something he could chance at the moment, when he so desperately yearned to be trusted, but then ...

Why hide something from the old guy, when she could yell it out and get it over with? And does she even realize how closely she's being hunted?

Brennan had felt the other shadow, always skulking behind, neither human nor specter, but intent on harm. It made him sick being or stepping close to it, and he avoided it like the plague, fervently wishing never to be pitted against it. He only hoped Freya wouldn't have to, either.

Brooding at the thought, Brennan was not conscious of Seamus talking to him. It was only when he realized three pairs of eyes were focused on him that he snapped out of his daydreams.

"Sorry. You were saying...?"

"I was inviting you to tell us a bit more about yourself, Brennan," O'Keeffe repeated. Though his tone was gentle, it was clear he was assessing him.

Brennan hesitated, uncertainty gnawing at him. *Can I trust them? Can I really reveal the truth to them, when I've only met them for a short while? Freya's already seen too much...* The medallion shining while they were teleporting came to his mind. What he carried was far more dangerous if it fell in the wrong hands. And yet, he'd been specifically instructed to speak only to the two Sages. Reluctantly, he decided to brave his chances with honesty – at least in part.

"I guess I should begin by being a tad more truthful..." He threw a sheepish smile to Freya, then admitted, "My name isn't Brennan Taggart. It's Dublin. Brennan Dublin."

&&&

Seamus started violently at the first mention of Brennan's last name, going pale. Coffee sloshed out of his cup and dripped over him, but he paid it no mind. Freya, however, noticed his demeanor had changed.

"Is everything all right?" she asked, but only received silence in return, as Seamus focused on Brennan.

The elderly man now understood why the features, the eyes were so familiar. He peered at the teenager closely, before whispering, almost in awe, "You mean your grandfather is the Wiseman Thomas Dublin?"

Freya and Sam shared a confused glance. How did Seamus know Brennan's grandfather? And why had Brennan lied about his name? Lastly, who –

"Seamus," Freya started tentatively, "who or *what* is a Wiseman?"

Her mentor had an oddly glazed look in his eyes, as though lost in a memory. In a daze, he stood and placed his cup on the desk, then dabbed at his clothes with a napkin.

Finally, with a shake of the head, he went back to his normal self and smiled. "It's true, I have not yet broached the subject with you. Wisemen, my dear, are humans with powers and, like Sages, they are almost extinct as well." The last bit was murmured in a whisper.

"Are they born with their abilities?" Freya asked, narrowing her eyes at her mentor's odd behavior.

"No. They..." Seamus trailed off, glancing back at Brennan. "At least not to my knowledge. Their powers get transferred from mentor to apprentice."

"Like a bank account?"

O'Keeffe had to laugh at that. "Yes, Sam, very similar to a bank account, though no paperwork is involved. It's all done spiritually, at a certain time of the year, in the presence of witnesses."

To Freya, he said, "When I say they are alike, I mean Sages and Wisemen wield the same forces. Both can speak and touch ghosts, giving them solid form whenever necessary, and fight them with ease. Their abilities are *almost* the same. And I do emphasize almost because the sources are slightly – only *slightly* – different."

As he warmed up to the subject, Seamus began pacing while explaining.

"Wisemen's abilities act differently, though they can be just as fierce. Why, twenty of them could battle armies of hundreds ghosts and, yet outnumbered, still win. Now, separate, Wisemen are less potent than Sages. But put one Wiseman and a Sage together, and you obtain remarkable power."

Freya and Brennan shared an astonished look. Noticing it, Seamus stopped his pacing.

"You don't believe me? And yet, you knew how to combine your faculties together at the harbor, Freya. How come?"

Freya was startled. "I-I had a hunch it may work," she stammered, not quite ready to confess she was hearing not one, but *two* voices in her head lately. "I felt a force in Brennan, but I wasn't sure of the result... I figured if we used our abilities together, we had a chance of escaping there alive."

"Exactly!" Seamus' excitement at what he was explaining gleamed on his face. He was so lost in his narrative that he didn't challenge Freya's instincts in that situation, but rather kept talking. "Your potential combined is what brought us back here safe."

"Seamus, but... How can we unite our powers when we don't even know each other?" Freya frowned. "What you're suggesting doesn't seem, well, possible with two strangers."

"Ah... But I didn't say you had *united* them, Freya," O'Keeffe corrected her. "I said you had *combined* them."

"What's the difference?" Brennan interrupted.

"Combining two different sources," O'Keeffe instructed, "means taking a few elements from one and from the other in order to make them act as one. The two, however, remain different. But *uniting* them means adding them to each other, dissolving them into one true entity. And –"

"They are one," Freya finished, gaping at her mentor.

"What?" Brennan blinked in confusion.

Freya tried to clarify what Seamus had explained. "If we unite our powers, there won't be any differences. Where yours begins and mine ends won't matter. They'll both act as one true energy. Whereas if combined, they'll be halves, because only a few elements have been put together."

"Exactly!" Seamus exclaimed. "And that's what makes the uniting of a Sage's potential and those of a Wiseman's so amazing."

"Mr. O'Keeffe –" Brennan started, but was interrupted.

"Seamus, please," the professor said.

"Okay, Seamus, can you explain why exactly we're so influential if united?"

"Your grandfather didn't tell you?" Seamus' eyebrows rose in surprise. "And yet, when we were both students, it was what we most debated on!"

Freya choked on the glass of water she was sipping, before coughing out, "You went to *school* with his grandfather?"

Seamus chuckled, admitting, "Yes, we attended Yale together while he was an international student. We realized the other's powers completely by chance, while getting ambushed by ghosts in the library one night." His gaze flicked to Brennan. "My only regret is I have been remiss in keeping touch with him. Your grandfather saved my life that day, and we became best friends, sharing everything. Which is why it's unsettling he would not share such wonderful conversation with you!"

"He might have had his reasons," Brennan muttered with an indifferent shrug. "Regardless, *why* are we so powerful?"

O'Keeffe seemed surprised by his nonchalance, hesitating for a brief moment before answering. There was something odd about the newcomer, something he was not yet sharing with them. Deciding to trust him, if only for the sake of the friendship he had with his grandfather, Seamus nodded.

"Right, good question, Brennan. Both your abilities come from the same place – your spiritual energy. But a Wiseman's ability is controlled – and generated – by powerful emotions. A Sage's, on the other hand, is influenced by the four elements – fire, water, earth and air. When fighting, a Wiseman uses the power of emotions, while a Sage uses that of elements. Together, these two forces make one true entity – one controls the inside, the other the outside." He paused and tilted his head at Freya. "Do you recall how on our first day here, you told me the story of the dragon and Estella?"

"Sure..."

"Then you understand that is how we Sages have received our faculties, yes? They've been passed down from generation to generation by not only blood, but also initiation."

Freya frowned. "What are you getting at?"

"Would you care to share the story with Brennan?" O'Keeffe demanded instead.

Rolling her eyes, the Sage turned to the newcomer. She was in no mood to play teacher, especially to someone who wasn't being truthful to them. With one last dejected glare to her mentor, she followed his instructions and related to Brennan the story of the creation of Sages.

When she arrived to the part about the book, she exchanged a quick check-in with Seamus, to see if he wanted to convey Brennan that information, as well. When he approved with a nod, she went on.

"And so, Estella's brother became nothing. The end," Freya finished a few moments later.

"Not quite," O'Keeffe interrupted.

Freya and Brennan raised surprised glances to him. After making sure he had their undivided attention, Seamus completed the last bit of the story.

"This part, I was unaware of despite my training, until I met Thomas, your grandfather. At the same time as Estella's brother disappeared, another event took place. Close to the hill, there was a boy, merely twelve, who always played in the area. His name was David and he happened to be there when Estella's brother opened the book."

Sam, who'd been floating further away in the room, joined the three, intrigued by the prospect of another boy.

"Attracted by the light that erupted within it, he ran to the top of the hill and arrived near the man, as he died. Though he was gone, the force had not yet retreated back to the prized artifact, and so it touched David. The first emotion David felt impregnated the remaining energy as it filled him, and so it happened that his own powers were only activated by his emotions."

Seamus paused, reading the shock on Freya's expression, and Brennan's avid curiosity. "The years passed by, and David grew and became, with each day, wiser and wiser. He didn't marry, for he preferred to live as a hermit. And after decades of training, he finally mastered all of his newfound faculties."

"The powers you mentioned before, like mine?" Freya interjected.

"Yes. So each ten years, David would then take an apprentice and pass some of his faculties to him. The apprentice would then cultivate them, until they grew, and after a certain age, passed it on to apprentices of their own...And so were the Wisemen created."

"But how was he able to share his powers over and over?" Sam countered.

"Because he only shared a little of them at a time. Seeing as they were ruled by emotions, after a certain amount of years, the spiritual energy evolved, until each apprentice surpassed the teacher beforehand."

Both Freya and Brennan had their mouths hanging open by the end of O'Keeffe's little speech.

Freya recovered first. "And you didn't share this with us – or at least *me* – before, *why*?"

Seamus lifted a palm in a pacifying gesture, "You didn't ask and, well, even if you had, you were not ready for it." To Brennan, he said, "Keeping that in mind, I do believe it would be time for you to share your story with us."

"Not yet."

Freya turned to Brennan, stunned not at the words, but at the flat tone in which they were spoken by the young man.

"Tell me first what you know of Isis's orb, and Osiris' scepter. Then, and *only* then, will I reveal everything."

Seamus was struck by the demand – and what it alluded to.

Chapter 14

"How are you aware of this?" Seamus narrowed his eyes, no longer forthcoming. "The secrets of the relics you reference were shared with only a handful of people, most of whom are dead now."

Brennan stood up to square off against the elderly man. "There is too much at stake here for me to waste my time. Do you have the answers, yes or no?"

Freya jumped to her feet, angling her body to stand slightly between the two, while Sam peered back and forth in confusion.

"Hold on a second," she held a palm up to his chest, to keep him at a distance.

Brennan glared at Seamus' obstinate silence, then his dark-brown eyes descended on Freya. "What?" he hissed through gritted teeth.

"First off, mind your attitude," Freya's voice dropped a few octaves. "Second, you're not here to make demands. You lied to us from the beginning, and that doesn't exactly make you trust-worthy."

Brennan's anger deflated in the next second, as quickly as it'd come. He dropped back down to the armchair, running his hands through his hair. "Please, you have to help me." His head hanging, he continued contritely, "Lying was the only way I could make sure no one *not* meant to hear this, chases us here. It was for my protection as much as yours."

There was a long moment of dead air, as Freya tried to look past his aura. The only conclusion she could draw was that his feelings were as real as his words had been.

"Very well," Seamus surprised them all by capitulating, though his sharp gaze never wavered from Brennan. "I will share mine, if – and *only* if – you tell me yours in return." It was only once he nodded his agreement that the elder Sage continued.

"Long ago, this is way before our time, or even our civilization existed... Back when the gods roamed the Earth, a legend arose. Are you both familiar with Isis and Osiris?"

"Ancient Egypt," Freya blurted, "They were husband and wife. Him, god of the underworld and her, goddess of fertility."

"Yes, indeed," Seamus nodded. "They were also rulers of Upper and Lower Egypt. As part of their royal duties, they had commissioned for each other a gift. Isis received an orb from Osiris, to represent his heart whilst he was in the underworld, and not by her side. Osiris, on the other hand, received a scepter from Isis, to keep him safe from harm whilst away from her."

He paused there, and directed a glance full of meaning to Brennan, to take over.

"My grandfather revealed they were called the relics of the Underworld. The two objects, together, could be used to control all spiritual entities," he said.

Freya stared between the two in shock, then at Sam.

"You mean... Like what happened to me?" Sam's whisper came out choked, and she read the underlying panic in tone.

At Brennan's blank expression, Freya explained, "Sam was immobilized by something earlier today, and it was as though he was frozen. Asger, the henchman of Cadmael whom we're up against, mentioned something about his master being able to send ghosts away. Is this related?"

"No," Seamus refuted categorically. "The gods' prized possessions could in no way have been located by that Viking."

"What makes you so sure?" Brennan arched an eyebrow. "Together, they could make one do anything to ghosts – including remove their mobility."

"Your grandfather may not have divulged this, but the orb and scepter were long ago cast away by Isis and Osiris. They were hidden, to avoid them ever ending in the hands of the wrong people."

Judging by Brennan's scowl, Seamus realized he was right – for whatever reason, Thomas hadn't shared the rest of the information. He hesitated for a brief second, wondering why, before continuing.

"All that has been left behind is a map. To this day, no one knows where the relics are hidden."

"Well, we have to find them," Brennan said, standing once more. Before Seamus could interrupt him, he continued, "My grandfather sent me here on this quest, with a tidbit of information. The map has two keys – a medallion and a book. I happen to have the former." He lifted the dragon medallion up for emphasis. "And I gather you have the latter."

Seamus and Freya shared a shocked look. Neither was willing to admit to it, but how could they break the standoff if they didn't?

It was Sam who came to the rescue, with his undeterred boyish charm. "Maybe we can settle this no-trust thing, guys. I mean, Brennan needs info from us. And he gave you pretty much everything he could. One thing I'm still not clear on is, who exactly was Brennan's granddad? Maybe since Seamus knew him so well...."

"Yes, Seamus," Freya added, folding her arms across her chest. "Do share."

"Well," O'Keeffe began, "Thomas Dublin is one of the greatest Wisemen that exists, but also the one who, in the old stories, trespassed the sacred Code of the Wisemen. You have to understand Freya, unlike Sages, Wisemen have rules. One of them is to not get married, and always live as hermits. Thomas was an exception. He fell in love with a peasant, whom he then married. He is the first to have risked doing so."

"Risked?" Freya asked, intrigued.

This time, it was Brennan who jumped in, though his expression was nostalgic. "Wisemen believe that if they get married, they lose all their abilities. None have ever chanced it." He shrugged. "My grandfather was the first, as Seamus said."

"And?" Freya pressed.

"And what?"

"Well, *did* he lose them?"

"Yes. I mean, not exactly," Brennan corrected himself, remembering his grandfather's last years. "The thing is, everyone reckoned he wasn't a Wiseman any longer because he never used his powers after he married... for their own good. He knew the remaining Wisemen, after the bloodlines had died out, believed with all their soul that if the first of their race lived alone, they all had to do the same, or else something bad would happen. My grandfather was smart enough to realize that if he used his abilities after his marriage, confusion would have reigned over the Code of the Wisemen for many decades."

"So he decided to *pretend* he lost them?" Freya interceded.

"Yeah. And guess how they repaid him?" Brennan's tone became bitter as he continued. "They ignored him, made a pariah out of the man that saved their beliefs. Even his own son rejected him. He was disgraced, all because he allowed them to keep their legends and superstitions."

Freya took in his haunted expression, the anguish in his eyes, then glanced at Seamus. She could read something in her mentor's eyes, a sort of resignation, almost a realization that dawned on him.

"Brennan..." Seamus trailed off, almost wishing to ignore the innuendo in the young man's words.

"Yeah?"

Seamus sighed and finally asked the question heavy on his heart. "Is your grandfather still alive?"

"No," Brennan shook his head. He blinked quickly, as though fighting away tears, then mumbled. "He died last year."

"I'm sorry," Seamus put a hand over his shoulder, squeezing in silent comfort. "This may not help, but since the years we spent as friends, I have never run into anyone more generous and open-minded than him. He was truly a great man, an exemplary human being."

"Thank you."

Seamus stepped away, then dropped heavily back on his chair. "Does that answer all your questions, Freya? Or do you have more?"

The Sage's gaze shifted from her mentor to Sam, then Brennan. "One more, actually. How did you become a Wiseman, if your grandfather's dead?"

Brennan frowned, as if not understanding the question. "Before his death, he taught me about the Wiseman abilities and passed his on to me, then showed me how to use them."

"Wait," Sam intervened, brow furrowed in confusion. "How did he pass the stuff on to you, if he didn't want people to know he still had powers? Seamus, didn't you say the ritual or whatever needs witnesses?"

"Indeed."

Brennan shrugged again and walked to the window. After a moment of looking out, he faced them and leaned against the wall. "We waited for the full moon, and the transfer took place in the house he lived in. I'm not sure how he got around the witness part of things. All I know is, his cabin was far from the village, and no one noticed the odd occurrence."

"What was it like?" Sam asked, his eyes shining with curiosity.

Brennan read the same question in Freya's expression, and said, "It was...interesting. Exhausting. My grandfather waited until the moon was at its apex, before entering a trance. I'd already been meditating for a few hours. It was during the trance that everything transferred to me. When I was conscious again, my grandfather smiled, and told me I was a full Wiseman."

"So unfair," Freya muttered with a glower to Seamus. "Meanwhile, I only get my powers little by little!"

Seamus shook his head. "Brennan's powers are tied-in with emotions, Freya. It makes sense that he would receive them at once, whereas yours require you to get accommodated to the elements."

She rolled her eyes in response, then softened her tone towards Brennan. "Then what happened?"

He shrugged, before continuing, "It was a few months before his death. So we spent time training, then one day out of the blue he told me about this legend of the relics of the underworld, and gave me the medallion."

He thumbed the piece of jewelry, as though drawing solace in some way from its presence. "The most I can guess is that together, this medallion and your book can form a map, leading us to where the objects have been hidden."

His gaze was demanding when it landed on Seamus, asking its due. The elder Sage nodded and said, "Yes, we are in possession of the other artifact. But what did Thomas say about the medallion, Brennan?"

The Wiseman gave a one-shouldered shrug. "Just that he got it when he was a boy, and guarded it all his life."

"Guarded?" Freya frowned and turned to Seamus. "Did my mother do the same with the book?"

O'Keeffe hesitated, then nodded. "Yes, she did. For the entirety of her life."

Something about his tone kept Freya's attention. "Did this book have anything to do with how she died?" Out of the corner of her eye, Freya caught Brennan straightening up, and felt his eyes on her. "Seamus?"

To her dismay, her mentor's expression turned blank. "You know I cannot answer that."

"You just did," she whispered, and faced Brennan again. "Maybe we shouldn't try to locate the relics, if both our families suffered because of them."

"You know *nothing*!" Brennan spat, his features darkening. He opened his mouth to say more, then seemed to collect himself and shook his head. He blew out a breath, then said, "I'm sorry, I haven't slept well. And the use of my powers earlier..." He trailed off, pleading for an apology with his eyes.

Freya looked at Seamus for help. "When you said Wiseman and Sages powers are different..."

"They also have various effects on your spiritual energy, yes," he confirmed.

Freya mulled the information over in her head, then filed it away for future use. To Brennan, she said, "Let me rephrase. Why do you think it's so important we find these relics? Did your grandfather mention anything?"

"Yeah, he did." Brennan's tone left no room for interpretation – the news would not be good.

"The prophecy..." The whispered words came from Sam, but he might as well have yelled them.

Brennan was across the floor in the next second, towering over the boy, his eyes intense as he asked, "What prophecy? What have you learnt?"

Sam backed a few steps, and Freya stood up. She shoved at Brennan's shoulder, pushing him away from Sam. "Oy! Whatever issues you have, or tiredness you're experiencing, don't grant you the right to be an asshole!"

Brennan clenched his jaw, before forcing himself to relax. "All right, you have a point. I'm sorry, Sam, I could have handled that better. But *what* do you know? This is important."

The boy glanced to Freya, then Seamus, before admitting, "When I first came to get you two, after seeing the Vikings... That night, Asger mentioned something about a prophecy. He seemed to believe Cadmael was in a race with it. That's all, I swear."

Brennan backed away, running a hand through his hair. "He knows, then. Someone must be advising him, someone that wants the relics too..." The words were spoken almost to himself.

Freya raised a hesitant palm to his shoulder, to draw his attention to her, but he flinched away out of reflex. She raised her eyebrows inquisitively, but dropped the subject. Brennan would share when he was ready to.

Turning his back to her, he said to Seamus, "There's a prophecy that evil will try to get the relics, to gain control of this place as we know it. And the only thing standing in its way will be a boy and a girl." His voice was earnest. "It specifically mentions a *boy* and *girl*."

"And if I gather your meaning correctly, you and Freya are it, because you are not yet of age?" Seamus asked, drawn in by the theory despite himself.

"Yes," Brennan admitted. "And my grandfather believed so, as well. He followed your movements, knew about Freya, her origins... I, for one, didn't believe it was an accident he died, because he was in perfect condition for a fifty-year-old. I think he was poisoned by somebody, but I don't have any proof of what I'm advancing."

As he paused, running a hand tiredly over his face, O'Keeffe took pity on the teenager. That, and he remembered something he needed to examine, to be better informed. When

Brennan stifled a yawn, but seemed as though he was about to continued his story, Seamus interrupted.

"No, Brennan. I think we are all a bit tired by now and we certainly need some sleep. How about we regroup in the morning?"

Brennan threw a look full of gratitude towards the elder Sage, even as the enormity of what had happened in that day crashed on him, all at once. "I guess sleep won't hurt," he whispered, already struggling against another huge yawn.

They stood up and stretched, then O'Keeffe pointed to the second bed in the room, which Sam had no need for – he never slept. "You're welcome to sleep here."

"Thank you," he seemed surprised, as though simple kindness was not something he was used to. "I truly appreciate it."

Chapter 15

The next morning, they stood around a big breakfast for three containing – among others –bagels, pancakes, toast, tea, coffee, bacon and some scrambled eggs. Each human piled their plate with food, and Brennan went on with his story.

"So, last night I was telling you about my granddad. See, he was killed, that part I'm sure of, but I never discovered who could've done it. No matter how hard I tried to investigate, my Wiseman status filled most of my free time." He took a sip of coffee, and said, "Like you, Freya, I stand against evil spirits. My powers, however, can't be used daily. Because they're triggered by emotions, using them engages large amounts of energy – the *vital* kind – from me. I tend to get tired easily when I use them for battles."

"But there is one faculty," O'Keeffe interrupted, "that does not require much – telepathy."

Freya dropped her bagel and turned to Brennan, eyebrows arched. "You can speak telepathically too?"

"Yes," he nodded. "Here, I'll show you."

Can you hear me?

Freya started at Brennan's voice in her head – he hadn't moved a muscle. She followed his example and replied telepathically, while maintaining eye contact.

Loud and clear.

Good. He paused, then added, *Thanks for not mentioning anything last night about what you know – or suspect.* This time, Freya showed no particular sign of listening. She broke eye contact with the Wiseman, and concentrated on her breakfast.

Brennan was a little startled at being ignored, but resumed his story nonetheless. Every few minutes, he'd glance at Freya out of the corner of his eye, but the Sage seemed focused on eating. It was imperative he convince them to help hunt for the relics.

&&&

Seamus, who had been eyeing the two closely, tried to hide his satisfaction. The sooner the two teenagers got along, the better for all of them – and the world.

The previous night, after Brennan passed out, he'd reviewed his notes, and the last letter he had received from his old friend. Brennan had been truthful, indeed. The two youths had a lot to achieve together, if what Thomas had divulged to him was true. The last passage of his letter kept floating in Seamus' mind.

> *I found this in a copy of your dragon book. It indicates that one day in the future, a Sage and a Wiseman shall unite their powers for the better of humanity. If that day ever arrives, the sun and the moon will be endangered, and only those two could save them. I will try to learn more… Keep you posted.*

O'Keeffe had almost forgotten the letter, what with the last few months, but he was now of the same opinion as Brennan. The Sage and Wiseman in question were Freya and Brennan, and the sun and moon were a code designating the orb and the scepter.

With a huge effort, he focused back on Brennan's words.

&&&

"... I fought ghosts by myself, mainly lost kids out for trouble," Brennan said. "But then, one day, I knew something was wrong. As I live close from here, I picked up a vibe coming from the harbor and I began to investigate. It took me days to figure out the real purpose of the Vikings. By then, I knew it wasn't a one-man job. I surprised a conversation between some ghosts, of two mortals that were going to intervene with fate. Curious, I decided to find out exactly who they were."

He focused the full intensity of his stare to Freya, "That's why I was at the airport that day – to observe you and see what you were capable of. Now, don't take this the wrong way, but I also wanted to make sure I could trust you before I showed up. This is why I left as soon as I knew I'd been spotted."

"Am I wrong in assuming you trailed us after the airport?" O'Keeffe asked.

"No, you're quite right... And I apologize for my paranoia."

Seamus waved the apology away, then smiled, "Well, all I can add to that is I'm glad you decided to trust us."

Brennan returned the grin, but only Freya spotted the tightness behind it.

So he's not *telling us everything?* Freya thought. *I wonder what else he's hiding...*

It was then that Sam, who'd been quietly listening to the entire conversation, interrupted. "One last thing. Why did you choose to show up when Freya was in danger?"

"Because it was then I realized that I didn't want to lose such precious allies."

Sam was satisfied with the answer, and resumed floating in the room.

And you couldn't let a chance like that pass, could you? Freya's sarcastic reply rang in his head. *An opportunity to play the hero who rescues the damsel in distress.*

Brennan glanced to her out of the corner of his eye. The Sage was still eating her breakfast, nothing in her appearance hinting at what she was actually doing.

No, I couldn't, could I? he countered.

When only silence answered him, he tried to casually read her, but her raven hair blocked most of her expression. In an effort to draw her out, and seeing as Seamus was discussing logistics with Sam, Brennan decided to continue with the telepathy charade.

You master this thing really well. An outsider probably couldn't tell you're communicating telepathically.

Freya was unsure of what to retort, so she opted for quiet.

The only clue is that you're stabbing your eggs really hard... You'd better quiet down, or Seamus will figure it out.

Freya scowled for no particular reason. The reason she was stabbing her eggs so hard was because the boy opposite her could be quite annoying, and he was unnerving her. She forced herself to calm down.

So... What exactly have you figured out? Brennan demanded.

Why would I answer that?

Why wouldn't you? I've been honest, don't I deserve some back, quid pro quo and all? Brennan waited, crossing his fingers under the table.

Freya threw him a dark glare, before concentrating on her toast. *You have almost the same powers I do and there's more to you than you're letting on.*

Mhmm... And? Come on, there must be more.

Freya rolled her eyes, before admitting, *The presence. You weren't the only one following me, were you?*

Nope. Someone else, too. I'm not sure who, but their vibe isn't exactly friendly, if you get what I mean. So stay safe.

By the time she glanced up at him, surprised by his words, Brennan was already addressing Seamus, "So, what's your story?"

"Well," O'Keeffe began uncertainly, "I've trained Freya since she was little. She—lost her parents in a car accident at an early age and I took her in. Her father was one of my best friends."

"I learned at fourteen I was a Sage," Freya revealed, "and since then, I haven't done much more than training over and over. I've almost mastered my abilities." As an afterthought, she added, "Ghosts like these Vikings shouldn't normally be this hard to put out of commission, but... There's something about them, and Cadmael." She paused, then grudgingly admitted, "We'll have to really work together on this, Brennan."

He inclined his head in agreement, while mentally saying, *You're not all you seem, either.*

You have no idea, she taunted in return.

"What about you, Sam?" Brennan kept at his quest for answers.

The twelve-year-old grinned. "Well, let's just say it's a *long* story." At Freya's glare, however, he hastened to add, "But I guess we have time. I met Freya on one of her missions."

Freya snorted and teased, "Sam, tell the story how it really happened."

"Fine," Sam grimaced, as if he tasted something sour. "Actually, it was Freya who saved me from getting my butt kicked by a fairly angry ghost." To Freya, he mumbled, "Happy now?"

"Perfectly." She grinned, and Brennan found himself mirroring it.

"Anyways, to show her my gratitude, I decided to help her on her mission. Umm, I don't remember what it was –"

"I had to confront some crazy Amazon ghosts who were going to reduce all men – immortal and mortal – into slaves for their own benefit," Freya intervened.

"That doesn't sound so bad," Brennan interceded with a twinkle in his eyes.

"Yeah, that's what Sam thought too," Freya said. With a mischievous smirk, she went on, "If I remember well, you had quite a crush on their leader, Sam..."

If a phantom could blush, Sam would've been crimson. But being a translucent spirit had its advantages. He only cleared his throat, then went on.

"Right-o, well... Anyway, I tipped Freya on the Amazons' hiding place."

"He was only able to do so because he'd been spying on their leader..." Freya interrupted once more.

Sam went on, ignoring her last comment, "And later on went there to support her and the professor – whom I'd met in the meantime – to fight the Amazons."

At this last statement, Freya let the laughter she was trying to hold back escape. When she finally calmed down, it was only to burst into another set of giggles at Brennan and Seamus' astonished expressions.

Finally, after a few more minutes of good laughter, she stopped and was able to speak, though she would break every now and then into silent giggles.

"Sam has a funny way of remembering things," she chuckled, before trying to sober up. "He didn't exactly *help*, if you get what I mean... He sort of got in the way. He'd just stay there, in the middle of the battle, and stare at the leader."

At this, Sam was offended and snapped back, "Hey, who's telling the story? You or me?"

"You, oh great master of stories," Freya allowed, leaning back against her chair and holding her palms up. A smile played on her lips.

Brennan chuckled softly. He'd been observing the two bickering, and now his golden eyes twinkled with amusement, all guarded expression vanished.

"Go on," he encouraged Sam.

"Yes, well, as I was saying before I was so *rudely* interrupted for the tenth time...." He waited for an apology that never came from Freya, then huffed. "I decided, after the battle – which, might I add, Freya won – to be their guide in the spiritual realm. I basically roam the Earth and warn them if there's anything strange they should take a closer look at."

"I'm impressed," Brennan said, looking at each of them in turn. "You've got a decent team here."

"Well, now that you have a feel for all of us," Seamus interrupted, "do you agree in helping out to defeat the Vikings?"

It's in my best interest. Rather than voice that aloud, Brennan nodded. "Sure."

Seamus seemed pleased by his answer, and took another sip of his coffee. "Then let us focus on more important matters now – such as how to defeat a hundred Vikings."

It was at that moment that Freya caught wind of some good news – finally. Tyr's voice in her head announced, *It has been done.*

Tyr! Finally! I got worried when you didn't get in touch.

The tiger sighed, sounding weary. *It was not an easy incursion onto the ship. But the Vikings are gone, you can be sure of it.*

How? Freya asked, taken aback.

They were sent back to nothingness.

But... how? Freya pressed, taking into account what Seamus had revealed of the huge power needed to do such a thing.

It is of no importance.

But–

At the guardian's warning growl, Freya backed off. *Okay, okay... I won't ask any more questions... At least not on this particular subject.*

Good, was the tiger's definitive reply.

Thank you so much, Freya said. *I really owe you one, Tyr.*

It was my pleasure, for your safety. There was a pause, and Tyr said, *I see you have company and will leave you to it. My spirit needs rest.*

Before Freya could ask the entity if it had known about Brennan, the connection was broken. The Sage tuned in to the conversation once more, having missed only seconds of it.

"*Three* hundred Vikings," Brennan corrected O'Keeffe. "There's a long ship coming with two hundred more."

"Nope," Freya intervened, grinning. "Seamus is right, we only have to worry about the hundred."

"What? How?" Brennan frowned, his gaze shifting between them.

"It's been handled," Freya shrugged, then bit back into her toast. The silence at the table didn't deter her from wolfing down the rest of her breakfast.

Chapter 16

Tyr entered into the palace of the gods, and crashed in front of the fireplace, groaning softly.

"You truly have overdone yourself," Isis stepped out of the shadows, and walked over. She knelt next to the immense feline, softly caressing its fur. "And endangered yourself."

Freya required backup. They would not have been able to win against three hundred phantoms, not with only the three of them.

"Four," the goddess gently corrected.

Tyr opened one glazed eye, moving its head slightly to contemplate Isis better.

Four?

"A new companion joined them yesterday while you were out battling those ghosts."

Osiris chose that moment to step in, his eyes immediately locking with his wife's. "The boy?"

What boy? Tyr half-growled, trying to stand up, and failing.

Isis pressed her hand in its fur, restraining, "Calm down, Tyr. The boy is no stranger, he is a Wiseman."

Dublin's boy, the one we have been watching?

"The same," Osiris confirmed. "He has already briefed them on his story – most of it, at least."

How did Freya take it?

Isis shared an amused look with her husband, then focused her twinkling midnight eyes on the entity. "Well. I confess they have a certain...chemistry."

Tyr surprised them all by snorting. *Of course they do – they're both stubborn as hell.*

"There is one more matter," Osiris deemed important to point out, ignoring the warning from his wife. "Brennan also warned your protégée of another shadow trailing her... We think he captured, if only subconsciously, the essence of evil."

Tyr managed to get to an upright position this time, though barely. *The demon showed up?*

"Yes," it was Isis who confirmed, in her soft spoken nature. "We have seen his presence, more than once in Freya's vicinity. Perhaps it would be time you told her the truth."

Perhaps... But for now, I must sleep, and recuperate my strength. After, I will decide.

Tyr then curled back down in front of the fireplace, and went to sleep.

&&&

Back at the hotel, the companions had moved into Freya's room for privacy. Her announcement that the number of ghosts had diminished – as if by magic – went by rather well.

Seamus, already aware she was getting outside assistance, only nodded. Sam seemed to believe she could do no wrong, and would always pull the proverbial white rabbit out of the hat at the last minute.

Brennan, contrarily, received the news with suspicion. "So you're telling me that, for months, I've been covering this, stressing about the extras, and now it's all fixed?" he challenged flatly.

"Yep," Freya grinned, but it didn't reach her eyes.

Though not a mind reader by any means, the Wiseman read loud and clear the Sage's vibes – which at the moment were warning not to ask questions. Her nearly-closed fists further indicated she'd defend the secret with her life.

"Okay then," he agreed. *Keep your secrets, for now.*

Choosing to ignore him, and the intense stare, Freya addressed her mentor. "Seamus, even if there are less Vikings now, how are we going to get rid of them?"

"Well, it certainly won't be easy, but we can come up with a plan," he said. "But first, let us review what we have gathered already."

His suggestion was met by a groan from Sam. "Can I skip this part?"

O'Keeffe exhaled loudly, tiredly rubbing his eyes. "In order to defeat your enemy, you have to understand him well. Thus, *no*, Sam, you are as much a part of this as everyone else."

"Can't you just tell us everything? You were up all night reading about the Vikings!" Sam's complaint drew raised eyebrows from the other teenagers, but Seamus shook his head.

"I may have done so, but it is their knowledge I wish to test, not my own."

Sam rolled his eyes, but didn't vanish. Seamus focused his attention on Freya and Brennan. "Let's get back to the basics. What exactly do we know about the Vikings?"

Freya's brow furrowed as she tried to remember what she'd learned about them in history class, though it had been a long time ago. After a few moments of mulling it over, she said, "They were great navigators, capable to find their way by the stars in an unknown sea and their fierceness mostly stood in that skill. They were also good fighters, especially with the axe."

When O'Keeffe gestured for her to go on, she added, "However described as barbarians, they were no such thing. At least the majority of them. Most Vikings, despite battling on sea and stealing from other boats – mostly merchandise-carrying – were quite clean, though maybe a little brutal." She paused, frowning. "Wasn't there a different race – or clan – of them, called the Jomsvikings?"

Seamus nodded. "Yes, they specialized as mercenaries and worshipped the gods Thor and Odin."

"Jomsvikings?" Brennan repeated, and Freya noticed a gleam in his eyes that didn't predict anything good.

"Yes," she said apprehensively.

Brennan spun away, unresponsive. Brow furrowed, he was deep in concentration, staring at the floor with particular interest, trying to place the name – and the sense of foreboding that filled him.

Freya shrugged at his odd behavior, and went on, "And if I recall my lessons well enough, these Jomsvikings only admitted among themselves men of proven valor. Another condition was that all members had to be between eighteen and fifty years old."

"Yes…" Seamus rubbed his chin and started pacing, sorting out his ideas. "However, there was one exception to the rule."

Freya raised her eyebrows in confusion. "There was?"

"Yes," O'Keeffe said. "The exception was a boy named Vagn Akesson who defeated a strong Jomsviking at the age of twelve."

"*Twelve*? How?" Sam asked, becoming quite interested with the subject.

"Every new member had to prove his valor by facing off against a seasoned Jomsviking. Vagn fought one of the strongest," O'Keeffe explained. "To this day, we can only guess at how he managed to do it, but he defeated him. Years later, in one of their great battles against the English, when their leader had fallen, Sigvaldi – the Jomsviking Vagn had defeated – seized charge and ordered the retreat. Vagn refused to listen to him, and persisted in fighting. When the battle was over, he was considered a hero, and Sigvaldi a pitiful coward."

"I never heard this story," Freya mumbled.

"That's because you weren't listening in class," Sam retorted back, an innocent grin spreading when Freya glared at him.

O'Keeffe nodded to Freya – ignoring Sam's comment – and then went on, "Now, what exactly do we know about this Cadmael?"

"Oh, you mean except the fact that he's a sadistic maniac who wants to take over the world and rule every spirit and/or human on Earth?" Freya retorted sarcastically.

"We know his name, for one…And that gives us more to work with than you might guess," Brennan intervened.

Freya opened her mouth to say something, but Seamus lifted a hand. His dark look shut her up, and gave the floor to the Wiseman.

"Cadmael's a Jomsviking, and one of the best," Brennan said, in a tone that implied he knew what he was speaking of.

"The man was a legend, and also the son of Vagn – his *only* heir. This battle you mentioned, I believe it took place around the same time as the Battle of Stamford Bridge, when the Viking Era practically ended. Either way, Cadmael was part of it and afterwards he retreated, along with a few dozen of the best warriors, on the sea. He wasn't seen again by the Jomsvikings."

Freya's eyes widened as she remembered the words Cadmael had mentioned that night, in the harbor – *They certainly don't expect an army of ghosts to try and beat them at their own game.*

Her thoughts were interrupted when Brennan added, "As the son of Vagn, Cadmael had a lot to prove. Always in the shadow of his father, there were rumors he was interested in the occult, or worse. So when he disappeared, no search parties were launched."

"That's quite a lot of information," Seamus beamed. "Well done, the both of you. And much of it corroborates what I've read in my notes – which, now that I think about, I should go get."

While he stepped out of the room, Freya was left to her own speculations. She was first awestruck at the amount of information coming out of her new companion, until another idea hit her. *How would he be aware of all this, unless...He's not who he says he is.*

Composing a cool expression, she tried to mask her suspicion, arching one eyebrow. "How do you know all this?"

"I'm well-versed in history," Brennan grinned annoyingly – yet again – then scowled as he caught wind of her emotions. "Hang on a second, what are you—" His eyes widened, then narrowed in a glare. "I'll have you know, I'm *not* working with the bloody Vikings! What the hell is up with you, to even come to that conclusion?"

Freya crossed the room in two strides and shoved against his chest in frustration. "First off, get *out* of my head! You have no right to read my thoughts!"

"Then don't be so emotional!" Brennan glared. "It's a Wiseman thing; I don't even do it on purpose!"

"And second," Freya continued, ignoring him, "It's a bit co-incidental you just happen to know all of this about our enemy!"

Brennan walked a few steps away, then spun incredulously. "I just told you Cadmael's a dreaded Jomsviking – that you'll probably have to confront in the end – and all you care about is how I know this?"

"Yes!" Freya glared.

Brennan's own fuming gaze shot daggers back at her. "What the hell is wrong with you? London will get attacked, and you don't even care?"

Freya moved so fast, in five steps she was in front of him, hissing, "I'm perfectly well aware of what I'm doing. Now answer me! *How* did you learn everything about him?"

Brennan gritted his teeth, glaring back in response. Freya lost her patience and smacked him on the head – hard. He let out a startled "Ow!" and scowled at her like she was crazy.

"Don't you get it, you idiot?" the Sage hissed furiously, her grey eyes burning into his.

Brennan stared with a look that clearly stated she was out of her mind. Ruled by her impulses, Freya punched Brennan in the stomach, but as she tried to hit again another time, Seamus entered the room, and immediately restrained her.

"That's *enough*, Freya!" He peering apologetically at Brennan, who was trying to catch his breath. "What is going on here?"

He then glared at Sam, who'd been quiet in the corner. "And why aren't you doing anything to stop them from bickering?"

The boy grinned. "Not part of my job description. Plus, it was *way* too entertaining!"

Seamus gave a disgusted shake of the head. Reassured Freya would no longer assault their new companion, he let her go. "Would you care to fill me in?"

"Freya thinks Brennan's a spy for the enemies," Sam summed up chirpily. "And she got mad he read her mind. And he's clueless about something."

Seamus threw him an annoyed glance, and the boy shut up.

"Explanations. *Now*." He demanded of both teenagers, folding his arms across his chest.

Brennan sighed, then turned to Freya, "My grandfather had a lot of historical volumes on Vikings. For some reason, he followed this guy, Vagn's story, quite closely, and realized Cadmael was his son. I didn't put two and two together until we started talking about Jomsvikings just now."

Freya's gaze hardened at the information, even as she stepped away from him, deeply in concentration.

"What's *wrong* with you?" Brennan burst out angrily, taking a few steps closer and grasping her shoulder. "In two days, an army will march on London, and you're not doing anything to stop them!"

Freya jerked herself away from his grip, and shouted at Brennan, "That's because he *isn't* marching on London, you idiot!"

Brennan blinked – then blinked again in shock.

"What are you –?" he began, but stopped as he realized what the Sage was implying. Her emotions were easy to read. His golden eyes widened in horror, as the concept of what Cadmael planned finally hit him. "You don't mean–?"

"How dense can you be?" Freya said, then walked away from him to the window of the room. She leaned her forehead against the cool glass, deaf to anything but the panic swirling inside her.

"*I'm* dense? What about *you*?" Brennan moved next to her, grabbing her shoulder and forcing her to look at him. "You begin punching me for no reason and somehow I'm supposed to read your mind?"

Her grey eyes blazed when they met his. "Why not? You have no problem reading my emotions, so privacy shouldn't be an issue!"

Brennan groaned and let go of her, then slid to the ground. Freya returned to her previous position, while he grabbed his head in his hands. They were mirrored pictures of despair, leaving their two companions confused.

On the sidelines, Seamus and Sam shrugged in tandem. It was evident, by Freya and Brennan's stricken expressions that both had realized something about their enemy's plot – and it was nothing good.

"Right, then. If you two are quite done with your drama, would one of you mind telling us what the hell is going on?" Seamus sounded like he'd lost the last bit of his patience.

Freya's glare flicked from Brennan to Sam. The ghost floated a few steps away at her ardent stare. "The problem is that Cadmael is a sleaze, and played us for fools. He had a perfectly prepared plan, and we played his game like he expected us to."

"What?" Sam gaped at his friend, but before he could ask something more pertinent, she was already explaining.

"He was never going to march on London," Freya said. "Cadmael's target was the coast of the island, from where he'd slowly but surely spread his faithful servants all over England. Think about it, Seamus. Even today, ships bring commerce and import-export all kinds of merchandises. That's easy Viking transportation, all ripe for the taking. If Cadmael gets to bring his scheming to an end, then England, and possibly the rest of the universe, will be doomed."

"But—how?" Sam asked.

This time, it was Brennan who intervened in a low voice. "The boats. They travel all over the globe, to Russia, Asia and America. Cadmael would've inserted his army in the boats, who would have entered ports unsuspected. If all of them materialized somewhere randomly, regular humans would know to suspect them, maybe even realize something was wrong."

"Entering through the back way ensures total privacy," Freya picked up the string of explanation. "Plus, it gives them all bodies of the crew to possess, which is probably what Cadmael wants, in the end. It would give him total power over entire countries' water transportation, and worse, their navy – if he gets ahold of a soldier or two."

O'Keeffe was incapable of uttering a single word. After a long, stunned moment, he asked, "How did you put all the pieces together?"

Freya sighed and looked at Brennan, then met her mentor's eyes with a wry smile. "Something didn't work out from the beginning. I mean, why London? What use would it be to a Viking leader, of all people? As I began to talk about the Vikings just now I realized that, indeed, they were the strongest at sea."

The Sage paused, choosing her words. "Plus, the night we went on the ship, Cadmael mentioned something about beating *them* at their own game. All I needed to do was add two and two together and, when Brennan mentioned this guy being a Jomsviking, it all made sense. He wants revenge on the British for having defeated his people in the Battle of Stamford Bridge. Except his vengeance won't focus only on one country, but rather the world. His thirst for power and ruling, and everything else, now makes sense."

"Also, how stupid we've been," Sam added. "I can't believe I didn't catch any of this, and I've been spying on them."

"As have I." Brennan muttered from the ground, avoiding looking at them.

Freya hung her head down, but then someone squeezed her shoulder. Raising her eyes, she met Seamus' soft grey stare and gentle smile. "You know my motto, my dear – never linger over the past and always look to the future."

Freya took a deep breath, drawing reassurance from his calm. A slow grin spread on her face. "And you can guess mine – kick as much ghost butt as I can!"

She turned to Brennan and stuck her hand out to Brennan. "You in?"

Brennan eyed her cautiously, trying to determine whether or not she was going to punch him again, or if he was safe this time. A quick scan of the Sage's aura showed only good intentions, so he took a risk and shook on it, "You bet!"

Freya pulled him to his feet, then they faced O'Keeffe. "You're right, and we don't have time to mope around. We'll work together, the two of us." She paused, then grinned wider. "And yes, I won't beat him up ... *If* he behaves."

As if you could, Brennan snorted mentally.

Ignoring him, Freya added, "All we need is a plan."

"And I might have one." Brennan's smirk was firmly back in place.

Chapter 17

"**N**o!" Seamus resolutely shook his head when Brennan exposed his idea. "It is *far* too perilous for the two of you."

"It's not," Brennan argued. "It's logical, maybe a bit risky, but it's something Freya and I can do together."

"You barely know each other!" Sam intervened, panicking as he saw Seamus was losing ground, and actually considering it. The last thing he wanted was for the girl he considered a sister to get hurt.

Brennan faced both O'Keeffe and Sam, squaring off his shoulders and widening his stance as though preparing for a conflict.

"We may have only just met," he started determinately, "but we are both meant for something greater than this. My grandfather believed it, and so do I. We *will* survive this battle, because more will come. Please, trust me on this."

O'Keeffe glanced to Freya, curious what she thought of it. To his dismay, she was nodding at Brennan's statement.

"Seamus," she said patiently, "it's the only way. If we don't do something soon, England will be in great danger – not to mention everyone else. I don't mind taking risks if they'll serve to save both."

"Freya...what if it backfires? You two can't possibly expect the plan to be perfect."

"No," the Sage shared a glance with Brennan, then smiled sadly, "but at least we will have done everything we could to stop them. Besides, you shouldn't worry. I've fought blood-thirsty pirates and survived. You think Vikings can stop me?"

O'Keeffe recognized the fire in her eyes, and knew that nothing would detract her from her goal. A part of him was painfully proud of her, even while the other trembled at the thought of the danger she was walking in. *Nonetheless...*

Let her try, the soft voice in his mind came again. *She has help, more than you can guess.*

With a sigh, Seamus conceded defeat. "Very well, we will do it your way. But please, try to avoid being harmed."

"Not a problem," Brennan acknowledged, then shook Seamus' hand firmly. His gaze was unwavering as he declared, "We'll do our best to stay out of trouble – as much as possible."

"Good. Then I suppose you had best go off to prepare."

Brennan and Freya watched as the elderly man and the boy left the room, leaving them alone for the first time in hours.

As soon as the door closed, Freya dropped the act and turned to the Wiseman, eyes narrowed. "All right, now spill."

&&&

"Why would you agree to that crazy plan, professor?" Sam wondered, unable to keep the question in as he trailed after the old man into his room.

Seamus threw him a distracted glanced over his shoulder, whispering, "Do you think Freya would have had it otherwise?"

Sam mulled it over, then admitted, "Yeah, I guess I can see it." After a pause, he said, "They'll work well together, though. They make a good team."

Seamus turned, amused, towards him. "Really? What gives you that idea?"

"Well... Once they get past the fireworks and all. I really thought Freya was going to kick his butt back there."

"You and me both, Sam," Seamus laughed, even as he turned his suitcase upside down for the notes he'd hidden there the night before.

He stared, once more lost in memories, at the letter he'd received from his old pal, Thomas Dublin. *Keep you posted*, it promised. Yet months later, Seamus hadn't received any further news, and his last letter had gone unanswered.

His shoulders hunched as he realized just how much his friend's death hurt.

"Professor?" Sam floated closer, hesitated, then grasped his shoulder. "Are you all right?"

Seamus peered up at him, blinking away the tears threatening to fall. "I'm feeling old, Sam. So old..."

"It must be that beating you got in the harbor." Sam forced a smile, trying to keep the worry off his face. "Why don't you rest for a bit? I'll keep an eye out for Freya and Brennan, and wake you when they're ready."

Seamus hesitated, then sighed tiredly. *A sleep would not be so bad, after all...* Too many things floated in his mind, like the fact Brennan was hiding something, as was Freya, and the danger awaiting them both...

Yes, sleep is a good idea, he tiredly reflected as he lay down on the bed. He was fast asleep before his head hit the pillow.

&&&

Brennan looked at Freya like she'd grown two heads. "Spill about *what*?"

She placed both hands on her hips and, tossing her ponytail back, glared at him. "Everything you didn't reveal before. Starting with your grandfather."

Brennan's expression closed, but before he could even voice the lie he'd been about to, Freya raised her index in warning. "Nuh uh. I've been patient, but I won't go into battle with you watching my back until I trust you. And right now, I don't."

Brennan exhaled loudly in annoyance, then walked to an armchair and plopped down in it. A yowl made him jump back up, gaping. A white fur ball dashed out of the armchair, and scurried under the other armchair.

"Artemis!" Freya yelled, forgetting all about the stack of questions she'd been about to ambush him with.

In all the craziness of the last twenty-four hours, she'd forgotten all about the cat. Or, rather, Artemis had forgotten all about her. Frowning now, Freya reached under the armchair, and picked the cat up in her arms.

"Where have you been?" she mumbled, scanning her for injuries. It didn't seem as though she had been outside, not that she was an expert in pets.

Shaking her head, she started heading towards the bathroom.

"Uh, *hello*?" Brennan called out from his sitting spot.

Freya retorted over her shoulder, "Oh you'll live. Wait there for a few minutes while I feed her." As she walked away, she added, "And *stop* smirking!"

Brennan grinned wider, annoyed by the girl's antics. When she wasn't kicking his ass, or otherwise pissing him off, she was pretty...tolerable. He watched Freya go into the bathroom, speaking to the cat as she gave it some canned food.

A few moments later, Freya retraced her steps and took a seat on the bed, across from Brennan.

"Good. Now, back to what I was saying. Let's start with something simple. Why were you following me?"

Brennan was surprised, though Freya detected a hint of something in his eyes that she couldn't place.

"Because you asked me to," he snorted.

"Ha ha. Very funny, Brennan," her tone implied the exact opposite. "Why did you *really* follow us after the airport, all the while trying to hide you were?"

Brennan leaned on the armchair, quite relaxed. "Weren't you paying attention? It was to make sure you were trustworthy."

Freya nodded sharply. "Fine, if you want to play it that way..." She trailed off, but within seconds Brennan was levitated into the air.

Freya watched him closely as he concentrated on breaking her hold. "Don't bother," she said. "We need you against the Vikings, and you'll only waste strength trying to get yourself back down. You'll be floating in midair as long as I want you to. And I can hold it for hours, you know."

Despite her calm words, the Wiseman was doing everything possible to avoid her gaze. So, she decided to go with the big bait. She reached out to the dresser and opened the middle drawer, rummaging through it. After a few seconds, her hand landed on the leather-bound book, and pulled it out.

"Was this the reason?" she asked him, her eyes hardening to clear crystal.

Brennan looked her way, and his gaze widened. The book seemed to have him mesmerized, until he finally gulped and nodded. "Yes. My grandfather was adamant that Seamus had it in his possession."

"How did he discover it?" Freya demanded.

"Seamus?" Brennan's brow furrowed. "I thought he told you?"

Freya clenched her teeth, before pushing past her emotions and muttering, "You'll notice Seamus doesn't always tell me everything. It's his roundabout way of protecting me." She rolled her eyes, before repeating, "*How*?"

Brennan raised his palms in a gesture of peace. "I swear I'm unaware of the full story, only what my grandfather said. He mentioned your parents had been great Sages, that together their powers were renowned, not only here in Europe, but everywhere. It was said they were so formidable, they'd been entrusted with two objects..."

"The orb and scepter you mentioned earlier?"

"No," Brennan contradicted her, then scowled. "Can you get me off here? I'm cooperating, and getting a headache for all my troubles."

Freya hesitated for a brief moment, before letting him fall down. Brennan raised himself in a half-sitting position, and shook his head. "It wasn't the relics. They've been hidden for millennia, or weren't you listening?" Without waiting for a reply, he rolled his eyes. "Your parents were rumored to hold the *keys* to the map."

"The same map that leads to the relics..." Freya whispered, her gaze shifting from her hands to Brennan's neck. "The book and medallion."

"Right," Brennan agreed, ruffling his hair. "Unfortunately, the rumors became truth, and people started hunting them down."

"My parents?"

"Yeah. Only whoever it was didn't know that your mom only had the book, and my granddad had the medallion." Brennan paused. "Thomas didn't have any proof, but he was convinced there was more to their accident than the police, or anyone else, let on... He even reckoned Seamus knew what happened, that he'd been there."

Brennan watched as the shock spread across Freya's expression, and she was crestfallen. "Listen, I didn't mean anything by it..." He tried to backtrack, but it was too late.

Already, Freya was shaking her head. "No, it's fine. I'm fine. Please go on."

He hesitated, but at the prompt of her glare, shrugged. "There's not much else, to be honest. Someone was after your parents. A few months after their death, my grandfather received a package. There was no sender, but inside was a yellowed page with dragon runes. He wrote to Seamus, to check it was what he truly thought it was... And Seamus agreed. My grandfather had no reason to suspect it was him that had sent it in the first place. But as the years passed, he realized the rest of the book was in Seamus' possession – it hadn't been destroyed along with your parents."

Freya swallowed past the lump in her throat. "And he told you all this?"

"Yep. And I came to find you. The end."

"Not quite." Freya rotated the cover towards Brennan, her eyes hardening. "What's the connection between this book and your necklace?"

Brennan paled considerably when he saw at close range the dragon on the cover, and he gulped at the power he sensed emanating from the worn leather. "Where did you get that?" he asked her shakily.

"Right," Freya snorted in disbelief. "You should realize, you were there. The hill of Dinas Emrys."

Brennan's golden-brown eyes widened as he pointed to what she held. "Please tell me that's not the book Seamus handed you on that hill?"

Freya frowned at the contrite tone in his voice. "Of course it is, don't be daft."

"*Shit*!"

"Hey!"

Brennan stood up, pacing nervously from side to side. His hand ruffled his hair in agitation, before he finally spun to her. "I wasn't the only one on that hill!"

"What are you talking about?"

"You were being followed by another."

It finally dawned on Freya, his earlier warning. "The evil presence you mentioned before..."

"Yeah. I strongly..." He trailed off, then started again. "I can't speak to the truth of this, it's only a hunch based on what I could read off the trail, but I think it's a demon."

Brennan waited for some shock from Freya, but she only took the information in stride, analyzing it, before nodding. "Guess that makes sense," she whispered, almost to herself.

"*Makes sense*? You're joking, right? Wraiths don't exist!"

Freya threw him an annoyed glance. "Of course they do. Ghosts exist, why wouldn't evil spirits? And guardian angels, for that matter?"

Brennan gaped at her logic, before folding his arms across his chest. "Let's make a deal," he suggested, but it was more of an order. "I'll explain the connection between the two artifacts when you start being honest with me."

"What are you going on about?" Freya narrowed her eyes.

"Don't play games with me, Freya. I'm the best player there is. You haven't told me all about you, either. And I'm done talking."

Rather than reply, Freya turned her back to him and replaced the book in the dresser. She ran a hand over the drawer, covering it with a hint of power. Once she was satisfied, she took out a pile of clothes to change into, picked up her hair brush, and walked towards the bathroom.

"Really?" Brennan called out, as she walked right past him. "You're going to ignore me now?"

Artemis stepped out of the bathroom, her dainty paws pressing into the rug. Freya smiled at her cat, then headed inside and closed the door.

"Real mature, Freya!"

Brennan's yell didn't faze her in the least. Ignoring him, Freya dumped her clothes in the bathroom, then headed back out and out the door. She tiptoed to Seamus' room, smiling at her mentor's sleepy form.

"Don't wake him just yet," she whispered to Sam, picking up Brennan's backpack. "We'll come back here when we're ready."

Then she walked back to her room. She threw the bag towards Brennan, then walked back to the bathroom. After locking the door, she stripped and took a hot shower, enjoying the feel of the water on her sore muscles.

Afterwards, she changed into clean clothes. She brushed her hair quickly, then tied it up in a ponytail. Examining her reflection in the mirror, Freya swore out loud at the dark circles underneath her eyes.

When this is all over, I'd love to get some proper sleep.

As she came out of the bathroom, Brennan sized up her outfit, stopping at her face.

"Where did you get the cut?" he pointed to her forehead.

Damn, Freya cursed mentally, but only teased, "That's another thing you won't find out today."

Brennan rolled his eyes, then headed to the bathroom. Within half an hour, he came out showered and changed, more awake than before. He was wearing clothes as dark as Freya's, and locks of wet hair fell over his forehead.

He looks almost cute – when he's not busy talking.

Freya pushed away the unwelcome thought. "Do you really think it'll work?" Her grey eyes searched for an answer in his, one he was unable to give.

"The plan? I'm not sure. But it's the only one we have." Brennan's eyes slid to her forehead again. "Seriously, where did you get the cut?"

Freya rolled her eyes. "Courtesy of Asger."

"Care to explain?"

She sighed and tapped the floor next to her. Brennan joined her as she started talking.

"Two days ago, me, Seamus and Sam went to look for clues at the harbor. That part should be familiar, since I'm pretty sure it was you following me there, too. Anyway, I found a piece of paper making some...allusions to a thing I wanted to find out really badly."

"About your parents?" At her shocked stare, Brennan chuckled, "A guess, nothing more. Don't get your panties in a twist, I'm not reading your mind."

Throwing him a dark look, she finished, "Anyway, the note also gave a meeting place. I went back at night by myself, and fell into one of Asger's traps. At least, I thought it was his trap at the time, but now I'm not so sure."

Freya chewed on her bottom lip at the recollection, wondering if the demon Brennan had sensed could've had anything to do with that particular encounter. *Either way, it's done now.* With a shrug, she said, "Bottom line is, I fought twenty Vikings, and by the time I got back safe here, I was exhausted. This scar is just one of many from that night."

Brennan was staring open-mouthed at her, and as he was about to add something, she warned, "Don't you dare lecture me on being foolish – or anything close to that. Seamus got there first and I got an earful."

Brennan shook his head, laughing slightly. "I was going to say that it was both brave *and* stupid of you to do that, but I'd better keep my mouth shut."

"Yeah, you'd better," Freya scowled.

"Since we're on the topic of sharing, how exactly has the long ship been *handled*?" Brennan asked, arching an eyebrow.

Freya's eyes changed to iron. "Don't push it, Wiseman."

They stared at each other for a few minutes, then Brennan backed off. "All right, I'll be fair. You asked me earlier about the connection between the book and my necklace."

Freya's eyes shone with something Brennan could only describe as excitement. "The truth is, I'm not sure, other than the fact they lead to the same thing. I've no idea to work either of them."

"But the necklace shone, when we used our powers together to get back to the B&B," Freya reminded him.

Brennan only shrugged. "Like I said, I've no idea how to work it. The only other thing my granddad said about it, and I quote, was *Its remarkable faculties will assist you some day in the future, but when you use it, do not forget who you are.*"

"So you're as clueless as I am?" Freya's shoulders slumped in disappointment.

"Pretty much, yeah. Aside from the fact they're keys to the map, I don't know how to activate them, if that's even what we're supposed to do. It's the truth, honestly." Brennan thumbed the dragon pendant for a few moments, then said, "But, for what it's worth, this thing saved my life a few times in the past. It's like it has some short of shield, or something."

"Maybe it's better like this," Freya whispered. She bit on her lip, meeting Brennan's brown-golden eyes. "Maybe we're not worthy of the information, or ready for it yet. If that's case, it's best for us both to stay away from what we don't understand."

The Wiseman said nothing, but she could read disappointment in him. Freya sighed, then got back on her feet. "Anyway, thanks for trusting me."

Brennan shrugged, following suit. "You trusted me with part of your story, so I figured it's only fair."

They shared one last understanding glance, then both headed to Seamus' room where they were to meet, before heading out.

Chapter 18

Seamus woke up to find Sam staring at him accusingly.

"What?" he muttered, rubbing the sleep out of his eyes.

"Freya and Brennan are almost ready," Sam said, floating closer as the elder Sage stood up.

Seamus blinked at him, realizing it hadn't been a trick of his imagination. Sam was really watching him with an almost-glare in his eyes.

"Why do you look like I killed your favorite puppy?" he asked.

Sam crossed his arms over his chest, his bottom lip jutting out. "Forget that. What are you hiding from Freya and Brennan?"

"What?" Seamus froze mid-stretch.

"You talked in your sleep," Sam muttered, avoiding his look. "It's not like I was eavesdropping... You said you should have informed Freya of the truth, about the uniting of the powers."

Seamus groaned, a heavy gust of air expelling from his lungs. He took his shirt off and, ignoring Sam, went into the bathroom to shower. After he was dressed in new clothes, he returned to the room where Sam was waiting.

"I won't stop," the boy pointed out.

"Yes, I realize that," Seamus muttered under his breath. Aloud, he confessed, "I didn't divulge all of it, Sam. The two of them can indeed do what I mentioned, but in order to do so, they would have to be unconditionally complete."

"What do you mean?" Sam frowned.

"For Freya and Brennan to have this remarkable potential I was talking about, both of them have to achieve spiritual completion. In other words, they have to trust each other completely, unveil their darkest secrets, be there for each other at any risk."

"That's why you didn't agree with their plan," Sam pointed out. "Because their crazy idea of taking on the ghosts, of using Cadmael's own strength against him, may backfire, and they're probably relying on what you told them as a plan B!"

"Yes..."

"But you have to tell them!"

"No, and neither can you." Seamus spun a determined expression to Sam. "They cannot find out, because to do so, is to put them in a situation they do not want to be in. This unity will not happen if they are coerced together. It has to be a voluntary choice on their end."

"Even if it may hurt them?" Sam's lower lip trembled.

"I thought of little else since they exposed their insane plan, Sam," Seamus whispered. "And I gather that eventually, they will get to this point. These two have a lot to deal with before achieving the spiritual completion. And, most importantly, they'll have to deal with each other."

"I thought they dealt pretty well with each other." When O'Keeffe raised a sarcastic eyebrow, Sam went on, "Except for the little incident we witnessed this morning, that is."

"Just you wait," Seamus warned, smiling smugly.

"But..." Sam trailed off, hesitating.

"Yes?"

"We really won't tell them?"

"No, Sam. We have to be patient until they figure it on their own and pray they won't need to unite their forces to defeat the Cadmael."

Sam nodded silently, but his face still expressed concern. A knock on the door interrupted any further debates, and in walked Freya and Brennan, all decked and ready for battle.

Seamus took in their determined expressions, and the knot in his stomach became heavier. He had to believe what he was doing was right. He'd be staying at the hotel, leaving the two teenagers to battle, while Sam would only play the decoy part.

Freya will be fine. She has to be.

"Are you positive you can fight this?" he asked both teenagers.

"Yes, Seamus," Freya gave him a reassuring smile. "Don't worry, it won't even take long. We'll kick some butt, then come back here, *alive*. I promise."

Seamus wasn't too convinced, but did he have a choice? Freya had always been pretty stubborn, and now with another equally stubborn friend, O'Keeffe wasn't sure he could hold her back.

"Freya, are you entirely sure you want to do this? It really is a dangerous plan."

"I'll be fine, honestly. Brennan's here to watch my back, and you know I can fight. We rescued you, didn't we?"

O'Keeffe nodded reluctantly, and Freya stepped to hug him before pulling away and heading to Sam next.

"So, no advice? No *be careful or else*?" she teased.

"What's the use?" Sam gave her a resigned smile. "You won't listen to me, so there's no point in repeating it."

Freya mirrored his smile. "Finally giving up?"

"Don't count on that," he threatened, waving a finger in her direction.

This time, Freya really laughed and hugged Sam tightly. "Take care of Seamus for me, okay?" she whispered in his ear alone. "Don't let him worry too much."

Sam held Freya at arm's length, and he shared a long look with her. Then, he engulfed her into another bear hug. "*You* be careful!"

"I will, don't worry." She released her friend and backed away.

Sam turned to Brennan next and pulled the Wiseman in a brotherly hug. While doing so, he stood on his tiptoes and whispered to him, "If she gets harmed in any way, I promise I'll possess your body for eternity."

Brennan pulled away and peered down to meet Sam's gaze. The young boy's expression was serious, but he knew it was because Sam was protective of Freya.

They were like brother and sister, thus he could rely to the emotion surrounding him. He too had a sister, but he preferred not to brood about her anymore. It was way too painful and he didn't need such emotions clouding his judgment at the moment.

With a head shake to Sam, he joined Freya. After a last wave and instructions to Sam and Seamus, the two teenagers exited the room and headed for the car.

"I hope they'll be okay," O'Keeffe muttered aloud.

Sam didn't answer. He only hoped Brennan would take his threat seriously, and get Freya back safe. With a sigh, he started to dematerialize. It was time to get his part of the plan over with.

&&&

The few dozen Vikings were sitting in a circle, close to the long ship. In their midst was the hideous Asger, giving them instructions for the next phase of their plot. Mid-sentence, a strong wind began blowing out of nowhere.

Soon after, Sam materialized in front of them. "Looking for something?" he taunted.

Before the Vikings could register what was happening, Sam was already gone.

Asger was stunned at the intrusion, but he snapped out of it and jumped to his feet. "Up, ye lazy arses!" he yelled to the rest of the ghosts. "Get *up*!" His loud bellow had the rest of the men scramble to their feet.

"Ssssmart decisssion," the shadows hissed.

Asger inspected right and left, already afraid of what he would encounter. He'd heard the voice of corruption speaking to his chief, on and off. The whispers of the obscurity had been taunting him, and now he was afraid they were coming to haunt him.

"My, you really are a coward," the voice snickered.

"Show yourself!" Asger yelled.

The shadows in the background blurred, then the demon came out. Skin black as night, eyes flaming red, he radiated evil. Even Asger stepped back in fright.

"W-what do you want?" he stuttered.

"Your sssoul!" he said, then burst out in cackles at his horrified expression. "Would you relax? I came to warn you. The Sssage is coming, and thisss time, you have one chance to get rid of her. Do not wassste it."

Then he dissipated, back in the same shadows he had emerged from. Asger shuddered, trying to shake off his unease. He'd heard demons spoke aloud with the hiss of snakes, cursed to be forever branded as creatures of the Underworld by the sound. *Except in their own minds.*

The acolytes rallied to Asger, waiting for his orders, weapons in hand. He snapped out of his dark thoughts and shouted order. "Split into groups, and patrol the harbor. Keep your eyes open! We'll have company soon."

&&&

Less than an hour later, just as Asger and his group were ready to march off, someone called out to them.

"Leaving so soon? Why, Asger, and I thought we were friends."

Asger froze, eyes flicking in panic, trying to locate the voice.

It spoke again, this time sounding amused. "Scared yet, little Asger?"

The Viking spun and stared at a concealed corner, gasping when Freya stepped out of the shadows.

He looked behind her, noticing she was alone, and recovered with a laugh. "You are one against a hundred. How exactly do you imagine you can battle us, one puny human girl?"

"By myself? No, not even I'm *that* crazy. But who says I'm alone?" Freya asked with a devilish grin.

Brennan joined her from behind, and Asger gulped. *Why wasn't I warned?*

He'd expected the Sage to be alone, but even with another person, they were outnumbered. *That is, depending on how powerful the boy with her is.*

Brennan and Freya only had time to mouth a good luck, when the phantoms launched at them, all brawn and no brains. Then they got pulled into a whirlpool of punches, kicks, defensive strikes as they battled back to back.

It was after his tenth victim went down, that Brennan sensed it – the evil, the obscurity in the vicinity.

Freya... He tested their newfound mental faculties, praying she'd respond.

Yeah? When he didn't reply right away, she added, *In case you haven't realized, I'm a bit busy here. What is it?*

Another pause.

You really aren't very patient, are you? Brennan muttered. *That presence I mentioned before... I sense he was here.*

Freya froze, then finished her punch, before evading another attack. *The demon?*

Yep. His darkness is everywhere. I figured you'd like to know.
I do. Thank you.

Narrowing her eyes, Freya continued hitting the enemies, packing punches with more intensity. She reached within for more power, letting it fill her as Tyr's nudge had done. She re-

fused to give in to the elements, baiting her once more, and re-
lied on her spiritual energy only.

Her arms became less laden, and she was able to avoid more
direct hits. A sixth sense nagged her to look behind. She spun
in time to watch helplessly as Brennan received a punch to the
stomach, and fell to the ground.

He'd been positioned at her back, and taken a hit meant
for her. Freya felt, in that moment, something she never had for
another human being, aside from Seamus – gratitude.

Getting rid of the Viking trying to hit her, she lunged at the
one heading towards Brennan. Freya managed to catch him off
guard and kicked him – both feet out. In doing so, she dropped
to the ground next to the Wiseman.

Their eyes met, and she grinned. "Come on, partner. Don't
drop the gun on me, now!"

She pushed off the cement and stuck her hand out, as he
had the last time they'd been in a fight together. "We can do
this, remember?"

Brennan's looked at the extended hand, then smiled.
"Right."

Freya helped him to his feet, and they bounced back into a
fighting position – back to back. "It was *your* crazy plan, anyway," Freya added with a chuckle.

The Wiseman laughed, then sobered up as more specters
neared them. The two youths fought with all they could master. Eventually, physical strength wasn't enough and Brennan
had to use his abilities as well, levitating the ghosts or stopping
them in midair, all whilst trying to protect the Sage's back.

Freya, on the other hand, focused on the ghosts and tried her best to stay out of reach of their axes. She got hit a few times, until she was covered in dust and blood.

She stole a quick glance at Brennan, but he was faring no better off. His eyes were tired, but still he was packing punches, delivering kicks, unfailing in his duty to protect her back. Freya admired his determination, even as she was coming to realize that the plan itself was not as foolproof as she'd thought.

Do not despair, a soft voice said in her mind – not Tyr's.

Did you hear that? Freya asked Brennan.

He stopped, scanned the area, then threw her a confused look over one shoulder. *What?*

Never mind, Freya mumbled mentally. Apparently, hearing two voices had become habit for her.

I wish you no harm, remember? The voice chuckled. *Tyr knows so.*

Uhh, Freya?

Brennan's tone made Freya block off all else, and take a closer look at everything around them. Instead of the sparse foes they'd been fighting, now more descended on them. In only moments, they were surrounded by ring upon ring of phantoms, with no possibility of escape.

Yet the new ghosts weren't attacking, but holding back and watching them.

I don't like this, Brennan said.

I second that, Freya added. *Though, on one hand, I welcome the rest.*

Brennan chuckled by her side, bumping shoulders with her. *What, you're not enjoying this?*

A girl needs her beauty rest, Freya rolled her eyes.

The silence surrounding them broke up their banter, and they both tensed.

Whatever's coming, I'm glad we're in this together, Freya admitted.

There was a long pause, then Brennan added, *Me too.*

Freya would've laughed out loud, if it weren't for the figure cutting through. Taller than the rest of the Vikings, with his head of blonde hair, Cadmael couldn't be mistaken for anything other than what he was.

A ruthless, merciless leader.

Time for part two of your plan, Brennan. And let's hope you were right.

The Wiseman could only hope the same.

Chapter 19

The chief of the Vikings wasted no time. Eyes on the teenager, he passed through his army, indifferent to how they parted their ranks for him, like water.

His blond hair was braided and hidden under the huge Viking helmet. He wore armor of leather, which protected his chest. His eyes were of cold iron, and a translucent aura surrounded him.

"At last, we meet," he rumbled as he stepped in front of Freya, a few meters only separating them.

"At last," the Sage agreed, sizing him up with an unreadable expression.

Brennan's presence at her back was reassuring, as was the fact he was covering her back. It made Freya more confident, and she straightened her shoulders – a futile effort, since the chief was nearly two feet taller than her.

"I am Cadmael," the Viking saw fit to introduce himself.

Freya snorted. "Well, in other circumstances, I'd be polite and all, expressing how nice it is to meet you. But, considering you're about to destroy my second favorite country on Earth, I'm afraid I'm *not* so pleased to meet you."

Cadmael remained silent, in a somber mood that would have been unnerving, if Freya had been alone. Brennan's strength at her back was a pulsating force, sufficient to empower her resolve.

She searched his expression, trying to guess his next move. But the Viking seemed content to study her, his massive eyebrows furrowed. An icy gaze to his men followed, as if to say, *This is what your fear?*

Freya smirked. "Don't always believe what you see."

"Really?" Cadmael took a step closer, hand on his axe's handle.

Brennan moved then, silently stepping to Freya's side and half in front of her. His body was the only protection she needed, apparently.

Cadmael looked at him as one would a fly, then met Freya's eyes again. "And what is it that I see according to you, girl?"

Freya shrugged, unfazed. "A sixteen-year-old mortal girl."

The Viking didn't appear surprised – nothing changed in his expression. But Freya had caught, for a split of second, something flicker in his eyes. It emboldened her, and she didn't look away.

"And what about you, Cadmael? Why did you return? Shouldn't you be somewhere dead by now?"

The chief laughed – more like cackled – evilly, and his hand relaxed on the axe's handle. "Let us say I had some things to finish."

"Such as?" Freya asked.

Careful there, Sage, Brennan said. *You don't want to upset the big guy so early on...*

"What could be more important for a Viking than leading his men to battle?" Cadmael's expression instantly changed, and a furious gleam blazed in his eyes.

Or maybe you do... The Wiseman threw her a warning glare over his shoulder, but Freya was too focused on the Viking leader to grasp it.

I got this, Freya assured him, placing a hand on his shoulder and pulling him back until he was by her side, instead of half in front of her.

It didn't escape her notice that Cadmael once more touched his axe, as if by reflex. *Interesting... He can't be afraid of us, so why the bad habit? Is he hoping to intimidate us with it?*

His cool laugh pulled Freya out of her thoughts. "You wish to know what kept me busy? Perhaps learning how to kill ghosts did," he said in a casual tone. "I gather you've not yet grasped the concept of what I can do. Let me provide you with a demonstration."

Freya raised an eyebrow, attempting nonchalance, but her insides were torn in apprehension.

"Don't listen to him," Brennan warned. "He's just bluff –"

Brennan didn't get to finish his sentence. Cadmael turned his back on them and drew his axe out, approaching one of his men. With a sickening swish, the blade went through the glowing body, cutting it in half.

Instead of the silhouette reconstituting – as it should've normally done – it shattered into pieces. Each dissolved into nothingness, vanishing to the beyond.

Freya bit her lip to stop her gasp, and Brennan stiffened close by. She refused to show Cadmael how the evidence affected her. *It's a good thing Sam's back at the B&B.*

She shared a look with Brennan. *Well, we have our confirmation. If Cadmael gets loose, he'll destroy all ghosts that oppose him.*

Or enslave them, if he ever gets the relics, the Wiseman reminded her. *And by controlling them, he'd have the bodies they'd possess...*

Right. Time to head this to its inevitable end.

"Aren't you missing something?" Freya challenged the large chief. He froze, and slowly turned to her. Surprise flashed in his eyes – he'd expected her to be cowering.

The Sage's smirk widened, enjoying his confusion. "So you have the ability to kill ghosts, big deal." She shrugged to emphasize her indifference. "It's your own men you're killing, making my job easier."

Cadmael's only reaction was an icy smile. "More will replace them."

Freya made a show of looking around. "Oh, you mean that long ship on its way here?" She had the satisfaction of seeing his grin fall. "Sorry, guess you didn't get the news. It sank."

Cadmael's fists clenched in anger, and he stepped closer. "Hang on," the Sage stopped him with a raised palm. "You're also missing something else."

A low growl started in his throat, but the Sage didn't let herself get intimidated. "You familiar with Isis and Osiris?"

Brennan watched in satisfaction as the chief's eyes widened, and the gleam of greed was impossible to hide. *We hooked him.*

Freya... Tyr's familiar tone warned in her head. *What are you up to?*

I'm glad you're better, Tyr, but umm... Kind of a bad time here.

An ominous silence settled, before the guardian tried again. *This is your idea? To bait him with the relics of the Underworld?*

Freya cringed at the fury in the tiger's speech. Then another voice, Brennan's, made its way through. *You ok?*

She guessed he'd seen her contrite expression, and wondered at the change in her. Freya nodded his way, *Fine.*

Freya, Tyr intervened, *if this is that boy's plan, you are insane to go along with it!*

Tyr... All due respect, we have to do something about this guy. Unless you have a better idea?

&&&

In the palace, the feline was ready to jump into a portal and head over to its protégée's aid.

"Not this time, Tyr," Isis walked in, Osiris by her side.

You cannot keep me here. She needs me!

The gods shared a look, then Osiris raised a palm in peaceful intent. "Brennan will assist her. You are aware of the prophecy," he added sternly. "It was the one condition we imposed when you requested we go along with this charade."

The entity was quiet, throwing daggers at the gods.

"Do not be upset," Isis begged, kneeling by its side. "Freya is stronger than you give her credit for."

I know she is!

"Then let her prove herself. Let her learn... So that she does not make the same mistakes you did."

Tyr looked away, back into the flames, where it could watch the Sage and Wiseman facing off against the Vikings.

"Be her guardian, give her guidance," Isis said, "but do not be a burden."

When they left the tiger alone, the gods knew it would listen. After all, its demand had a price.

&&&

It is too late for me to undo what you have started, Tyr's warning rang in Freya's head. *Please ensure that when you stop him, you stop him for good.*

Freya frowned at the change. A heavy feeling settled in her stomach. She'd promised Tyr to avoid reckless actions, yet there she was, putting her life in danger once more. *I'm all open for further solutions...*

There is always a way. Remember all you learnt about ghosts... Replay the movie of their arrival in your head...There is always something you could have missed.

With that, Freya lost the connection with her guardian. She tilted her head to the side and met Brennan's confused look. *I'm fine.*

The Sage then turned Cadmael, trying to figure out what Tyr meant. Their plan, to succeed, had to be played just right.

"Is there a point to this line of questioning?" the Viking was asking.

"About the gods?" Freya folded her arms across her chest. "Quite. You ever hear of an orb and scepter the two gods created, something called the relics of the Underworld?" She paused for effect, then chuckled and shook her head. "Who am I kidding... Of course you have."

"I do not know what you allude to," Cadmael growled, stepping towards them once more.

"Of course you do," Brennan snorted. "Man to man, that *is* what you left your people behind for, isn't it? Two *trinkets*."

The men around the chief started muttering amongst themselves as the Wiseman's words echoed over the calm wind. There was only one sure way to break their loyalty to Cadmael, and that was through destroying their respect for him. If they got to see the chieftain as a lesser leader, then Freya and Brennan had a chance.

Despite the unhappy murmurs, the Vikings kept to the ranks and didn't budge. It was almost as though...

Brennan... Freya bit her lip as a thought occurred to her.

I gathered as much. They're waiting for a signal from him.

Then we better make sure he doesn't give it!

"Trinkets, you say?" Cadmael laughed. "You truly are children. They are relics of powers, and it is said the person who possesses both can control all corporeal spirits. With those *trinkets*, I could rule the dead – and living."

Freya and Brennan shared a look.

"You really are pitiful!" Cadmael stated spitefully. "Trying to gain more time? Do not be so surprised, I am a master strategist at war, after all. And I applaud your efforts. So considering you will be dead in the next hour or so, I suppose I could entertain your silly notions of success."

"Gee, thanks," Freya muttered under her breath.

"Tell me, mortal," Cadmael addressed Freya, "what do you know of the Battle of Stamford Bridge?"

Might as well humor him? Brennan pointed out uncertainly.

"Short version or long one?" Freya taunted, taking the Wiseman's advice in stride.

"Short," Cadmael said, giving all signs of impatience. His hand moved over the handle of the axe once more.

This feels like Seamus and his bloody lectures, all over again. Freya crossed her arms over her chest and sighed. "After a stubborn battle with losses on both sides – though greater on the Viking side because of them being unarmored – both King Hardråde and Earl Tostig fell. The battle was prolonged by the arrival of the Norwegian reinforcements for the Vikings, but in the end, the Vikings were defeated. The king of England, Harold Godwinson, made a truce with the surviving Norwegians on the condition that they were never to attack England again."

Freya's summary was followed by a curt pause, but Cadmael recovered from whatever trance he'd been in and declared, "You are well informed, yes. It is true that we lost the battle, and I was among some of the survivors. Along with a dozen of my men, we took a long ship and headed for the west. It was in one of my dreams that I received the illumination."

"Here we go..." Brennan muttered.

"The soul of my lost king appeared to me and revealed I was to go to an island where, in time, I would receive a great gift. But I was to go alone. I accepted and found myself on the island. It took me years and years to prepare, and when I was finally ready, the image of Thor, the god of lightning appeared in my dream and my training such began."

Training? Freya glanced to Brennan for an explanation, but he only shrugged in response. It was news to him, as well.

"After many quests, it was time for me to give the greatest sacrifice of all to Odin, the supreme god – my life. And so I became a ghost, and was granted the gift to kill."

Freya fought back the urge to check with Brennan, then she cocked her head at Cadmael. He seemed to be deep in his memories, but she had to get the end of the story, before they acted against him. Seamus had said, after all, they had to know their enemy in order to defeat him.

"So, when was this? Twenty years ago?"

Cadmael snapped out from whatever reverie he was in. "It was about a hundred years ago. And when I returned, it was only to see that all those which I had lived with were like me, dead."

"And you didn't wonder how ghosts came to populate the Earth?"

Cadmael frowned. "As if that matters. We are immortal, and as long as that lasts, we cannot be killed." His fist tightened on the axe. "Unless it is by my hand."

Ready?

Freya saw out of the corner of her eye Brennan nod, and pushed deep within herself for the fierceness she'd tasted before.

"Well, think again!" Freya yelled to the Viking leader, and shoved her palm through the air, extending it towards Cadmael. The Viking leader was thrown backwards as the element did her bidding.

The other Vikings immediately closed ranks on her and Brennan, but luckily her blast had thrown their chief far enough. It would buy them some time to kick ass.

"That's one way to piss him off!" Brennan yelled.

Freya grinned over at him, then jumped into the fray next to her partner. "Time to put those muscles to use, Wiseman!"

It was the last either of them would speak for the next moments.

Chapter 20

Freya groaned, aware only of the soreness of her muscles, and the headache forming in her mind. They'd been battling nonstop, and both she and Brennan were feeling worse for the wear. The one thing that kept them going was the ghosts' numbers dropping, as their souls received their beatings.

Originally, ring upon ring of Vikings had surrounded them. With some effort on their part, they were left with only an inner and outer ring to fight off.

Both Wiseman and Sage had used their spiritual energy to fight, as well as their physical force. Freya had stayed away from the elements, fearing that using them in her state of weakness would only lead to another problem she'd have no time to fix.

She could sense Brennan behind her, wrestling with another opponent. He'd been enjoying the fight almost too much at times, as if he'd been in dire need of the release. Her thoughts went back to what he'd suggested – finding the relics. *If we had the blasted things, we'd be able to put an end to this now.*

A hit to her ribs had her bend over in pain, gasping. Freya inhaled deeply, then rose and slammed her fist in the Viking's chest. Armor or not, he flew backwards – and took another two with him.

Despite the success, Freya's vision blurred for a second, and she had to shake her head. Brennan was in no better state at this point; she was surprised he was even still standing. Both youths were getting spent, their mix of physical and magical exertion finally getting to them.

They were both aware it was do or die. No assistance would arrive, from human or ghost alike. The only benefit – and disadvantage – was that Cadmael hadn't yet returned. Freya and Brennan had counted on getting his axe to put an end to the show, and his delay was causing them to doubt their own plan.

Both were so lost in their respective altercations, they didn't notice the ghosts pushing between them. The maneuver separated them into two different camps, rather than the cohesive unit they'd been resisting as.

As she finished one attacker, Freya observed Asger advancing, axe in hand, somewhere to her left. It struck her as odd that he was bypassing trying to kill her – after all, he was no friend of hers.

He must be after something else!

No sooner had the thought struck her that Freya peered to her left, and gasped. Brennan was confronting three opponents at the same time, twisting and turning, evading their punches and landing some in return. In so doing, he was oblivious to the danger coming his way, his back to Asger.

He was an easy target for a trained barbarian, but the Sage wasn't about to let a cowardly Viking get to her partner. *Especially not after he had my back for the last few hours.*

Moving as swift as a wolf, Freya headed towards them. In a few steps was on Asger's heels and got rid of another two Vikings. "Looking for something?" she asked him.

Asger spun to her, axe raised high and ready to strike. Freya blocked his hit with her own, crouching down to punch. Packed with a good dose of spiritual energy, the hit sent the henchman flying backwards, straight into one of the ghosts trying to knock Brennan out.

Freya then placed herself back-to-back with the Wiseman, in their original position.

Thanks for that, Brennan threw gratefully.

Don't mention it.

Freya narrowed her eyes on the remaining Vikings surrounding them. Even their meager numbers caused her to groan, as strength seeped out of her.

We can't do this all night, she complained to Brennan.

I know, he said, and sighed heavily behind her. *Just a few more moments, all right? Hang in there. Cadmael must be plotting something, else he'd be all over us.*

Yeah... We didn't quite take into account his narcissism, Freya pointed out.

Brennan was just as covered in sweat and blood as Freya was. His breathing was ragged, every muscle sore as he tried to throw off the last few phantoms.

Slowly but surely, both youths became easy targets for the Vikings, the last of which pounced like vultures on fresh prey. Brennan was knocked down by a quite well-built specter, as Freya fought to keep both of them safe.

The moment she deemed herself incapable to handle one more blow, a breeze came over her and everything seemed to still. She half-closed her eyes, breathing in the smell of the salted air.

Do not surrender, Freya, Tyr's warned in her head. *Cadmael is not as certain as he was before that he can crush you easily. Please do not allow him to be right.*

I can't anymore. I'm drained, and I still have to fight the biggest and baddest.

The tiger refrained from pointing out it was exactly what it had feared, all along. Instead, it reassured, *You cannot stop, Freya. The fate of the world lies in your hands. If you abandon, who will save it?*

Brennan could.

Does that appear possible, right now? The tiger's challenge had Freya glance to the side.

Through half-lidded eyes, she saw the beat-up Wiseman panting to regain force. With a groan, he dragged himself back to his feet and lifted his fists. Freya could sense his fatigue, mirroring her own.

As tired as you both are, you know he cannot do it alone. And neither can you.

Freya realized it was the truth, but the lethargy trying to overcome her was overwhelming. On the edge of her consciousness was another sensation – of impatient fire, earth, air and water. Energy burned in her veins, a flame that craved to burst to the surface.

Her half-closed eyes snapped fully open. *What is that?*

Your spiritual power, Freya. The more you hold it in, the more the elements yearn to show you how you can use them. It is not only a matter of playing with air, or having strong punches. There is more to it, awaiting to be unleashed.

Freya frowned, another idea dancing in her thoughts. *What Seamus mentioned... About sending the ghosts back to their graves...*

You have that potential, hidden deep within you. You do not need an axe, or anything else.

Freya would have had a hard time believing it, were it not for the burning intensifying, even as the feline spoke. Her eyes changed to fire, the silver glow surrounded her once more, and her fingers tingled of electricity.

She spun to Brennan, noticing his eyes widening. "It's time to end this!"

Ignoring the Wiseman's bewildered manner, she struck the Viking stepping close to her. Ducking under his too-slow retaliation, she kicked his stomach. Her spirit and body fought as one, fuelled by an energy outside of her grasp, yet within it.

&&&

From the sidelines, Brennan took a deep breath. He peered closer at Freya's aura, and his energy answered in kind, replenished by her intensity. The silver glow extended to him, and his dark-brown eyes glinted.

The medallion around his neck glowed softly, the blue eyes of the dragon reflecting the moonlight – or the blaze in Freya's eyes. All Brennan knew was the pain in his muscles was gone, replaced by adrenaline – pure and simple.

Tensing his body as one would a hard-wired machine, Brennan held up his palm and stopped a Viking's punch. The man's eyes widened, but the Wiseman was already retaliating with his free fist. The ghost flew into a barrel, and Brennan turned to the next. He dispatched him just as easily, and kept up the face with the few remaining ones.

The Vikings fell one by one, until only one ring of the army was left. Brennan and Freya shared a look.

Fifty-fifty? Freya asked him.

Brennan grinned in answer. *First one done gets Cadmael? You're on!*

A competition was exactly what they needed to keep their will up. Freya engaged the right side, while Brennan fought the ones on the left. They gave their best shots, and in ten minutes, had their adversaries down.

As he finished the last one, Brennan turned to Freya and announced proudly, "I'm done."

His victorious smile slid off when his eyes fell on Freya sitting on top of a pile of knocked-out phantoms – her bounty.

"How did you –?"

"Oh, this?" Freya smirked, pointing to the mountain of Vikings underneath her. "What can I say? I'm full of surprises."

Brennan shook his head, chuckling softly, but then he froze.

"Um, Freya?" he tried.

"What?"

"Ghosts," he warned, pointing over her shoulder.

"Don't be silly, Brennan, we knocked them all out. They'll be unconscious for at least a few hours, hopefully."

Brennan shook his head violently. "No, no. *Ghosts!*" he insisted, pointing frantically to something behind Freya.

She rolled her eyes at his antics, but listened, if only to humor him. Her smug expression dropped, replaced by a groan.

The ghosts they'd knocked out before where now getting up, ready for another round.

"I guess I forgot the part about paranormal beings getting over injuries fast, didn't I?" she muttered aloud.

"Yup, looks like we both did."

Freya backed away, as did Brennan. They shared a glance, the same thought crossing their minds. *If we want to get Cadmael, we need to get out of here.*

Agreed, Brennan said. *No way can we fight him, if we're dead tired. Unless that's his plan.*

Could be, Freya scowled, then nodded. *Let's get out of here.*

They were about to run into hiding when Freya spotted the chief. She stood frozen on the spot, unable make up her mind. He was in the background of the ranks of Vikings, thus another sea of them stood between her and the ultimate fiend.

Freya's gaze shifted to Brennan's retreating shape, now a few meters away, and distancing himself further. He was under the impression she was behind him, but her feet had her rooted to the spot. The Sage made the mistake of looking to the Viking once more and noticed his victorious smile.

Hell, no. The decision was impulsive, but she couldn't care less. *This is the same guy that kidnapped my guardian* and *my friend. No freaking way he's getting away.* Jumping forward, she launched herself towards Cadmael.

Brennan, a few meters away, caught the shift of energy and spun around. "Freya, *no!*" he yelled, immediately backtracking to protect her back.

Cadmael detected a shadow moving out of the corner of his eye, then he was kissing the ground. A furious Freya was in front of him, fists clenched and panting.

"Ah, so you've finally recovered," he spit as he stood up. "Let us stop playing games. Show me what it is exactly that scared the hell out of my men."

"They didn't need to be scared," Freya retorted in a cold voice. "They were *born* that way!"

Cadmael launched forward, ready to strike, but was stopped into midair. He scrutinized Freya, assessing his adversary for weaknesses. *My victory will be sweet indeed.*

"Piss off!" Freya yelled as her foot connected with the Cadmael's abdomen. Despite the armor, her energy impacting him was enough to send him flying backwards.

Cadmael hit a barrel, but landed on his feet, in a crouch. He straightened up slowly, then rolled his shoulders and smirked. Then he was on the move, heading towards the Sage, hand on his axe.

The chief's gaze moved to something over her shoulder, but Freya didn't react. She waited a few more seconds, then spun and punched. The Viking that had been trying to knock her out ended up flat on his back, not grasping how it had happened.

Freya turned to Cadmael, growling low. "Play fair!"

"Fair is not part of my vocabulary," he replied.

"Then you'll learn it!" Freya yelled, and jumped forward.

Cadmael waited this time, and caught her foot before it reached him, one-handed. With his other, he twisted it viciously, throwing Freya head first to the ground.

She extended her hands and managed to roll on her back, protecting her face. The move proved to be lucky, as Cadmael's heavy boot connected with her right forearm – instead of her nose. Though she stopped his boot from trampling down on her, Freya couldn't stop the sand from reaching her eyes, and she was soon blinded.

She managed to avoid a fatal blow only by following her instincts, and Cadmael was once again thrown in the air.

Freya got up fast, blinking furiously to have her vision restored. In the few moments that took, two enemies headed her way, but all she could see were blurry shapes. She prepared to block more hits, but instead the blows never made contact.

She rubbed her eyes and her view cleared. Blinking, she scanned the area, only to notice the two ghosts sprawled on their backs. Her eyes landed on Brennan, only a few meters away, and she mouthed *thanks*, to which he responded with a grin.

Freya was then able to concentrate on Cadmael, who was in a semi-kneeling position. She advanced towards him, narrowing her eyes when he didn't move.

The Sage had a hunch something was wrong, mainly due to his cold gaze fixated on something behind her. She was also very aware that if she twisted around to humor him, Cadmael would use the chance to escape.

"Enough, chief. Your army is done for, and there's no way you're getting your hands on the relics, no matter what training you had. Your little plot's been dismantled by two teenagers." She paused, then shrugged. "How about you surrender?"

"I think not," Cadmael sneered. "This is only the beginning."

Before Freya could do anything, he dematerialized in front of her. "*No!*"

She kicked the ground in frustration, clenching her fists. A quick look around confirmed the rest of the specters had vanished as well. If only that was all... For no matter where she looked, searching, hoping to locate him, her eyes didn't fall upon the one person she desperately sought.

"Brennan?" Freya murmured aloud, her words echoing eerily in the night.

The Wiseman was nowhere to be seen.

Chapter 21

"Brennan?" Freya whispered into the empty surroundings.

Her gut clenched painfully at the realization she'd failed in protecting his back. Tears stung her eyes. The Wiseman had been kidnapped while she was clashing with Cadmael, a ruse designed to weaken them.

Dammit, I've been so blind! Another realization, just as strong, hit her. For Brennan to be safe, she had to retreat from the battle... Meet Cadmael and surrender.

Do not give up, Tyr encouraged.

They have Brennan, Tyr. Can you help me get to him? A flash of hope ran through Freya, quickly extinguished at the tiger's next words.

How I wish that was possible... The entity sounded wistful, and sad. *After what I did with the long ship, I cannot re-enter the Earthly realm as before. I lost too much, at a huge cost to my own spirit.*

Freya angrily wiped at her cheeks, erasing all trace of tears. *I can't confront Cadmael while Brennan is in danger. He had my back when I needed it, and I couldn't return the favor. The least I can do is make sure he gets out of this alive.*

He is not in danger, little one.

How can you say that? The Vikings have him, and there's no way I can get to him in time!

I may not support you physically, but I can guide you. Close your eyes and feel.

Freya did as she was told and, shutting away everything else, extended her senses in the area. She could almost picture Tyr in her mind's eye, guiding her along a path...

See with his eyes...

Freya cast her spirit like a mist, crawling across the distance, as she had done before at Dinas Emrys. This time, she encountered the faint vibe of ghosts, followed by a beating – a human pulse.

Brennan? Freya called out mentally, afraid of raising the attention of the other spirits. Yet she needed the Wiseman to answer her, to point her out to his location.

There was silence for a few moments, then a sign of life.

Aye.

Brennan! Are you all right?

Do I sound all right to you? he grumbled. *My neck hurts like hell, I'm blindfolded, bound by ropes and –*

Okay, okay, I get the picture, Freya interrupted. *Could you do me a favor? Try to use your abilities.*

What for?

So I can find you, Freya explained, trying to rein in her impatient temper. *It's the only way. I can't figure out your vibe among all these ghosts. But if it's more intense, then I'll be able to. It doesn't have to be a huge burst, even something small will do.*

Brennan was silent for a few seconds, then, *All right, hang on.*

Freya concentrated, scanning the mist for any trace of his essence, and soon she felt something. It was a faint burst of energy in the southeast corner of the port.

I found him!

Opening her eyes, she shut off the communication with Tyr, but kept linked to Brennan's vibe. She jogged that way, trying to keep her footsteps as silent as possible, until she arrived at an old warehouse hidden past the most abandoned of ships.

She crouched towards the open door and peeked inside. No glowing shapes that she could see. *Let's hope this isn't a trap*. Whether it was or not, Freya wasn't willing to let Brennan pay the price. She allowed the vibe to guide her in the gloomy darkness until she stumbled upon something soft.

"Ouch," someone said.

Freya reached out in the obscurity and fisted some hair. "Brennan, is that you?" she whispered.

"Yes, and will you *please* be careful with the hair?"

"Sorry," she apologized, letting go immediately. Freya extended her palm and murmured, "Release."

The ropes keeping Brennan tied loosened, and he was able to get up and remove his blindfold. "This doesn't help. It's even worse in here."

"Let's get out of here," Freya said and reached out for his hand, grasping it in hers. "I have a bad feeling about this."

Brennan froze for a beat, then squeezed back. He nodded in the dark, but then, remembering she couldn't see him, agreed, "Yeah, you and me both."

They'd only managed a few steps forward – or the way they guessed was forward – when Brennan tugged on Freya's hand, stopping her dead in her tracks. "Something's wrong."

And then, darkness was no more.

Light bulbs suspended to the ceiling turned on, and they were bathed in brightness. Freya squinted around, trying to see what they'd landed in.

She and Brennan were right in the middle of a large boating warehouse. Opposite them, and encompassing them, Vikings began stepping out of the shadows.

Take Cadmael. I'll handle the rest, Brennan suggested to the Sage, and let go of her hand. He was already sizing up his opponents.

Remembering what being separated did to them, Freya shook her head. *No, I don't want you to get hurt. Stop playing the hero, Brennan, and let me help you.*

For a few seconds, he didn't reply. When he finally did, his tone was all business. *I'm not kidding. Our plan's shot to hell, and the only way to stop this is to get rid of Cadmael. Call it a hunch, but I think you're the only one that can do it.*

Freya chewed on her bottom lip, her gaze shifting everywhere as she sized up the numbers they were up against. *I am not!* she denied, a bit too vehemently. Then, an idea struck her. *We could unite our powers! According to Seamus, the potential we would generate would be enough to get rid of all of them!*

Brennan gave a bitter laugh, but didn't look her way. He shifted so his back was to her. *No, Freya, we can't. I'm surprised you, of all people, didn't catch on that Seamus omitted a lot when he revealed that.*

What are you saying?

There's a condition to get to what he promised. I haven't worked out what it is, but I have a gut feeling it's important.

Freya was silent, at a loss. It wouldn't be the first time Seamus had kept something hidden to protect her... And in his defense, their plan never mentioned uniting their powers. The elder Sage had no way of knowing how bad it would all turn out.

Dammit!

Glancing at the Wiseman behind her, Freya was conflicted. She didn't want to let him fight the rest of the Vikings alone, considering how tired his aura showed he was. But they couldn't let Cadmael escape either. If he did, he'd just go somewhere else and reattempt his crazy plan.

And with him free, the relics won't ever be safe.

Sensing her hesitation, Brennan reassured her aloud, "I'll be okay. You go."

"No," Freya shook her head.

Let me help you... It was the melodic voice, once more.

A soft breeze caressed her face, and Freya inhaled its sweet scent. As though animated by another person, she turned and walked towards Brennan. Her palms rose of their own accord and touched his necklace, under his bewildered gaze.

As soon as her fingers brushed the dragon, a flash erupted from within it, as silvery and pure as the aura that had surrounded Freya. The two teenagers shared shocked looks as the glow enveloped them.

&&&

The demon scowled, hidden in the darkness of a corner. He'd hoped they would die, and he could pick up the artifacts from them, then force them to reveal the location of the relics. Now, it was apparent their bond had only grown.

Damn the gods and their mingling! he cursed, then turned to leave.

It would be best, at this stage, to go with his second option. Let them acquire the objects for him, *then* dispose of them. After all, the Wiseman was hell-bent on retrieving the relics... *Why not let him?*

With a cackle, the demon dispersed into nothingness, letting the Vikings fend for themselves. They'd been only pawns in his game, and had no value left to him.

Fetch, mortal fools, fetch! he chanted to himself, in a better mood.

&&&

Freya and Brennan locked gazes, grey against brown-golden, and nothing could tear them apart. It was as though the bubble they were in stopped anything else from entering. A warm sensation crawled over their skins, akin to a blanket being thrown over them in an icy storm.

Then, as soon as it had appeared, the blaze extinguished.

Freya was filled with the certainty of what she had to do. Her fingers slipped off the necklace and she stepped back. She met Brennan's eyes and whispered softly, "Take care."

Then, she sought Cadmael, noticing him gazing at them curiously. As soon as she caught sight of his blonde hair, Freya leaped forward.

Evading the Viking that tried to catch her, she advanced to the one that mattered. Right before she reached the chief, she was stopped by Asger. The hideous creature stood in front of her with his axe, and Freya had to roll her eyes at his determination.

"You're never tired of getting beaten up?"

The only answer she received was Asger trying to cut her in half.

"I guess not," she muttered.

After sending a well-placed kick in his abdomen, Freya extended her palm and yelled, "Stop!"

Air froze around the henchman, immobilizing him the same way the ghosts had paralyzed Sam not so long ago. Leaving a floating Asger in the dust, Freya pursued her way to Cadmael, not watching her own back.

The sting was so sudden Freya stumbled and fell to the ground, gasping for air. As soon as it showed, it disappeared, and she blinked, disoriented.

What the hell was that?

There was nothing in the vicinity that could've hurt her, nor had she caught wind of a spiritual attack. A flash of blonde hair grabbed her attention once more and she hurried to it, forgetting about the pain.

&&&

After Freya's departure, Brennan stood frozen on the spot, bewildered by what had taken place.

He emerged out of his trance rather brutally – a Viking punched him in the stomach, and he sprawled on the floor. Despite the gasping sensation, Brennan got up and blocked the next strike.

Viking after Viking moved to attack, and he had to fight against the soreness of his muscles, the demand on his body. *This is not the time to slack off.* He was in the middle of a particularly fierce battle, when smoke enveloped him and his adversary.

The Wiseman searched with his spirit, but couldn't sense Freya close by.

Freya? he tried mentally.

When she didn't rebuff him with her usual snark, he started panicking, fearing for the worst. After all, he'd sent her to battle the fiercest of the Vikings.

Freya? Dammit, Sage, answer me!

Another beat of silence answered, then, *Not really a good time, Wiseman.*

Finally! Brennan elbowed the Viking in his face, breaking his nose. Once he fell, he let out a sigh of relief that she was alive. *I thought you were in trouble or something. What's the update?*

A few bruised ribs, a sprained ankle, an open cut on my forehead, and limping. You?

Finishing off the last Viking, Brennan massaged his shoulder, wincing at the ache developing. To his surprise, no other ghosts were around him – not that he could see much past the fog. To Freya, he said, *Few bruised ribs, a nearly dislocated shoulder and a deep cut on my arm.*

Guess we're lucky then.

There was dead air for a few moments, then Brennan felt a sharp burn in his stomach. Scanning the area, he couldn't see anyone, yet the attack couldn't have been in his head.

Where the hell did that pain come from? he wondered, rubbing the area.

What pain? Freya questioned, sounding out of breath.

Brennan's brow furrowed, then his eyes widened as he realized something. *Freya, did you just get punched in the stomach?*

Possibly, why? Something about the way she expressed the thought made him picture her doing so through gritted teeth.

Never mind, I'll explain later.

Another ache developed in his stomach, on the heels of the first, then his head began hurting. This time, he knew why – or, at the very least, guessed.

The moment Freya had touched his necklace, a bond had been created among them, making one of them feel all the emotions the other endured. It must have been yet another of the medallion's properties, designed to protect its wearer.

Fearing for Freya's safety, Brennan closed his eyes and began meditating. He found her in a small amount of time despite the mist. Stumbling from the lost energy, he shook off the blues and headed her way.

&&&

Freya squared off against Cadmael, breathing heavily. The meeting wasn't going so well, considering she was tired *and* the chieftain was one hell of a good fighter. This was no mere boy or brainless henchman she was sparring with, rather a warrior intent on killing her.

Her ribs ached all over, and some of her previous cuts had reopened, but she couldn't – *wouldn't* – stop. Each time she landed on the ground, Freya forced herself back up.

She'd tried using her spiritual energy to give a little something extra to her punches. But the damn Viking's axe kept neutralizing her attacks, leading to more wasted energy than anything else.

It didn't help that his men kept interfering. Evading another hit from a Viking that had emerged out of nowhere, she wheeled to the chief angrily.

"That's *it*, Cadmael!" she yelled at the Viking, her eyes beginning to blaze. "I'm getting sick and tired of your army and your smug ass. It's time you get back to beyond – for good."

"Have you not grasped the truth yet, girl? You cannot kill me, for I am already dead. And you cannot stop me, either."

"Don't be so sure about that," Freya hissed, a fire burning in her. Her fists clenched, and this time, when the elements called, she was no longer saying no.

Cadmael's words were a fog. "You cannot do anything, foolish mortal girl."

"But a girl with powers," came a voice from nowhere.

Freya threw a look over her shoulder, and smirked. *My knight in shining armor, to the rescue.*

At your service, Brennan beamed.

Taking advantage of Cadmael being distracted, the Sage launched herself in the air, and kicked him hard to the head.

Having misjudged her leap, Freya stumbled as she landed, falling on the ground in the end. Her head smacked the concrete hard, and for a few moments, she saw darkness. As she blinked back to her surroundings, faint sounds of a battle floated to her.

Freya managed to get herself back up in an upright position. Turning, she saw Brennan facing Cadmael, the latter apparently winning.

What are you doing? she asked Brennan, afraid for his safety. A larger target than she'd been, the Wiseman wouldn't be able to last as long.

Buying you some time, he retorted.

Freya nodded gratefully, and closed her eyes for a split of second. She soon snapped them open at a blow in her chest, and her head went dizzy.

Tyr, what's happening? Why do I feel like this?

Calm down, child. That is what Brennan hesitated to share, earlier. When you touched his medallion, an unbreakable bond was created between the two of you. Your emotions are now shared.

Ouch! Freya winced. *And our pains...*

She glanced to the Wiseman, and gasped. Brennan had fallen on the ground after a particularly strong punch from Cadmael, and wasn't getting up. The Viking chief, meanwhile, was advancing with the axe in hand, ready to finish him.

Don't forget...The strength is within you both... Tyr's tone rang in her head.

"Leave. Brennan. *Alone*!" Freya yelled, standing up from her spot on the ground.

The burning announced itself before it reached her extremities, the tingling intensity, and her entire body electrified. The Sage extended her hand and yelled, "Stop it!"

It was as if fire and water had collided. Thick smog emerged out of nowhere, and Freya heard Cadmael's muffled, "You cannot stop me, poor girl!"

"I don't believe that," Freya said.

Before she had a chance to prove it, Freya was thrown into a wall, and felt the impact in her ribs. The dizziness spread to her muscles and she fell to the ground, barely supporting herself.

Two boots ended up in her vision, and Freya raised her head to see Cadmael in front of her, smirking evilly, enjoying his victory. Before she could do anything, he advanced to her and his spirit entered Freya's mind.

"No!" she cried out, crumpling to the ground. She was holding onto her head, screaming in protest at the invasion of her personal domain.

Cadmael was taking possession of her spirit, a slimy intrusion, forcing her mind open to pry inside. Everything within the Sage rebelled at his presence, and her spirit reacted – a soft, silvery glow enveloped her.

Panting against the exertion, Freya moved up, inch by painful inch, until she was standing up once more. With one last groan and mental push, she rejected the Viking's spirit brutally.

When her eyes met Cadmael's, Freya could read the surprise, the consternation at having failed. Fear began to show in his iron eyes, but the girl that was now in front of him was no longer the teenager he'd possessed for a few seconds.

Her aura pulsated, as strong as a human heartbeat. Its emanating strength had him stumble back, eyes widening. He sensed his end at bay, saw it in the fire from her lit eyes. This was a Sage, a fully grown and trained one.

Somehow, the intrusion had caused Freya to reach maximum capacity, and her power was completely released. It filling her with a strength she hadn't felt before.

Freya took one step, then another towards Cadmael, her palm extended. She could almost feel a ball of electricity form at the tip of her fingers.

"No!" he yelled. "You cannot have the same ability I do!" He looked around, his eyes searching something impossible to find in the fog. "Demon, you *swore*!"

Freya smirked, and her voice was icy cool when she spoke. "I have no idea which evil you are praying to... But you are no longer a ghost, Cadmael. Merely a lost spirit. So let me show you the way *out*."

She didn't allow him a chance to answer. Instead, she brought her palms up, reaching deep for the energy – and calling the elements to her. *I'm ready.* Their strength was in every breath she took, in each step. Freya envisioned it colliding with the Viking's non-corporeal form, and saw him...gone.

Cadmael screamed, but it was a distant faraway echo. Fierce force spilled from Freya's extended hands, sucking everything in its powerful vacuum. And the Sage had no idea how to stop it.

She was aware of the phantoms perishing one by one, hit by the wave of force, disintegrating into nothing. And yet, Freya could barely stay awake. Internally, she became dimly aware that was losing the battle – she couldn't manage the intensity, the power. As her eyes closed, she felt life being drained from her.

Soon, I will join them...

Freya couldn't stand up anymore. She fell to her knees, her arms still extended.

Sense the power, do not try to control it. Tyr's words were close to her ear, and Freya turned her head slightly to her right, and saw the mighty tiger behind her. Her eyes pleaded for it to help her, but the protector only smiled wisely, *I trust you, Freya.*

The Sage's eyes shone of a profound fire burning in their depths. Freya lowered her gaze to her hands and the white – almost blue – blaze escaping them. She concentrated her focus on the overwhelming energy leaving her, and the intensity, the spirit within, and let it overcome her.

Somehow, it felt as if she was finally in control. Freya was able to stand up, and straightened her back. Then, her eyes opened, and she was falling.

&&&

Brennan snapped to conscience at the same time Freya battled the leader. He watched, bewildered, as the force escaping from Freya disintegrated Cadmael into nothingness.

Asger was next, followed by the fog, and finally, the remaining Vikings. His gaze went back to Freya and he could've sworn seeing, for a moment, a white tiger in the background. As he blinked, the animal was gone, only a figment of his imagination.

The following moment, the brightness ceased, and Freya fell. Brennan hurried to her and caught her before she hit the ground, drawing her in his arms. Her body was warm as if she had a fever, and though he thought she was unconscious, her eyelids fluttered open.

Brennan gasped softly.

Freya's grey eyes were burning, and they were so intense it was as though they were searching his very soul. He didn't wish her to be aware of his past, but he couldn't escape that ever-seeing gaze.

"Are they gone?" Freya whispered, and blinked once. The intensity disappeared, and her eyes regained their original silver color.

"Yes," Brennan whispered. "You did it, Freya, you did it!"

She smiled weakly, then went limp in his arms.

Chapter 22

Freya was falling, hard, and she couldn't pause. She tried to stop herself, but simply couldn't. When she came to a stop, she was surrounded by darkness – thick, overwhelming.

She was awake but yet, not. Her eyes opened and were met with brilliance – a shining, silvery light.

A voice surrounded Freya, begging her to return, and a nagging at the back of her mind argued she had good reason to. And yet, the glow in front of her was so attractive, her feet kept walking closer, of their own accord.

When she was within its grasp, it enveloped her, like a warm cocoon. *I don't want to leave here, ever again,* Freya mused serenely.

"Come back, Freya," the voice on the outside coaxed.

No, I don't want to. It feels... too good here.

As Freya floated into space, enveloped by the light, she saw something move out of the corner of her eye. A shadow, slithering closer. Her eyes widened and, under her bewildered stare, a shape formed. It was the silhouette of a man, with ebony skin and glowing red eyes.

"At lassst, we meet," his deep rumble of a voice was reminiscent of an animal.

"You're the wraith," Freya stated, shivering with the truth of her words.

"Yeesss," he hissed, "It isss I. Raksssh is my name, and I have been chasssing you for too long now, sssilly girl."

Freya glared at him despite her fear. The blaze enveloping her was giving her courage. "I'm not a child!"

"Oh yesss, you are..." he laughed. "You're the sssame ssscared little girl, in the backssseat of the car, watching as your parentsss die in front of you." He paused, enjoying her stricken expression, before adding, "I ssshould know. I wasss there."

"You're lying," Freya murmured, her throat dry. "My parents..."

"Your parentsss were *weak*! Giving up that power, the relicsss, for love. For *family*." The disdain in his tone was apparent with every syllable.

He stepped closer, not letting her analyze his words. "Be better than them. Ssstep out of that beacon, and help me get the orb and ssscepter. You can benefit, too..."

"Never!" Freya glared, stepping out of the cocoon of light, as his words finally penetrated. "How dare you lie about my parents' death, to manipulate me? I'm a lost soul in need of a puppet master!"

The demon stared at her for a beat, before laughing that low, animalistic laugh. "Manipulate you? Dear girl, why would I bother... When I can sssimply ussse you to get the objectsss?"

"As if I ever would."

Again, that unnerving stare, as though Raksh knew something she didn't. Then, he smiled. "Never sssay never, Sssage."

Even as he was going to add something, a roar echoed around them. In the distance, a shape appeared. It was coming closer, all stripes of white and black, getting larger every moment.

"Tyr!" Freya recognized the entity before it had fully reached them.

Stay away from him! With one last push of its powerful back muscles, the feline lunged in the air and landed between the Sage and the demon.

And you... I should have killed you when I had the chance.

"A ssshame you did not." The fiend retorted, and with one last glimpse at Freya, full of meaning, it dematerialized.

Freya?

The Sage turned to Tyr slowly, as though emerging from a daze. Shivers overtook her entire body, even as her mind refused to accept what the monster had revealed.

Freya!

The teenager fell to her knees, hugging herself tightly. "What's happening?" she shivered, panicking. "Why am I so cold?"

It was as though something within her was trying to burst to the surface, some memory deeply hidden, and she was afraid. A sharp ache erupted in her stomach, and she screamed.

Freya!

Tyr disappeared, as though pushed away by something. The agony was overwhelming, and Freya couldn't stay awake. She felt like fainting, but then a murmur rose from deep inside herself.

"I will not give up."

Another voice, weaker, denied, "I can't go on."

"I will *not* give up." The first one grew fiercer by the second.

Freya snapped her eyes open, and repeated, "I will not give up. I will not give up. I will *not* give up."

It grew stronger and stronger as she repeated it, almost a chant. A fire started in the pit of her stomach, and she enjoyed the warmth it gave her.

"I. Will. Not. Give. *Up!*" she shouted more forcefully.

A silvery light enveloped Freya wholly – coming from the deepest of her heart – and she was peaceful and serene. Her eyes closed, and her body, replenishing in the Sage's healing, fell into a restful slumber.

&&&

Freya woke up with a throbbing in her head. She opened her eyes and blinked in confusion, before realizing she was back in her room at the B&B. She wondered how she'd arrived there, before realizing Brennan must have brought her back.

The last thing she remembered was Cadmael's scream, and an impression of loss and draining energy.

Something else nagged at the back of Freya's mind, a dream... Or had it been a nightmare? Her brow furrowed in confusion, but try as she might, it wouldn't come back to her. When she closed her eyes, all she saw was the warm glow enveloping her, all she felt was her own healing process happening.

Dismissing the annoyed nagging, Freya lifted her head off the pillow and looked around. Seamus was asleep on the armchair closest to the bed, but there was no sign of Sam. *He's probably out doing this thing.*

On the other side of the room, Brennan was sprawled over the other chair. A lock of hair fell over one eye, and he had his arm bandaged from elbow to hand. Freya smiled fondly as she recalled his unwavering strength, belief in her, and his protection. Despite his arrogance, the Wiseman had a good heart.

How long have I been knocked out? Freya wondered, noticing for the first time the darkness outside.

Three days, Tyr answered, and Freya caught its relief.

What? She tried to stand at the surprising news, but the room spun around her. At the ache throbbing on the side of her head, Freya groaned and dropped back on the pillow.

How are you? Tyr asked.

Freya took her time, evaluating her body and trying to see if she had anything broken. Satisfied, and a bit surprised to notice the damage was less than she remembered, she said, *Sore, my head hurts, my body aches all over, but other than that, perfectly fine.*

You sound surprised.

I guess I am... I mean, shouldn't I be in more pain?

The tiger was silent a moment, then admitted, *Yes. But when you tapped into those new faculties, deep within you, you accessed what full-fledged Sages only do. This means your body is now able to generate spiritual energy to heal itself.*

Freya realized her mouth was literally gaping open, and closed it. *I guess that's good.... Right?* She glanced unsure at Seamus, then Brennan, lingering on the other boy and his arm. *Can Brennan do that, too?*

No. His Wiseman abilities would be depleted if he tried to heal himself.

Then... Freya hesitated, chewing on her bottom lip. *Could I heal him?*

Again, no. At least, not at this stage.

Tyr's short answer only caused Freya to frown. Her gaze stayed on Brennan, wishing she could do something to help him out.

It was Brennan who brought you at the hotel, Tyr revealed, as though reading her mind. *He and Seamus have been by your side ever since, only leaving for a few minutes to get something to eat.*

Freya glanced back at her mentor, then the Wiseman. *I... Why exactly was I knocked out?*

Because you acted foolishly out there, was the reprimand. *That entire idea was doomed from the start, and you could have died if it had not been for...* Tyr paused, as though biting its tongue.

For what? And why would I have died, Tyr? I only...

Freya stopped as she remembered exactly what had happened – Cadmael, Brennan, the two of them fighting... The Wiseman unconscious, and then her burning anger, and letting the power escape her.

She lifted her palms in front of her face, inspecting them in wonder. None bore any scar at all, and if she didn't have the memory carved in her mind, she wouldn't have believed being capable of such potential.

Tyr? she asked uncertainly.

Yes?

Is Cadmael gone? And the ghosts, are they all...?

The feline was quiet for a long time, then said, *Yes, they are gone. All of the Viking ones. And the world is safe now, but you could have paid a great price, Freya.*

Why? How could I have died?

You risked very much by listening to your instincts. I didn't expect, when I advised you, that it would lead to such an onslaught of force.

Tyr paused, and Freya could detect the regret and fear in its voice. *The spiritual force you released stole some of your vitality – the energy that keeps you alive. Because it was your first time, you were unaware of how to focus its deadly energy on only one Viking. Thus, with each ghost that perished, you could have lost more and more, until finally there was no more. But somehow, you reined it in, and the result was that instead of dying, you were only knocked out for a few days.*

Freya was quiet for a few minutes, letting the information sink in. Once done, she became aware of the tiger's hesitation about something.

Tyr? What are you hiding?

Nothing! I told you everything. Despite its words, Freya was under the impression her guardian angel was omitting something.

No, you haven't. What was it that truly saved me?

Tyr remained stubbornly silent, and Freya thought it wouldn't answer her question. But finally, the deep voice rang in her head. *I meant to say you could have died out there if it had not been for Brennan who, without wanting to – or even grasping he was doing so – lent you some of his own essence.*

What? Freya was astounded, her eyes flickering to the Wiseman. *Why would he do that?*

Because the bond that is now forged between the two of you cannot be broken.

And without further exploring the subject, Tyr ended the connection.

Freya was unsure of how to react, a mixture of emotions dancing within her. Relief she had succeeded and not died, happiness she was now awake, and...fear for having been so close to death. Mixed within all that was a great deal of gratitude towards Brennan.

She closed her eyes once more and inhaled deeply. It was then Seamus stirred and opened his eyes. When his gaze fell on Freya, he breathed out a huge sigh of relief.

"Thank heavens you are awake," he whispered, tears shining in his eyes.

Freya reached out for his hand and stroked it gently. "Shhh, don't worry, I'm okay. I told you I wouldn't go down easily." Any anger she might have felt at the incomplete information he'd given them, washed away under his concerned gaze.

Seamus moved off the chair and knelt next to the bed, bringing her hand to his lips. "Freya, I owe you an apology. When you two left, I should have –"

She squeezed his hand, and smiled. "I know, Seamus. We couldn't have united our powers, even if we'd had to do so. Our plan didn't rely on that, and there was no way in hell we could've predicted it would get so completely off-track. So, really, none of that is your fault."

One lonely tear trailed down Seamus' cheek, and Freya reached out with her free hand and wiped it away. "You are my guardian, and you have my best intentions at heart. I finally get that, you know." She blinked back her own set of tears. "And I'm sorry, for acting out and pushing for answers. Being a Sage means jumping through hoops, and while I don't get to have the conventional training... I get that, to some extent, I won't always know why you do the things you do. But I will *always* trust that your actions are meant to protect me."

Seamus stared at her for a beat, as though not really believing his ears. Then he reached over and hugged Freya daintily, so as not to hurt her. In her ear, he whispered, "Thank you."

He pulled away and smiled, finally mirroring Freya's mood.

"Well, well, sleeping beauty finally woke up." The words were spoken from the corner of the room.

Freya turned her head to the other armchair and smiled at Brennan. "Yep, and the knight in shining armor slept well, I suppose?"

Brennan chuckled and walked over. He perched on the free side of the bed and gave his trademark half-smirk to Freya, his brown-golden eyes gleaming. "Glad you're okay. I was a bit worried when you didn't wake up at the same time I did, you know. But then again, you *are* a girl, so..."

Freya arched an eyebrow, trying hard not to laugh. "And, what, being complicated is my prerogative? Is that what you're saying?"

Brennan shrugged. "I *was* going to say special, but complicated works just as well."

"Hey!" Freya mock-punched his shoulder, then snorted with laughter.

It was at that moment Sam flew through the wall, brow furrowed and muttering to himself. He saw Brennan up and hurried to him, not noticing Freya was wide awake.

The truth was, in all the days Freya had been knocked out, Sam had grown used to checking with Brennan for news, not even watching the bed for fear of seeing his almost sister dead.

"How is she? Did she show any sign of waking up?" he asked the boy worriedly.

Before Brennan had a chance to reply, Freya chuckled, "She's up and better than ever."

Sam turned to her and gasped. "Freya! You're *awake*!" His excited yell was only outmatched by the force of his hug.

"Ouch, Sam," Freya whispered. "Breathing...Need air..."

"Oh, sorry!" He quickly let her go. "Forgot about the injuries."

Unable to keep his joy controlled, the boy jumped up in the air, doing a weird dance, all whilst dancing and singing. The others broke into laughter, and soon Sam calmed down.

"So, how are you really feeling?" he asked, floating at the bottom of the bed.

"Just fine, I told you," Freya repeated.

The three men in the room raised their eyebrows sarcastically and Freya sighed. "I'm all right, honestly. A bit sore, and my arms and legs hurt like hell, but fine otherwise."

Brennan nodded and lifted his arm. "Yep, I hear you. So do you remember what happened?"

"Yes..." She hesitated, glancing between him and her mentor. "Most of it, anyway."

Seamus returned to the armchair, but leaned forward, elbows on his knees. His expression was stern, worry still coating his eyes. "Freya, you know it was very foolish of you to do what you did. Though those abilities do belong to you, and you will be able to use them at extent, you have not been trained in controlling them properly."

Freya winced. "Yeah, I figured as much. Honestly, Seamus, I didn't have much control over my actions. It just...happened."

"Be that as it may, I didn't give you that book so you could try out new things and end up killing yourself." He paused, softening his tone. "Please, Freya."

"I promise to be careful going forward. But, Seamus…"

Catching onto her hesitation about something, O'Keeffe dropped the lecture and instead asked, "What is it? Something you wish to add?"

"Actually, yes. I think I've finally discovered why there are ghosts on Earth."

Three pairs of eyes were glued to her as she went on, "Cadmael mentioned something about the gods Odin and Thor. He said they'd granted him the gift of killing spirits. My guess is that, when Cadmael returned among the living, a portal was opened."

"And through the portal came the other specters?" Brennan finished for her, already in agreement.

"Yes."

They were all silent for a few minutes, then Seamus spoke. "Well, gods are popular meddlers, so it is the least of our surprises. It is good to have the last missing piece of this puzzle."

Freya, Sam and Brennan nodded, but the Sage had one last query.

"Seamus… Brennan has been a full Wiseman from the beginning, but… Am I correct in guessing that after this battle, I've earned my own Sage stripes, as well?"

Her mentor inclined his head in assent, smiling gently. "Yes, you are. What clued you in?"

"I'm not in as much pain as I'm supposed to be," Freya muttered under breath, making them all laugh.

Nodding understandingly, O'Keeffe chuckled, "We will let you get some sleep, and come back later."

Freya watched as they went to exit. At the last minute, she called out to Brennan. "Could you stay a while longer?" When he hesitated, she added, "Please? I have a question."

Brennan closed the door after Sam and Seamus, then returned back to the edge of the bed.

Freya waited until he looked at her, before saying what had been on her mind. "Thank you."

Brennan tilted his head in confusion. "What for?"

"For lending me the energy that kept me alive... Does Seamus...?"

"No, he doesn't know about our bond. I only told him that you took out the ghosts, and went into a deep sleep for a couple of days." He paused, before continuing, "And to be honest, I didn't actually have a choice," he smirked slightly. "You're quite demanding for such a tiny body. Plus, the moment you touched my medallion, the bond that was created between the two of us... Well, it's not only very strong, but also *extremely* persuading. It practically commanded I save you. So I guess, if one of us is in danger, the other one has to do all they can to support them."

Freya nodded, then cocked her head to the side and wondered, "Brennan, are you coming back with us to Scotland?"

"No, I'm afraid not."

"What about the map, and the relics?"

The Wiseman was silent for a bit, glancing away wistfully. Then, his gaze settled on Freya. "You may have been right about that, you know. If we're meant to find them, we will. But my place is here, and I'll be of better use here than in Scotland. Besides," his smug smile widened, "what makes you think I need a girl as a partner?"

"Why, you little shithead!" Freya yelled as she threw a pillow at him, hitting Brennan square in the head.

Laughing, he jumped off the bed and hurried out of the room.

As Freya shook her head, the door creaked open and Brennan's head popped in. "Though to be fair, I'm a *big* shithead, you know..."

"Get *out*!" Freya screamed, laughing as Brennan hurried to close the door before another pillow reached its target.

Freya, now completely awake, decided to have another look at her book. The medallion Brennan possessed had proven to be of huge value to them, with a secret force they'd been able to tap into. Perhaps the dragon manuscript had its own secrets... Secrets that could lead to more powers being bestowed upon them. Either way, it was worth a glance to search for a clue about anything in it.

Using her powers, the Sage summoned the burgundy book, and it landed on her lap. As she touched it, Freya sensed the electricity run through her fingertips. The magical creature on the cover shone faintly, almost as if inviting her to open it.

Taking a deep breath, Freya flipped the cover over. The first page was empty, with no writing on it. She turned it over and, this time, writing decorated the next page.

Freya leaned in slightly to try and decipher it, but realized it was in another language. She frowned, scrutinizing it closely, before remembering where she'd encountered it before.

"Dragon runes." Her awed whisper was loud in the room. Seamus had shown her examples in the past, enough so that she could recognize them without issue.

It's no wonder my powers increased since I've had this!

Dragons were known for using the elements, another reason why Sages had the affinity. Their written language was also said to speak to the mind and spirit of humans. *I've been learning the secrets without truly reading this,* Freya thought. *The runes react to me, and I to them. They must've been whispering me the truths I was seeking since the very beginning.*

Feeling slightly excited, Freya flipped the pages frantically and found the rest of the volume was in the same writing. Her shoulders dropped as she recognized the key to unraveling the secrets of the book, was in her possession, but not her control – or Brennan's, for that matter. *At least not yet.*

After one last glance within, Freya closed the book and squinted at the cover once more. Silver on red, the fantastical beast seemed to be smiling at her.

"Many secrets are hidden within you, but I will eventually unveil them all," Freya murmured, making a promise to the dragon that had once upon a time created the artifact.

She called air back and returned the book to its hiding place. Exhausted by the simple use of energy, Freya curled up in a ball and closed her eyes. Within moments, she drifted away to dreamland.

Epilogue

Two days later, Freya and Seamus were packed, with Artemis safely nestled in the sixteen-year-old's bag – and ready to go back to Scotland. Sam chose to remain with Brennan, to ensure the Vikings wouldn't return. He planned to join Freya and Seamus home within the week.

It was so the three humans ended up back at Heathrow airport, from where Freya and O'Keeffe were to take a plane back home.

Back full-circle, Freya thought, looking around at the ghosts and the inside of the airport.

She was now able to walk without support, and the only things that reminded her of the adventure she'd survived were the scars on her legs and arms. Scars now hidden by the red sweatshirt and black jeans she was wearing.

Freya stopped near the line-up for boarding the flight. They'd handed in their luggage, and Brennan had accompanied her and Seamus.

"Young man, I thank you for your assistance on this mission," O'Keeffe said to Brennan, extending his hand.

The Wiseman shook it and grinned. "You're quite welcome, professor."

"I do hope we will meet again," Seamus added, squeezing stronger for emphasis.

Freya snorted behind him, but tried to cover it with a cough. She doubted they'd be meeting again soon, but after all, who knew what the future held? Absorbed in her reflections, she didn't grasp the look O'Keeffe exchanged with Brennan, nor the small smile playing on the young man's lips.

With one last wave, Seamus got in line and turned his back on them. This left Freya and Brennan alone to say their good-byes.

After looking everywhere but at him, Freya finally met Brennan's brown-golden eyes. "Well, I guess this is *adios.*"

"Yeah, I guess so," he grinned.

"So, goodbye then?" Freya offered, extending her hand for him to shake.

Brennan shook his head at her gesture, but grasped her hand in his anyway. At the last minute, he tugged on it, which caused Freya to collide with his chest. The Wiseman wrapped his arms around her for a tight squeeze. His steady heartbeat thudded against Freya's cheek, and she closed her eyes, enjoying the moment.

Too soon, Brennan released her and stepped back. To Freya's surprise, he then bent over and kissed her on the cheek. "I prefer see you," he whispered in her ear.

When he pulled back, their eyes locked for a split of second, and Freya thought she saw an amused gleam in his golden ones, but also a promise.

"Freya, hurry up!" Seamus called out, and she glanced over her shoulder to see him waiting in front of the boarding door, making small chat with the hostess.

When she turned back to Brennan, he was gone.

"Brennan?" Freya searched around, but he'd left no trace behind. People bumped into her, hurrying to get to their plane before it took off.

Shaking her head, she muttered, "You're never going to change, Brennan Dublin." After one last look around, she walked over to Seamus and climbed aboard the plane that would bring her home – to Scotland.

&&&

"All is good that ends well," Isis said, walking over to Tyr with her husband.

Yes, goddess.

"I am glad not to have met your protégée in person," Osiris added. "It is much too early for one such as her to end up in the Underworld."

Agreed. Nonetheless, you both observed what happened with the demon.

The couple shared a look, then Isis asked the question on both their minds. "What are the chances Freya will remember the dream?"

None. It was the vehemence of her mind, closing down on her painful memories that pushed me out of that same dream... She does not want to remember, thus she should be safe. For now.

"You can keep watch over her," Osiris allowed. "It matters much to you. But be wary of the demon. Should he get to you, he would have a direct line to us. Perhaps, in the future, you should try to keep your excursions to Earth to a minimum."

Not to worry. I have found a...shortcut, of sorts.

Bowing to the gods, Tyr then stalked off, to ensure its protégée had a smooth flight.

&&&

In the plane, seated in a comfy blue chair near Seamus, Freya peered outside the window into the waiting hall of the airport. She was absently petting Artemis, who was quietly nestled in her bag.

Her eyes narrowed at an annoying light that was shining in one of the windows. She could've sworn catching a glimpse of brown hair, then a side-ways grin, and sat up straighter, anticipation at the pit of her stomach.

Nothing happened.

She sighed, thinking of Brennan.

"Oh, you'll be running into him sooner than you might believe, Freya," Seamus said.

Freya started, her surprised eyes meeting O'Keeffe's. "How did you guess I was thinking about him?"

He shrugged, picking up a magazine to flip through. "Intuition, I suppose."

Freya flushed at his innuendo. "It's not like that. I wasn't thinking about him because I...because he..." She blew out a breath. "I'd just rather not run into him again."

Seamus nodded, but she could tell he didn't believe her. Annoyed at him – and herself – Freya turned back to the window.

"I mean, don't get me wrong. He's a good Wiseman," she said, "but his ego is way too oversized sometimes. One time working with him was plenty for me."

As she stopped talking, Freya wondered, *Why am I yapping about this, anyway?*

It may have something to do with a certain boy, Tyr teased her.

Don't get your hopes up, tiger, he is definitely not my type.

As you say, Freya, was the wise reply.

Dead air followed Tyr's last statement, until the entity spoke again. *Why do you keep looking outside the window?*

I– *beca– argh!* Freya stammered, before finally snapping, *Stop reading my mind!*

A soft chuckle followed her words, and she decided to ignore it. She couldn't help but wonder if – *maybe* – Tyr was right.

"I do *not* like him!" She didn't even realize she'd spoken out loud until Seamus looked her way.

"Like who?" he asked innocently.

Damn, that came out loud! Smacking herself on the forehead, Freya whispered, "No one, Seamus, just... no one."

She felt his curious eyes on her, and turned to him. "What?"

"Nothing." His gaze shifted over her shoulder to the airport, then back to her face. "I was simply reflecting on how good a companion Brennan has been. I have to admit, without him, our mission may have very well failed."

Freya scowled, but grudgingly had to admit, "Yeah, I guess that's true." When Seamus smiled victoriously, she hastened to add, "But nonetheless, he has a big ego!"

"Don't all boys?" he countered.

Freya pondered the matter for a few seconds. "Maybe. Anyway, I doubt we'll meet him again soon – if ever. His life is here. Ours is all over the globe. The chances are pretty dim."

Why am I still stuck on this? I thought I didn't give a damn.

Tyr couldn't resist answering. *Maybe you do more than you admit.*

Freya refused to dignify the suggestion with a response, instead focusing on petting Artemis. She closed her eyes as the plane began to move, and therefore didn't make out Seamus' voice, barely above a whisper, say, "We'll see."

As the monstrous bird bounced forward, Freya focused her attention back to the waiting hall, and the annoying light flashed in her face again. She squinted past it, trying to see where it was coming from – then her eyes widened.

Brennan was standing at one of the windows waving good-bye, his permanent half-smirk firmly on. It was his medallion, catching the sun's rays, that had annoyed her so.

As she gaped at him, the Wiseman beamed widely, and mouthed something. Freya didn't catch his words, but the action was enough to make her chuckle.

She shook her head, then leaned back against her chair and closed her eyes. In spite of her earlier complaint to Seamus, she replayed Brennan's words, and this time understood what he'd meant – five little words that held a huge promise.

See you soon, sleeping beauty.

End of Book I

**Turn the page for a
sneak peek at Book II...**

Preview of Book II:

The Dragon's Manuscript

"Sweet!" the Sage grinned, then turned to Seamus. "When are we leaving?"

"Not yet. We still have to wait for one more person to arrive."

"What?" Freya looked bewildered.

"We will need some assistance with this one," O'Keeffe announced.

"What for?" Freya protested. "I speak Spanish and we can handle whatever conquistador there is all alone."

"No, not this one," Seamus continued, stubborn as can be.

Freya placed her hands on her hips, full-on frowning. "Do you know something I should?"

"Not at all. Just a bad feeling."

Freya groaned, then threw him a suspicious look. "Hang on a second... Who exactly did you have in mind?"

"Brennan."

Freya was too shocked to say anything. That insufferable, arrogant prat was coming with them?

A nightmare. This has had to be a nightmare.

"No. Bloody. *Way*!" she reacted, finally regaining control of her voice.

"You can't say no, Freya," Seamus chuckled. "He's already on his way. In fact, if I'm not mistaken, his plane has already landed. He should be here any minute now."

"Seamus! I can't work with him! He's an–"

O'Keeffe lifted a hand to silence her. Ignoring her petulant look, he said, "Before you go on, I am pleading with you to please make an effort. For the sake of the mission."

Grudgingly, Freya nodded. "I'll make one if he does too."

Five minutes later, there was a polite knock on the door, and Freya groaned, sinking into the chair.

This should be interesting... Seamus thought as he watched the expression on his pupil's face.

Continue reading![1]

About the Author

Alexa Whitewolf is a dog-loving, caffeine-addicted, all-around traveling enthusiast. Author of three series of fantasy, paranormal and young adult, she spends her nights dreaming up new stories and her days fighting reality. She lives in Ottawa, Canada, with her husband and two mischievous furballs- Zeus and Achilles. Check out her website at www.alexawhitewolf.com !

Read more at https://www.alexawhitewolf.com.

ALSO BY THE AUTHOR

The Avalon Chronicles series
Avalon Dreams
Avalon Wishes
Avalon Nightmares
Atrox - A Novella

The Sage's Legacy – YA series
The Dragon Medallion
The Dragon Manuscript
Relics of the Underworld

Moonlight Rogues series
First to Fall
Second to Surrender
Third to Tumble
Last to Love
Moonlight Rogues: Origins

Standalone novels
Blood Ties, Love Binds
Unconditional Love
Blazing in a Storm of Ashes (Coming Soon)
More novels coming soon!

Sign up for my readers' group **at
www.alexawhitewolf.com/contact** and receive
a copy of *Unconditional Love* for **FREE,** as
well as first dibs on cover reveals, discounts,
giveaways, prizes **and more**!